P9-DCZ-815

The Dream Interpreters

Prepublication Praise

"Once I started it I couldn't put it down. The novel captures the power, the tragedy, and the humbling absurdity of the analytic process better than I have read anywhere. The social setting conveys how vulnerable analysts, like all human beings, are to struggles over power, rivalry, and narcissism. All of the characters come through as flesh and blood people."—*Richard Simons, M.D., psychoanalyst, co-author of* First Encounter.

"Through its lines and lenses the novel transmits an experience of what it feels like to be in the scene as a patient and therapist. . . . It really does transmit the action of psychoanalytic sessions in a way that the ordinary style of description of psychoanalytic sessions tried to do but can't."—*Lester Luborsky, Ph.D., psychoanalyst, author of* Principles of Psychoanalytic Psychotherapy.

"I am impressed that the individuals come to life in a way that rings true. The interplay (the plot . . . that gives a novelistic structure) is sufficient without being intrusive . . . and besides, it has enough tension to pull the reader forward . . . *Unfolds* has come to me to be a primary operative word for analyses. And the hours do unfold as you write them . . . The multiple voices for how analysts think also exposes, unfolds, in modest tone of substantial wisdom"—*Warren Poland, M.D., psychoanalyst, author of* Melting the Darkness.

"The book is a truly remarkable accomplishment . . . I was amazed at how faithfully the novel renders analytic work. To do so in verse and in seven different clinical situations takes rare ability as a clinician and as a writer. . . . I thoroughly enjoyed encountering the cast of characters . . . I was also quite intrigued by the events as they unfolded. . . . All together I found the novel to be not only a unique and original piece of fiction, but compelling reading as well." *Theodore J. Jacobs, M.D., Psychoanalyst, author of* The Use of the Self.

". . . the main thing I want to say is that this is a book of *depth*, of human depth, of compassion for the plight of *being* human. Perhaps "insight" is the word I'm looking for here applied to the individuals in the book, for them, insight and compassion abounds. But it's something else that I'm trying to convey, a wisdom larger than insight, a profound sense of the struggles of life, as those struggles reverberated in each of us."
—*Janet Sternberg, author,* Phantom Limb.

The Dream Interpreters
A Psychoanalytic Novel in Verse

Howard Shevrin

International Universities Press, Inc.
Madison ● Connecticut

Copyright © 2003, Howard Shevrin.

INTERNATIONAL UNIVERSITIES PRESS ® AND IUP (& design)
® are registered trademarks of International Universities Press, Inc.

All rights reserved. No part of this book may be printed or repro-
duced or utilized in any form or by any electronic, mechanical or
other means, now known or hereafter invented, including photo-
copying and recording, or in any information storage or retrieval
system, without permission in writing from the publisher.

Library of Congress Cataloging-in-Publication Data

Shervin, Howard.
    The dream interpreters / Howard Shevrin.
        p. cm.
    ISBN (invalid) 0-8236-1425-5
    1. Psychotherapist and patient—Fiction. 2. Psychoanalysts—
Fiction. 3. Dreams—Fiction. I. Title.
PS3619.H485D74 2003
813'.6—dc21

                                                    2003041672

Manufactured in the United States of America

For
my wife
Aliza Shevrin
fellow wordsmith
companion
and
lover

Contents

Acknowledgments

Most novels are born in travail at a desk with only a few close by hearing their birth cries. Then gradually the newborn is visited by a widening circle of relatives and friends. With encouragement and some disciplining, the newborn grows up and ventures into a world of strangers where its acceptance is chancy at best. This novel is now at that point. It has been strengthened for the challenge by the loving attention and interest of my wife, Aliza Shevrin, its first reader, who was present throughout the newborn's gestation and to whom this novel is dedicated. Thereafter the novel has benefited from a widening circle of readers to whom I express my profound appreciation and thanks. These include Winnie Siegel, Janet Sternberg, Richard Simons, Warren Poland, Theodore Jacobs, Lester Luborsky, Sidney Warschausky, Sylvan Kornblum, Rhoda Krawitz, Louise Kaplan, Elizabeth Coleman, James Kern, Sue Kern, Bobbie Levine, Amy Shevrin, and Daniel Shevrin.

My special thanks are owed to Arnold Richards, editor of the *Journal of the American Psychoanalytic Association*, who not only read the novel but championed its access on the Internet Press for Psychoanalysis and opened the pages of his journal to advertising the novel. I would also like to thank Todd Essig, president of the Internet Press for Psychoanalysis, for his willingness to make the novel available on his Internet service where it was the first such electronic book. Finally, I owe a special debt of gratitude to Margaret Emery, Editor-in-Chief of International Universities Press, who has seen some promise in this fledgling and is willing to be its godmother and usher it into the world beyond its cradle.

Howard Shevrin
Ann Arbor
December, 2002

ix

Foreword

If there is a hero or heroine (some might say villain) in this novel, it is psychoanalysis itself. This is not to say that this novel is not about people and their various plights. Each of the characters is involved, as patient or analyst, in a psychoanalysis—an undertaking uniquely developed to deal with people caught up in their individual plights. Rather, the movement of the novel, as it progresses through a succession of hours and shifts from analysis to analysis, is intended to reveal the inner pulse, the rising and falling tides of a psychoanalysis. Thus the stringent form of the novel—a pure succession of hours in verse in which one only learns about events through the analytic hours rather than having the events "opened up," as when the intimate setting of a play is transformed into a film with its enormous capacity for spectacle and detail. The true events of the novel *are* the psychoanalyses in progress.

Psychoanalysis is, in fact, more like a play divided into scenes and acts than it is a film. It is in spirit closer to the Aristotelian classic unities of time, place, and person than it is to the more "opened up" Elizabethan or modern theater. Psychoanalysis religiously observes these unities in the form of a strict succession of hours, length of hours, setting, and an economy of persons—just two and always the same. Yet, we know from our experience of Greek theater that these unities can work to intensify the drama, to strip character to the bone, to probe an action to its deepest sources in the human heart, and thus to discover what is human in us all in what is true for one person. Similarly, the psychoanalytic form is a powerful lens, gathering and concentrating experience—trivial, shameful, regrettable, painful, proud, vain—into a single beam of light illuminating what is furtive and obscure in our desires and their failed or unforeseen fulfillments.

Why verse? Psychoanalytic discourse is like none other. There is a formality of interchange in which, paradoxically, the most intimate revelations occur; there is an emotional distance in which, paradoxically, exceedingly powerful emotional demands are made; there is a one-sidedness in which, paradoxically, both parties risk much of themselves, although in different ways. How else but in verse to capture the paradox of these seeming antinomies, the simultaneous presence of the sound *with* its echo, the light *in* the shadow, the voice *of* the silence? Psychoanalytic discourse is to ordinary discourse as metaphor is to prosaic speech. It thickens ordinary meaning by its very form, much as putting a frame around a can of soup arrests its usual function and invites an act of contemplation. Only verse can provide these resources. And beyond that, there is the beat itself, the pulse, the undercurrent of organic vitality stirring in us the mute recognition that a life is at stake, that this is a *living* theater in which a repetition of the same plot is the undesired yet inexorable outcome, like a refrain in a folk ballad or a chorus in a song. Only verse can do this.

The practice of psychoanalysis is not in the hands of the gods, or of master poets, but in those of often quite ordinary human beings who have attempted with greater or lesser success to prepare themselves for their profession by long study, undergoing an analysis themselves (the training analysis, three of which are depicted in the novel), and submitting their apprentice work to careful oversight by a master analyst. Flaws and limitations persist. The finely fashioned tool of psychoanalysis, an instrument like no other, can be rendered blunt when the hand wielding it forgets its cunning. This too is in the novel.

Finally, psychoanalysis is that rare hybrid—an art and a science at the same time. As a science, it is uniquely qualified to explore the intimate inner life of a human being and to discover therein its principles. It has discovered much that is new and made explicit much that was intuitively anticipated. But it is also a clinical art, a praxis, in which inspired improvisation can count as much as careful application of theoretical principles. Above all, it undertakes to apply reason to the irrational, with difficulty inducing it to drop its subterfuges, while conceding the vulnerabilities of reason and respecting the vitality of the irrational. Psychoanalysis, therefore, is hard to learn and hard to practice. It lends itself to caricature and to dilution. At its best, however, it can raise human beings engaged in its pursuit, either as patient or analyst, to a pinnacle of humanity. This, too, I hope is in the novel.

The scientific discoveries of psychoanalysis can be, and have been, reported in the scientific literature where they have encountered more than their share of controversy; the art of psychoanalysis can be conveyed in case reports, taught in seminars, and exemplified in supervision. But there is still another task. It is, as Lewis Mumford said of another novel, to "achieve the deep integrity of that double vision which sees with both eyes—the scientific eye of actuality and the illuminated eye of imagination and dream."

Psychoanalysis deserves this effort, and this novel is that attempt.

A Note to My Psychoanalytic Colleagues and My Patients

To my psychoanalytic colleagues I need to say that no matter how true to psychoanalysis I have tried to be, portrayed in this novel is my version based on my experience and subject to my limitations. I can only hope that these limitations are not so crippling that they will be unable to see their own experience in what they read. In the unlikely event that some might think they catch a glimpse of themselves in these pages, let them think of it as looking into a fun house distorting mirror. The image belongs to the mirror and its inventor and not to the world of objective truth. But like all fictional creations, they are shaped as they are in order to carry forward the meaning and purpose of the work, that, like all fiction, seeks to bring into being its own version of truth.

To my patients—past, present, and future—I need to say that I have not knowingly depicted any patient or revealed any confidences. In whatever mysterious way the raw material of experience is refined and newly minted in the creative act, I can attest that what emerged from my pen over the years I wrote this novel often surprised me by its novelty. In a true sense, my patients inspired this novel but do not exist in its pages. They were the muse, but not the material.

List of Characters

The Analysands	in Analysis with	and Married to
Emily Patterson	Paul Dreyfus	---
Frances Dreyfus	Victor Kleinman	Paul Dreyfus
Marlena Kleinman*	Bernard Freeman*	Victor Kleinman
Serey Potmose	Greta Denkman	Michael Potmose
Victor Kleinman	Kurt Denkman	Marlena Kleinman
Paul Dreyfus*	Josef Fouchault*	Frances Dreyfus
Donald Prescott*	Paula Veroff*	Ruthie Prescott

*training analysis

Others referred to: Allan Fabrikant, a researcher; "Rupi" Rupenthal, a training analyst; Chuck, president of the institution; Betty, Chuck's wife.

The Argument

The action in this novel takes place in a large psychiatric institution located in an eastern Tennessee city during the sixties. The place is undergoing an upheaval because a new director of research is being sought. There is a strong internal candidate, Dr. Victor Kleinman, who is a psychoanalyst and gifted theoretician. He is supported by most but not all the psychoanalysts, and opposed by most researchers who see him as knowing nothing about research. The politics surrounding this search weave in and out of the seven psychoanalyses that comprise the main action.

Part One

Emily Patterson
and
Paul Dreyfus

1

Out the window was a small parking lot.
He could see his old beat-up Chevy
With the rocking chair front seat, rusted floor.
It got him around, he thought, a starchy pride
Stiffening an otherwise ordinary boast.
She was silent again, her pouf of hair
Hiding her small peaked face, button eyes, thin lips.
There was something of the Japanese wrestler
In her posture, walk—short, stocky, full-chested.
Her small wistful face out of proportion
With her deep chest, full thighs, thick calves, large feet.
There it was, he thought, a classic body type—
(He knew "classic" was not quite the word, but—)
Her head too small to manage that wild body,
Her eyes bewildered by the sweep below
Of breast, belly, muscle and genital.
("Paradoxical"—that was much better.)
He sensed his annoyance and impatience.
His eyes swept along the figure on the couch.

"Last night I met this guy at a party.
Real neat. And I said to myself, 'Oh, no—
Not again.' I decided I'd better leave.
So I left with Gloria. We went to my place
And talked and talked—you know—nothing talk.

I asked her about this guy. Surprise! Surprise!
She had slept with him. Leave it to Gloria!
I'm going to go out with him tomorrow night.
This is terrible isn't it? I don't change,
Do I . . . ? My mother called again last night
Before I went to the party. She was drunk
Or drugged up. But so loving. I cried
When she told me Dad had cursed her out again.
I just had to get away from all that!
Well that's the way it has to go, I suppose."

"*Has* to go?"

              "I don't know why I said that.
Really. It just came out—has to go. . . .
Tomorrow I start grading stupid papers—
Moron kids. How can anyone help them!"

"Please tell me more about the moron kids."

"Sweet, lovable, maddening, lazy and dumb."
The adjectives tumbled out innocently.
And once again she fell abruptly silent.

He considered his options, his tactics:
She wishes to be loved, not challenged. True.
But behind that is such unhappiness,
A drunken mother, a cruel father . . . or—
Her own madcap versions of her parents.
She paints in broad strokes, unsubtle colors.

"I'm getting tense. I can feel it all over.
My neck, shoulders, gut, even my legs."

"What comes to mind about that?"

                         "Nothing at all.
Just tense. This couch is uncomfortable.
Sags in the middle. This analysis
Breaks my back!" She guffawed, an explosive
Violent laugh.

                "What thoughts occur to you?"

"Nothing . . . nothing . . . at all. Just a bad joke.
Actually, the couch is really O.K."

Is she ready for an interpretation?
Or is it still too soon—just three weeks
Since she began. His thoughts turned to Fouchault,
Soft-spoken Fouchault. His smooth interpretations
That eased into his mind out of nowhere
Yet fit, clarified, resolved yet troubled
Like a thrown rock leaving patterned ripples
On the surface while stirring the bottom.
He had to be careful, his first patient.
She troubled him. Sensuous waves pulsed
Forth from her, enveloping him, stirring
Feelings, yearnings that clouded his insights.
He struggled like a swimmer to reach shore,
To escape that strange, fluid uncertainty
She drew him into, so that words seemed feeble
To contend against her wayward surges.

"What thoughts occur to you about your silence?"
A safe and useful way to mark time.

"Nothing—except I know I should talk more.
Doctor Dreyfus, I'm not happy with my life.
I'm young, not bad to look at, talented.
But I'm wasting away—just like spilt milk
Pouring out all over the floor, while I—I starve.

That's how it feels."

"Spilt milk? Your thoughts?"

"You know, don't cry over spilt milk. Don't cry.
No self-pity. That's why I'm in analysis.
I had this dream last night. So many dreams
Since starting here! I was hiding in a tree,
Feeling the leaves tickle my face, looking
Down at a rabbit munching on lettuce.
Then there were many rabbits, large and small,
Racing around. It became exciting.
The tree started to shake like in a storm.
Rain began whipping my cheeks, my body—
And then I woke up all sweaty, frightened.
I don't like such dreams. They seem such a waste."

"What led you to recall your dream just then?"

"I don't know. It just popped into my head.
When I was a kid I hated climbing.
I envied the kids who monkeyed up trees
And even walls. Oh, I longed to look down
On things from a window, or a hilltop . . .
Rabbits disgust me. Not cuddly at all.
They're little frightened trembly machines.
I saw a Spanish hunting movie once—
Horrible!—These men sent ferrets after them,
Snaky creatures that could squeeze down rabbit holes.
They'd grab the rabbits by the neck, bring them down,
While they made these awful screechy sounds.
These ferrets would land right on their hunched backs
And tear them apart, while the men smoked their
    pipes.
I know where I got that silly dream from!
Last night I saw this mouse scurry by me

As I went to the john down the dark hall.
Scared me for a minute. What a relief!"

"What was the relief?"

"Turned out to be a mouse."

"The relief doesn't also apply to the dream?"

"I don't think so. Why should it? What do you think?"

Questions! *My* patients ask *me* questions! he thought.
They don't reflect, associate . . . I bet my wife
Makes a better patient for that Kleinman.
He felt a dull throbbing in his chest
Like an answer to an unasked question.
"You woke up frightened from the dream, sweaty.
Perhaps you wish to go no further with it
Because something distresses you about it."

"I don't know what you're getting at, really.
Is there something more you want me to say?
I'm getting tense again and so shaky.
I wish sometimes you had a blanket here—
I'm like a rabbit—and you're the ferret!"

He felt uneasy, excited, challenged.
A clear, obvious transference remark.

"How am I the ferret?"

"You ferret things out,
Don't you? That's neat!" She laughed explosively.
"Yesterday I saw Tom again. He's sick,
Lonely, wants me to move in with him. Hell,
I can't take his sweetness, his pain, his sadness.

He's like a velvet pillow, soft and cozy.
Why can't I stand him?" She arched her body
Momentarily, sank back, fidgeted.

A ferret and a velvet pillow, he thought,
The rabbit and the deadly predator.
She changes her aspect like the hornéd moon—
Shakespeare? No. Maybe Keats. Yes, possibly.
And he must change to the opposing twin.

"Down this hall from me is this bright young kid.
I love to tease him. He's all books and term
Papers. I'm sure he's a virgin. Often
I fantasy undressing him as he reads,
Telling him to keep on reading, as I
Remove his shirt, one sleeve then the other
Very gently. Then I unbuckle his belt,
Zip down his fly, lift one leg then the other,
Slip off his pants. And he doesn't miss a word.
Untie his shoes, ease them off quietly—
On he reads. I draw his socks off by the toes,
Slowly. Finally I tilt him gently
To one side and slide his shorts half down.
His ass begins to show. It gets exciting.
I tilt him the other way. Pull his shorts
Down all the way. He's naked. Then I leave.
He's still reading. I never see his penis. . . .
Oh, I'm getting to feel restless, cranky.
Say something to me! Are you still back there?"
She suddenly turned her head and looked at him,
Her face, not angry, but frightened, tear streaked.
She turned back.

                    "I'm sorry. That's a no-no."

"What prompted you to look around?"

                                     "Like I
Said—are you still there? I get to feel so—
Forlorn . . . floating out to nowhere at all.
Where am I heading? Tell me. Where? Today
I bought a kite—just on impulse. Haven't
Done that since I was a kid. Watched it loop,
Lift off, tug at the string like something alive.
It didn't want me to hold it back. I—
Why am I crying, Dr. Dreyfus—why?
A silly kite. I felt like opening my hand,
Letting it go free. But I couldn't. No.
A fierce anger took hold of me instead.
I tugged hard at the string. It nosed downward,
Went into a spiraling dive and crashed.
A kid ran over and brought it back to me.
The spine was cracked, the paper ripped. I cried.
What is the matter with me! . . . My damn mother!
She kept my picture hanging on the wall.
Stupid picture—How I hated, hated it!
I was seven, in a pink polka dot dress,
Holding a bouquet of flowers, smiling—
Smiling like an idiot—my front teeth gone.
If you look close you'll see I'm crying—
Really—'Oh, how sweet dear Emily looks!'
All of them in front of me—laughing, smirking.
'Now smile Emily, do smile. Oh, look at
Those missing teeth!' I'd burst into tears.
'No! No! Emily—no tears. Smile, atta girl!'
My mother, father, brother and sister
Making me feel like a pet poodle on
Parade! And she wouldn't even take it down.
There it hung year after year. Oh, how I'd
Scheme to steal it or hide it or break it.
But I couldn't. It would mesmerize me
As if it were a—reincarnation!
Often I'd go up to it when no one

Was around and kiss the tears only I saw.
'Emily, I'd say, sweet Emily, be
Patient. Your teeth will grow back in.
I know. When I was older I'd go up
Smiling and show my teeth to her, saying,
'See, sweet Emily, they've all come back in now!'
I'd cry for her, sweet Emily, as I'm doing
Now. And I'm twenty-seven, Dr. Dreyfus.
I don't know where this is all leading. Please
Say something."

What could he or should he say?
She was talking better now than earlier.
Freeman encouraged facilitation
Not interpretation early in treatment.
Facilitate.

"You expect something from me?"

She turned her head toward the wall and sighed.
She was silent again. He felt uneasy.
It hadn't worked. Emily's thoughts turned
Toward tomorrow—Saturday—and her new date.

"It's time for us to stop."

She rose slowly,
Smoothing her bodice over her heavy breasts
And left, saying, "Good-bye" in her sweet voice.

2

She arrived, her sweet smile in place, her perfume
Stating a fact as real as her name and age.
Someday it would need to be analyzed,
He thought. It was a communication
After all, he thought further. But of what?
The sweet smell of hate—the phrase jarred him loose
From his thoughts which were drawing him inward
Toward his querulous obsession with craft.

"Good morning, Dr. Dreyfus. I hope you're fine.
I'm feeling fine, except for coming here.
Odd how coming here makes me feel nervous,
What's the saying, 'As nervous as a bride?'
Just yesterday I was telling Gloria
How I cried on Friday—real tears and you know
I can't remember over what! Crazy!
Absolutely crazy! Do you recall,
Dr. Dreyfus, what I cried about . . . ? Oh, well,
Today's another day. . . . This is so strange,
My lying here, not seeing you and talking.
I feel like a record turning round and round.
You put the needle on at the beginning
And fifty minutes later you take it off.
I bet you think I'm a broken record—
The needle gets stuck and I go on and on,

Saying the same thing . . . doing the same thing."

Her voice trailed off. He heard the ominous
Overtones in the last phrase. She acted out
No doubt. Freeman's lips would be thinner
When he was told about this later today.
Tuesday was not a day for supervision.
He liked it better on Friday, wrapping
Up the week and plowing ahead on Monday.

"Yesterday I got a call from my brother.
Imogene is pregnant again—their fourth.
Can you imagine being pregnant? I can't.
Who needs it. Don't get me wrong. I love kids.
I teach a batch of fourth graders every day.
I love their untouched minds and tell-tale hearts—
They can hide so little . . . not like big old me."

Again her voice trailed off. He heard the broad hint.
He could guess. He would continue to listen.
He felt a stirring of anger toward her.

"My mother said it's best to be knocked out
When you give birth. Too much pain, blood, and stuff.
For me it wouldn't be pain or blood—
No. I would go nuts from the body worry—
What's happening to me? What's happening inside me?
My belly swelling up, my belly button
Inside out. I've seen that on my sister.
The fetus kicking—imagine! Not yet born
And already kicking your guts out of you! Ugh!"

What was she describing, he pondered. Pregnancy?
Maybe. It was also intercourse, he thought,
Violent, body damaging, intercourse.
Listen carefully, he counseled himself.

"Gloria plays Russian roulette with her boyfriends.
She hates the diaphragm. She calls it the
Toilet plunger. The IUD gives her
The creeps—it reminds her of an insect.
Foam you can forget—she hates injections.
And the pill is just too much to remember.
So what's left? Rhythm. And dear old Gloria
Just ain't got rhythm! But she does have luck!
And some of the old-fashioned guys use condoms."

He thought, she was too bright to be so coarse.
It was a price she was paying, or was it
Intended to make him think badly of her?
"You go into such detail about Gloria,"
He finally let himself say, "and you?"

"Me?!" she exclaimed as if that pronoun
Were as irregular as unexpected.
"I use the pill but I'm frightened of it.
You read such horror stories every day,
Heart attacks and strokes, uterine cancer.
It sends shivers up my spine. But then again
The odds are one in a million. Better
Odds than crossing the street. It makes it all
So natural. It's like taking an aspirin
Daily so you won't get a headache. Does
That answer your question? I'm not Gloria.
Dumb, yes. Crazy, no. . . . It was so hard to sleep
Last night. I felt things crawling in my bed,
Like bed bugs, or beetles—horrid! In fact
I got up, put on the light, and looked. Nothing
Of course. . . . Maybe a bread crumb or two. I love
To eat in bed and read—a big sandwich
And a Coke. . . . Falling asleep is such a
Lonely thing. So quiet and dark. No one
Around. At home it was always lively

To all hours—radio on, telephone ringing,
Parents carrying on in the kitchen.
Now it's like going to sleep with snow falling
All around you in a dark forest, quiet
And cold . . . not weather cold, but lonely cold.
I can shiver from loneliness, my teeth chattering
And goose pimples like hives all over me."

Paul stirred uneasily, Saturday night,
His own cold season of the heart. And here?
He stared at his dusty shoes and glowered—
When are they going to fix that walk out front!
Of course, he could walk around it on the grass.
But he always forgot—dust unto dust.
What in heaven's name led him to these thoughts!
The final comeuppance—leveled with the earth.
Nothing fancy anymore, just flat out.
Eternity taken on your broken back.

"Sometimes in here I feel utterly alone
As if you had tiptoed out quietly
Because you find me so boring. And when
You don't say anything for a long time
I want to say, 'Are you still there?' . . . Are you?"

Paul shifted in his chair, setting both feet
On the floor and coughed.

                        "I guess you're still there.
After all," and she fell silent.

                        His office
Came into full view like in a wide angle shot
As he drew his eyes away from her,
Taut and rigid on the couch, and looked up

Toward the door with its crazy wooden Rorschach
    grain,
And then to the bookcase alongside, pennants
Of bright color waving from the book jackets,
The gaiety of their colors belying
Their somber contents, the desk cluttered like
A workman's bench with the odd paraphernalia
Of the intellect: doodled pads, broken—
Pointed pencils, scrambled stacks of notes,
Incomplete drafts, message scraps and an orange
Left over from lunch, a paper cup empty
And doodled over like a tattooed body.
The humiliating clutter of his mind
Fully visible, he thought. How could he help her,
He, of all people, picking his way, nose up,
Through a garbage dump where wild fantasies
Jerked up from behind tin cans and bottles
Like marionettes with dirty, pock-marked faces?
He blamed her. She dragged him down. Where
    would she
Lead him, this wild lost staring innocent?
Her tangled soul and gaudy mask were too much
For him. These were fevered impressions only;
How could he cool them into interpretations
That could bring her turpitude into awareness
And free her from her baroque excitements.
Paul's eyes returned to the figure on the couch.
She had not stirred.

                    " 'The enemy is ourselves.'
I read that somewhere, Dr. Dreyfus. 'The
Enemy is ourselves.' That sounds exactly
Right. One time I thought I'd throw myself off
A bridge. I had looked down and saw myself
Shimmering like in a distorting mirror
At the fair. My whole self was wavy, murky,

The outline blurry. My God, I thought, that's me
Down there. I'm not up here at all. Up here
Is just a cut-out. Down there is the real me.
I felt such an urge to toss the cut-out
Me into the river where it would be
Spun around and crumpled and carried off
Leaving that other shimmering me in charge.
It would not be death but resurrection.
I can't stand my cut-out self! It walks, talks,
Works, makes love, wets its pants, cries 'Momma,
    Momma'
Just like those Christmas dolls for little girls
Who have everything. I loathe my life, hate it
With a true passion. How did it happen to me?
How did it ever. . . . Tom and I went out
For a beer Sunday night. I looked at him
And cried. He thinks the world of me—this cutout.
Where does he come off doing that! No thanks.
He asked me why I was crying. I said that beer
Makes me sentimental. He shrugged and looked
    down. . . .
He was such a quiet guy. We danced far
Apart, he looking over my shoulder,
I trying to draw him out. But he was so
Preoccupied, I finally said, 'Who
Are you dancing with?' He was startled into
Looking squarely at me and said, 'Dana,
That's who.' And then totally flustered, he
Blushed, began apologizing and stopped
Dancing. 'How do you know *my* middle name
Isn't Dana,' I said, making a little joke.
He brightened up, 'Is it really,' he said
In a high-pitched, boy's voice. God, I thought,
He was probably a kid. But he wasn't!
He told me all about Dana and as
He did so, he fell a little in love

With me. Or so I thought. Don't you think that
Happens between people, like with that powder
In *A Midsummer Night's Dream*, wake up in love
And you'll love whoever first comes your way.
His eyes glistened and he moistened his lips
As he talked rapidly about Dana
This and Dana that. How I longed to be her.
I wanted to see a picture of her
But he didn't have one. He said
Pictures lied. I invited him to my place
For some coffee and a nightcap. By now
He was bubbling with Dana and I was
Green with envy and getting short of breath
Which I do when I get anxious. He was
Telling me how Dana made love, shyly,
Only in the dark and always partly dressed.
'How silly,' I said. I *heard* myself, I did,
Dr. Dreyfus. I began to see his game.
But why all this build up, this shaggy dog
Story—just to make me? Just to screw me?
I felt like going to sleep, but he wouldn't leave,
So we made love and then I went to sleep."

Sleep, he thought, is the opiate of the asses.
God, he was angry with her and with himself.
Why the latter, he wasn't sure. And the former?
He wasn't sure either. Of only one thing
Was he sure. The time was up for the session.
As she left she had trouble with the door,
Pushing it closed when she meant to open it.

3

His research had absorbed him utterly
Until it was time to see Emily
That hour. It had been all statistics—
The brute boring drudgery of science.
But Paul had welcomed its minutiae
As relief from all the crowded feelings
Elbowing each other for his attention.
Some had to do with Emily. One had
Only to be quiet, he told himself.
He called for his patient. She had not come yet.
He sat down to wait while his mind returned
To the figures which were beginning to tell
An interesting story, or so he thought.
Always the doubt, the worm in the apple.
Had he overlooked something important?
A decimal, like a rabbit dropping,
In the wrong place can destroy a finding
Greeted with great joy the day before, or
A certain control had not been thought of,
A step left out by mistake. He had learned
To his distress that science, or at least
His science, was a crippled, hunchbacked beast,
Half-blind, squinting effortfully at things
Well beyond its gaze, dimly making out
A vague shape, too quickly given a name.

Psychoanalysis was such a beast too,
Hiding its infirmities—or were they
Only his own? A pain clutched at his heart.
He was a failure. And then he rebelled
At the thought. Not for him the abandoned
Prose of the clinical writers inflating
A few observations into a theory,
The theory into demonstrated fact,
And thus psychoanalysis rose up—
A rickety tower of fact and fiction
From which bright guild pennants flew, hiding the
    flaws.
The foundation must be deep, solid, strong,
The structure itself sturdy, otherwise—
A house of cards like those he made and blew down
As a kid. . . . He was getting nowhere, nowhere
In his analysis. Maybe no one
Really knew how to do it. Maybe Fouchault
Was as lost as he was with Emily.
Sure, you can always be silent. John Wayne
Made a career of that. Silence, the first
And last refuge of the stumped analyst.
He knew better. He had to know better.
A tremor of panic made itself felt
A moment before the thought: where was she?
She had quit, that's what! Had quit him flat!
The clutching pain returned. To lose a case,
That would raise his stock in the Institute.
Dreyfus loses case. Cash in your chips, stranger,
The game is over for you. But it's the only
Game in town and I'm in deep. The phone!
He jumped across the desk to pick it up.
It was Emily. "I'm awfully sorry,
Dr. Dreyfus. I can't explain on the phone.
Be there in fifteen minutes." That would leave
About twenty minutes. His mind raced ahead

And behind the reasons for her lateness.
Last hour? She had been used by a man again.
But she invited it. Look at those creeps,
She was saying, and me innocent, yearning
For love, being tricked, deceived instead.
Yes, and the analysis? Same goddamned thing!
What was she getting from me? Boiled potatoes,
That's what, served up cold, all eyes and no mouth.
The lateness? A despairing protest. But I
Was what she deserved—to be mocked, laughed at,
Like her family did over her missing teeth.
Missing, missing—women missing and men
Holding on for dear life—'Hold on, stranger,
Don't get your balls in an uproar!' He grinned
Fiercely at the unforeseen admonition.
What made him such a stranger? But he was
A stranger. Hadn't he said so to Fouchault,
Even though jokingly? In Zigmundland no jokes.
The truth may duck and hide but it will out
At the seams. How did Freud put it? Lock up
Your lips and the truth will ooze from your pores?
He suddenly felt kidnapped by his thoughts—
Soon she will be here. He must free himself.
A curious resolve had settled itself
In his mind. Fuck Freeman! Fuck facilitation!
Hadn't Fouchault told him he had understood
His patient? He thinks he does at that. So—
The phone rang. She was here and on her way.
Paul's courage dwindled as he recalled his
Mutinous ways in the face of loneliness.
The word caught him in the midriff. No time
To wonder further, but a great sadness
Was loosed in him like a dark feathered presence.

"Dr. Dreyfus, can you ever forgive me?
You won't once I tell you what I did, I—

I—forgot and then remembered and
Then I didn't want to come—ever again.
I was in Grand Park when I remembered.
And then I felt sick. Still plenty of time
To get here . . . just . . . just . . . impossible.
My feet wouldn't take me here. I sat rooted
To the spot—this bench I was sitting on
Next to this zonked wino mumbling in his cups.
I found myself trying to listen, God knows why.
The only words I could make out were names—
Billy and Susannah. He said 'Susannah'
In a special way—drawing out the 'Su'
And the 'ah.' Was he, Billy, and Susannah
A girl friend or even a wife? Oh! then . . .
I can't . . . it was dreadful. I mean I was . . .
Wanting to be that Susannah so my name
Could be drawled so . . . lovingly. I fled from
That bench, glanced at my watch, and found a phone."

Paul thought back on the call, "This is Emily
Patterson. Dr. Dreyfus?" Their two names,
Male and female. But that feathered sadness
Lifted him above these cunning details
And he saw the whole aching plain of being—
Her being and his under a grueling sun,
Merciless, as it enunciated
Every syllable leaving nothing
To the reticence of shadows. Paul said,
"How hard to have your weaknesses revealed
Here for me to see, and yet how fearful
Not to come and have your weaknesses
Demean you."

                    Emily broke into tears
Which gushed from her eyes. At first she tried
Staunching them with a Kleenex. It was as if

The limp Kleenex was swept away
By a torrent. She gave over to her tears,
The Kleenex falling to the floor.
                                    "Really,
Dr. Dreyfus, you are not furious
With me? I wasn't going to come . . .
I wasn't . . . I couldn't take it anymore . . .
I was wasting your time . . . same old story . . . "

"How is it the same old story?"

                              "I don't know
Really . . . except it feels that way. Always
Something wrong about me and I don't know why . . .
Never that one thing for me I need . . . no.
But why should I expect it anyway?
What am I going on about?"

                              "No idea?"
"Well, that kite. I get a picture of that kite.
Funny that was also in the park, that kite
I bought on impulse and broke, God knows why.
It's all so mixed up . . . like a crazy dream."

"The kite was doing fine. . . . "

                              "Until I jerked it—
I know . . . I did it . . . I had to . . . sappy kite.
Do you believe what I just remembered?
Of course, a park! I ran away from home,
You know, like little kids do when they're hurt
Because no one understands them? No one did.
It was summer, no school and I wanted
To stay up. But Mom sent me up to bed.
I never protested. I was too good
For that. I smiled, went up and then sneaked out.

Smart work for an eight year old—and I wasn't
Coming back. That night had been the last straw.
My Mom just didn't want me underfoot
While she sat drinking and dreaming of her youth
Or something. Dad was always fixing the car.
He'd shoo me off because I'd get dirty
And, 'Your mother wouldn't like that. So git!'
Can an eight year old hate and feel so rotten
They just don't want to be? I guess so. When I
Ran off I was just glad to be away
From all that. It was still broad daylight out.
In the park older kids were playing, even
Some kids my own age with nicer mothers.
Adults were strolling and young people were
Lolling on the grass, couples half-playing,
Half-serious. They puzzled me. Sometimes
An older woman would look me over
As if trying to place me, following
Me with her eyes. I just stepped away, happy
To be out. Soon enough I found a friend,
Older, who I wasn't supposed to play with
Because he was nasty and foul-mouthed.
He was surprised to see me out so late
And I fibbed, saying my father was with me,
Off talking with friends somewhere in the park.
Bruno didn't much care in any case.
After awhile it started to get dark
And Bruno boasted how he didn't have
To go home but I did. I stuck out my tongue,
Boasting back that I didn't either—so there!
I added for good measure that my father
Wasn't there either. He was impressed with that.
Finally, he said, 'Em, let's be secret spies.
You'll see, it's fun.' I had no idea
What he had in mind. But it was thrilling
To be included by Bruno. I asked him

How we played the secret spy game. He said,
'Em, lots of secrets everywhere. Just watch.'
And he disappeared into a bank
Of dense bushes, waving for me to follow.
I did to find Bruno flat on the ground,
With his finger to his lips and pointing
With his other hand through the thick bushes.
I could barely make out two figures, one
On top of the other, moving furiously.
I was suddenly very frightened and wanted
Desperately to run. At the same time
I was glued to the spot, unable to move.
I could see how the man was on the woman,
Shoving at her and her head was twisted
To the side like a doll with a busted neck.
Bruno whispered, 'They're screwing!' 'They're what?'
    I asked.
'You know, screwing, fucking! Making babies.'
I knew my face was all red and I had
Difficulty breathing. I was getting sick,
But still my eyes remained glued to the scene.
I didn't so much as blink. Why was he shoving
So hard at her? Then I saw he was
Shoving something into her, but I didn't
See where it was going. Everytime
He pushed she moved up and moaned.
He was jamming something inside her,
Hurting her, but she was liking it. Why?
Making babies? When I looked at Bruno
He had his penis in his hand. It was
Stiff. I broke from the bushes and ran as fast
As I could with tears streaming down my face."

Paul glanced unhappily at the small clock
On his bookcase. It was past time to stop.
"We must continue next time," he said softly.

She rose slowly from the couch, a bewildered
Look on her face. She left without looking back.
He picked up the wet crumpled Kleenex and
Deposited it gently on his desk.

4

Paul sat fidgeting at his desk, sipping
Stale coffee from a Styrofoam cup, biting
The crisp edge as he tried to read his notes
From the previous session. Gibberish.
He could not make head or tail of them although
He had written them down right afterwards.
His mind was an utter blank. He could recall
Nothing. For a terrifying moment
He imagined it was a brain tumor
Or tertiary syphilis. Had he not
Once had a chancre at seventeen?
Strange, because he was still a virgin then.
But who really knows how syphilis spreads.
He bit through the edge, spilling coffee down
His chin and onto his shirt and tie. He rose
Angrily from his desk, pitching the torn cup
On the floor, grabbing a fistful of napkins
And blotting up the coffee draining down
His tie. "Slop-pot," he hissed, fuming at himself.
He slumped into the deep chair behind the couch,
Glanced at his watch and groaned—four minutes only
Before he must call for her and then what?
Back onto the high wire without a balance bar.
He shut his eyes, breathed deeply and cupped his
    hands

Over his eyes. He found the cupped darkness restful
At such times. There was no comfort in things
Or people. Only in sleep or the dark
Shell of sleep. When he called for his patient
Dreyfus had calmly sunk into a grim state.

Emily entered briskly, a frown on her face
Rather than the usual sweet fixed smile.
And once settled on the couch, she announced:
"I'm feeling better, Doctor Dreyfus, and
I don't know why. How do you explain it?"

Paul almost lost his balance, but managed:
"In what way have you been feeling better?"

"About myself mainly. I've had more zip
And much less interest in sleeping around.
Maybe I'm growing up. But it's confusing.
That's why I wanted you to tell me why.
What happened last time? I left very sad,
But about what? I can't remember much
Of what I said. You were very nice somehow.
Oh! That's right! I was late. No! That wasn't it.
I didn't want to come. Yes. That was it.
And you weren't angry. You were very nice—"
Emily broke off because she was crying
And with the tears came clear remembrance.

"Why was I always alone, Doctor Dreyfus?
What brought me back to the hour was
Loneliness. That tramp, even he had someone
On his lips—'Su-san-nah.' Damn, damn. 'Su-san-nah.'
Why not 'Em-i-ly'? So I came back here ...
To you. . . ." Emily's voice broke again as she
Struggled to continue. "I'm not a
Happy person, Doctor Dreyfus. I'm a

Frightened person, if you must know, really
Frightened. Sometimes literally—of things . . .
So many I can't count 'em. Insects, snakes,
And . . . and . . . merry widows—I mean black widows,
Those awful things. That's not all, Doctor Dreyfus,
I'm a terrible sex fiend—I'm awful
About it. I have a love–hate relationship
With sex. . . . God! Last time! I told you, didn't I,
About that time in the park? Those couples . . .
Why is it all so eerie—like twilight?
You know that park when night comes on, it was
Scary for me. Everything changes itself.
Or that's what I thought for the longest time.
That day-time things changed into night-time things.
They only looked the same but they weren't.
And when I was very young I even thought
People changed. Their voices got darker, lower
And their faces also got darker—fuzzier.
But they were always clumping up at night.
People clump up together when it's dark.
And it gets hard to tell who's who. The sun,
Doctor Dreyfus, keeps things clear and separate.
I prefer it that way . . . I do chatter on
When I feel good. Don't mind me. Doctor Dreyfus,
I had a dream about you last night, the first one.
You were rowing on a dark lake only
I couldn't see the boat, only your arms
Moving back and forth. Very muscular arms.
Although I couldn't see your face I knew
Somehow it was you. I waved and waved and waved
But you kept on rowing. Except I
Could see your eyes clearer and clearer like two
Fires burning into me as I waved.
Of course rowing reminds me of the park.
You were like a ghost on the water,
Especially those eyes . . . moving your arms

Back and forth. . . ." And Emily became silent.

Paul found it hard to credit her report
That she was feeling better. She seemed
As scattered as ever. No doubt it was
Some flight into health. He wished the hour
Were over and he could lie down himself
On the couch to rest. The dream did intrigue him.
Certainly the transference was taking
Since there he was in the dream, or perhaps
It was the transference neurosis itself
Beginning. Highly unlikely he thought.
What he felt mainly was her loneliness
And his own bitter bereft condition.
Again the tormented doubting of his own
Ability to manage this cosmos
In perfect miniature called analysis.
This Lilliputian stage on which Gullivers
Innocently destroyed all proportion.
What Gulliver was in this dream? Himself?
But who in fact was he? Muscular arms
Moving back and forth? Fiery eyes burning?
He wished she would free associate more:
"What else occurs to you about the dream?"

"Why do I get so tense when you say something?
I want you so to talk but when you do
I get so nervous I could scream. . . . The dream?
I was off thinking of something else—that guy
I met awhile ago—his girlfriend's name
Was Dana? The one who worked me over?
He made love like a marionette! All jerky,
In spasms as if he were having a fit.
I wanted him out of me real quick."

                                        Paul

Knew she was angry at him; instead her anger
Fastened on this stand-in. He had missed something
Still another time. Almost desperately
He addressed her loneliness, "In the dream
I am leaving you without waving back.
How do you feel in the dream?"

                                        "Scared, lonely."

"Yes?"

                "Yes, what? I don't know what else to say.
It's the same old story. I don't need to dream it."

"You were saying the dream reminds you
Of the park. But there are two different parks,
The recent one you were just recalling
And the other one from the past—the one you were
Talking about last time."
                                Emily placed
An arm across her eyes. "You mean with Bruno?
The time I felt so overlooked at home
I snuck off into the park at night looking
For company and wanting them to miss me?
I sure found company with Bruno! Well, they
Never missed me. But I'm feeling good now.
I don't care about the dream except for you
Being in it. Something about fiery eyes
That reminds me about here ... yeh ... because
Here it's only your voice. I see you a bit
At the start and at the end. Only your voice ...
I don't want to think anymore about that ...
Unless you want me to."

                                That's great, he thought,
An analyst who gives instructions! "You are

Obviously thinking of something but
Afraid to say it," he ventured.

                    Emily
Began humming a tune he thought he knew.
It was *Melancholy Baby*. To the point.

"Doctor Dreyfus, is it really possible
To talk about sex here? I mean not just
Telling about it, but really *talking*
About it—like two adults . . . man-to-man?"

Paul flushed, noted the man-to-man, but waited.
She went on, "The fact is I do have feelings
About you. Those arms in the dream aroused me.
And I think of you at the oddest times.
The other day in the park I wished you
Had been there with me. I wanted *you*
To be on the bench alongside of me
Instead of that wino. It was so nice out.
The sun was shining. You could count the leaves
On every tree. The wind was playing tag
With scraps of paper, rustling them about.
And I wanted to be on somebody's lips,
Alive instead of dead weight coming here,
Lying down and talk, talk, talk about me
And all my insufferable troubles.
Why did I think it was so terrible
To want you there with me in the park that day?
But I did. Once I had that daydream I . . . I
Fled the park. And one thought kept pounding,
    pounding
In my head—I must kill myself, kill myself.
I ran here as fast as I could go.
I expected you to throw me out not
Just for being late but for wanting you."

Emily clasped her hands over her abdomen
And Paul noticed how white her fingers became.

"It looks like you seek . . . a loving response
From those who always seem to turn you down.
When you were a kid, from your parents like
In that memory, and from Bruno who
Exposed you to frightening things, and from me now.
It makes you feel so lonely and worthless."
Paul had weighed his words. He now felt uneasy.

Emily unclasped her hands and placed them
Palms up alongside her body. Paul thought,
A mute appeal. Then the wild idea
That the stigmata would appear in those palms.

"I *am* worthless, Doctor Dreyfus. I'm sullied
From head to toe."

Paul frowned at her somber words
Said flatly as if describing the weather.
He signaled to Emily that the hour was up.

5

Outside Paul's window the sun was dipping west.
It was a hot, high summer day, blistering
The soft pavement in the parking lot. Paul sat
At his desk, strewn with discarded attempts
At finishing a diagnostic report
On a schizophrenic patient. His heart
Was not in it. At two he would be seeing
Patterson. His heart was not in that either.
Where was his heart these days, he mused vaguely.
Gone hunting in the highlands came the response,
The phrase utterly meaningless to him.
Ah, yes! Bobbie Burns. *My Heart's in the Highlands.*
Have I read it? Should have. Oh, for the mountains!
The cool, high, distant imperturbable mountains!
They doan know nofin', they just keep pilin'
Up high. He hated his thoughts when they turned
Wry and facetious. Something for Fouchault
The master analyst to figure out.
Soon Patterson—why suddenly "Patterson"?
His mind closed on that question. He noted
It was time to call her.

                           She was wearing
A fluffy sweater, baby blue, and a tight
Dark blue skirt. She could hardly move in it,

Making her way to the couch with hobbled steps.
His heart sank. More lurid escapades. More
Acting out to account for. She just wasn't
A good analytic patient. He was stuck.
Yeh! And neither was he, come to think of it,
Was his next derisive thought. So, baby,
You and I are in the same boat—and her dream
Of last session came back: he was in the boat
Alone. With growing discomfort, he saw
How he was fighting his own attraction
To her by casting in his lot with hers:
They were both poor, unhelpable patients.
No veiled and sinuous Salomé was she,
Nor he a gawking, scheming Hadrian—
(Was it Hadrian or another name?)
Always a tail end of doubt attached itself.

"I did something, Doctor Dreyfus, I haven't
Done in a long time. I got stupid drunk
All by myself in my room with the phone
Off the hook. I was going to get stinko.
And no one was going to disturb me.
Straight vodka. Goes down like water. You're bombed
Before you know it. I had tests to grade
And I was supposed to call my mother—
Something about going up for a visit.
Fat chance! I won't visit that asylum—
My father polishing the car, my mother
Watching TV as she sips her brandy
Watered down a bit so it takes an evening
For her to get crocked. But that's not what
I want to talk about. It's the treatment—
It's getting to me. One minute I want
To quit and the next I want to be here
More than any place else in the whole world.
You know, Doctor Dreyfus, I've lost interest

In all other men. I got blotto last night
Because I had to stop thinking about you.
I can't believe this!"

                       Paul drew in a sudden
Breath of air involuntarily, almost
Giddy with the opportunity opening up
For working on her transference feelings.
But a familiar sinking feeling forewarned
Of gross ineptitude, of likely failure.
His eyes seemed caught in the fluffy tangle
Of her baby blue sweater.

                    "As I got drunk,
I reasoned with myself. 'Now, Emily,
You're stuck on Doctor Dreyfus because he's nice
To you, doesn't get angry, or try to
Make you. That's all it is.' As I got drunker
I thought, 'But why doesn't he try to make you?
I've heard of doctors getting it on with their
Patients. A real big no-no, but it happens.
Not Doctor Dreyfus, no, not Doctor Dreyfus.—
He's such a powerful character, so righteous—
A man of unassailable integrity.'
I even started making up a song:
'Unassailable, Unavailable You.'
Didn't get further than the title though.
I zonked out. . . . But I can't say that I blame you
When I think of what I'm really. . . ." And
She interrupted herself.

                    He waited
For her to continue.

                    "No use. No use,
Doctor Dreyfus. The milk is spilt all over

The goddamned floor. Humpty-Dumpty
Can't be put back together again.
It says so in all the nursery rhymes—
And they have more truth in them than
A stack of bibles. 'Goosey, goosey gander,
Whither do you wander? Upstairs and downstairs
And through my lady's chamber.' I always said
'Wan-der' to rhyme with *gander* and never knew
Really what Goosey was doing in her
Lady's chamber." She giggled, her mood changed.

She was transported back to her childhood
Riding a simple Mother Goose broomstick,
He wryly noted.

                    "My father would read
Mother Goose and many other things to me.
I'd sit on his lap while Mom washed the dishes.
I could hear her singing in the kitchen.
I would be a little brat. I'd shout out,
'Stop singing! I can't hear Daddy reading.'
Mom would appear in the kitchen doorway
And reply, 'Have you thought of reading somewhere
Else? When I work I sing.' So Daddy and I
Went upstairs into their big quiet bedroom,
Far from the kitchen. We'd sit at the edge
Of the bed and he'd go on. It was quiet
And so comfortable. I'd fall asleep,
Amazed the next morning to wake up
In my own bed. I missed Daddy's reading
When I got older. We didn't do much
Together after I was about eight.
God! I was chubby back then—fat really.
I was the first to wear a bra in my class.
Not that I was that proud of it, you can bet.
You know, Doctor Dreyfus, I was never,

Never at home in my own body. It just
Grew and grew all around me and I was caught
Inside, wanting so to be little again
Before the chub came on and the big bras.
I so wanted to be a ballet dancer.
Can you imagine me, a ballerina?
More like a cow jumping over the moon . . .
What do men want—of us women, I mean.
I was also thinking that last night, deep
In my cups. Doctor Dreyfus, you're a man—
What do you want of us females anyway?"

Paul was startled by this sudden turnabout
And punted, "There was much on your mind last
    night."

Emily straightened her skirt over her hips,
Sighed and continued, "Was it the vodka,
You think, or did I have a lot on my mind
Anyway and the vodka uncorked it?
You know, I'm still a little high today.
I'm all over the place. You, Daddy, Mom,
Nursery rhymes, getting fat, being a ballerina,
Wanting to know about men and women. . . ."

"What does that all suggest to you?" Paul asked.

"The riddle of the Sphinx! No—I'm kidding.
Somewhere, at some point in my life, sex reared
Its ugly head, only I never thought
It was ugly, just too much to handle . . .
And . . . and something that was not for me. . . . It
Never has been. I've never had . . . a climax,
Close at times, but no cigar. I just can't.
When I thought of you last night I wondered
If with you, I could. But I shrank from the thought.

That would be incest, wouldn't it?"

                              "Incest?
Why incest," Paul wondered aloud, caught
Off balance.

          "I don't know, I don't know.
Except that's what I always thought—incest
Was when you went wild, couldn't stop yourself,
Maybe like 'incessantly.' That word,
'Incest,' it always made my mind go blank.
I know what it means in the dictionary.
That doesn't help. It's like a word in a
Nursery rhyme, like *wander*, or *Humpty*.
Or *Dumpty*, for that matter. What can they mean?
But they mean a lot. Doctor Dreyfus, I'm lost."
Her voice had become high-pitched, shrill, frightened.

Paul wished he were on a mountain looking down
On all this complicated topography
Instead of stumbling on foot along the same paths,
Following close behind as she so often
Changed direction and veered off on a new path.
"You've been lost a long time," he ventured, "longer
Than you can fully remember or care to.
Certainly since you started to get chubby,
But perhaps before then too." God! He heard
Echoes of Fouchault in his speech, its rhythms,
Its tone, and even its phrasing. Better Fouchault
Than Dreyfus right now. "You want me to help you
Welcome sexual excitement, but you fear it
Because I would be the wrong man for you.
And yet you are sorely tempted by the thought.
But also notice how you have lost interest
In all other men. Perhaps other men
Have just been stand-ins, unsatisfying

At that, for the real one who is—how was it?—"

"Unassailable and unavailable?"

Paul felt he had gone too far riding Fouchault's
Coattails. She would see through his playacting
To the perplexed lost soul he really was.

"Do you have any idea how many men
There've been? Don't let me count them up, please
    don't.
But nothing happened. Nothing ever happened.
And I don't want any more of that ever.
So what now, Doctor Dreyfus? What now?"
She said the last vehemently.

                        And Paul
Drew the hour to a close with some sense
Of achievement, borrowed though the power had been.

6

"Sex, Doctor Dreyfus, is my enemy—
Planted right in the middle of my gut.
I fight with my sex drive like a wrestler,
No holds barred, all's fair in love and war.
But I'm always being blind-sided.
I think I've knocked it out of the ring when
It's at me again, pinning me to the mat.
I sometimes wonder if it's just sex, or—
No. What else can it be? Do you mind,
Doctor Dreyfus, if I'm pretty frank with you?
Lay it all out on the table? I mean,
Flat out? You don't have to answer. I know
You're stuck back there with all of your three ears,
So have a good listen. . . ."

                              Emily paused.
He could see tears gathering in her eyes
Silently at odds with her tough guy talk
And the prurient role she had assigned him.
He was on the ropes himself, dodging hooks,
And uppercuts, and wild roundhouse punches
From all directions. Fouchault had the hook,
Right around his guard. He was sure Kleinman
Was aiming an uppercut at his chin,
And Francie was wildly roundhousing him.

Her's was the blow he most feared and deserved.
Here they were, two punchy fighters. Yet he
Had to be her second, in her corner,
Strengthening her, mending her, sending her back
For the next round when he wanted to shout,
"Stop fighting! Let me throw in the towel!
It's no use. You're bound to lose. Save your skin!"
Surely, he thought, this was the wrong metaphor
For both of them. Wrestling, fighting. Bad. Bad.

"You know when I first decided to come here
It was because of Gloria. She was
Sleeping with a married psychiatrist.
I thought I'd have myself one too. Why not?
I'd slept with about everybody else in pants—
White, black, young, old, gay, straight.
But I knew it wasn't the whole story.
Gloria always fussed about enjoying sex.
It was the greatest thing since sarsaparilla.
Never for me."
                Emily's posture changed.
She placed her arms alongside her body,
Her palms pressed against her tense thighs,
Her chin tucked into her neck, her legs tightly closed.
Dreyfus observed her folding inward, away
From him. He was drawn out of his absorption.

"Did you note how you changed your posture?"

"Did I? I suppose. It's quite automatic.
What about it?"

                "You were talking about
Not enjoying sex."

                    "Was I? I suppose so . . .

Doctor Dreyfus, I don't belong here at all.
In the waiting room I feel like an oddball.
All those housewives and bright young men sitting
Nervously, flipping through old *New Yorkers*,
Or their noses stuck in fat paperbacks,
An ear cocked for the receptionist's call.
It's all a pretense on my part, an act.
How can anything like this help me now?
I sit there feeling sweaty and grimy,
If you must know, like a cheap, two-bit whore
Trying to pass herself off as a sicko,
A sad middle-class neurotic female
Who does the wrong things only in her head
And maybe masturbates to those fantasies,
What Gloria calls solo banjo picking.
I'm different. Have been different for a long time . . .
You said something last time that stuck with me.
It was about that funny song I made up—
'Unavailable, Unassailable You.'
You said . . . wait . . . I've forgotten what you said . . .
I can't believe it! It's gone, vanished.
I must have big holes in my head, big deep holes
Like craters or mine shafts. . . . It's gone completely."

Paul was searching for words himself, unsure
Of what he had said that would have such import.
And then he remembered. It became clear
Why she had forgotten. "Those holes in your head,
Craters or mine shafts, you say? Quite striking
To put it that way even as you mean
To convey how lacking you are."

                              "What's that?
Doctor Dreyfus, sometimes I can't follow you.
Craters and mine shafts are just deep empty holes.
That's me."

        "But they're not, are they? Are they?"
Paul heard himself uneasily, sensing
How much he wanted her to see her worth
As he often failed to see his own.
He knew it would only make her angry.

"Sometimes I think you're a man after all.
Why can't you tell me what you said last time?
Oh, why should you? It's I who forgot it.
So strange because it made such sense to me.
It was a whole paragraph. Not like you . . .
I've been such a homebody lately,
Cooking, cleaning, singing in the kitchen,
Spending more time at school with my kids,
A tough bunch with hard heads. Teaching English
To them is like driving nails into stone walls . . .
I came across some letters I once received
From an old boyfriend. He really liked me
It seemed. He spoke about my mind, my smarts.
He thought I should be a writer. Imagine!
Me! When I first received the letters
I almost threw them out. Just a line, I thought.
For some reason I saved them. Yesterday
I found those letters moving."

                        Paul wondered
If his was the head too hard to penetrate.
At first he was caught up in all the sex.
Violent sex. Promiscuous sex. Whorish Sex.
His own unspent cravings. Could he with her . . .
Get an erection? So that's where that leads,
He commented sardonically to himself,
Deciding that the sex as such was his
More than her preoccupation.

                        "Tell me

What moved you about those letters?"

                                     "Nothing
Especially. Maybe because he missed me.
The guy wrote, not once but several times
And I answered, except the last time. Why
I don't know. Well, I got caught up with Fred.
That was it. He was a gay beautician
Trying to go straight. Only oral sex with him.
He was so afraid for his precious penis!
He wouldn't let me suck him off ever,
But any guy he picked up in a john
Was O.K. How do you figure that one?
He used to nip my pussy with his teeth
And then bury his nose in my muff like
A puppy snuffling after a nipple.
I would play with his oily thick black curls
Thoroughly without feelings, all detached,
Sometimes wondering in the midst of it how
In heaven's name this head got between my legs.
I didn't mind the free hair-dos, I mean
At his shop. A bad joke, Doctor Dreyfus."

"It sounds as if sometimes you think your whole life
Is a bad joke, including this analysis."

"The joke's on me and it isn't a one-liner.
It's a whole TV comedy series,
Life with Emily or a better title,
Emily Screws It Up from Start to Finish.
Tune in next week for more of the same. Much more."

Paul heard the paradoxical self-pity
Which raised defeat into sanctimonious
Victory, hiding its triumphant banners
Behind black pennants at half-mast. He grew

Uncomfortable at its familiarity.
"It looks like you can't laugh at a joke unless
It's on you. That praise from an old boyfriend
Was discounted. You always lead with your chin,
Even when you're being invited to dance."

"I know what you said! All those guys are stand-ins
For 'unavailable, unassailable' *you*.
But I was sleeping around long before y—
You gotta be kiddin'! Are you pullin'
A Freud on me? My Pop? That old reprobate!"
She burst out laughing, a deep, rich belly laugh
Resounding through the office like the deep tones
Of a bright-belled horn, its notes dispelling
What she had just uttered like a comment
That ends discussion.

                Paul was confused
By her leap and then her outburst. And yet
Her laughter did not trouble him. Emily
Placed her arms under her head, a broad smile
Settling on her lips as her eyelids lowered.
He knew that in good technique you first explored
The transference and only then the past
Which should emerge spontaneously, extending
And confirming what had first been revealed
In the transference. He had muffed it again.
She would now destroy the link by making
Fun of it and of him. His must have been an
Inexact interpretation, enough
On target to alert but not sink in.
But what the hell is the matter with her,
Why must she always screw things up, even
His interpretations? He felt like her
Old boyfriend sending her letters for naught.
But he felt his anger reached deeper still,

Beyond her seeming mockery of him
That he could take and even join in.
It was the way she looked right now, relaxed,
Even dreamy, on a high satisfied
Plateau of pure self-intoxication,
Enjoying something he could never fathom—
He in his trudging through that rugged terrain
Of his being, a hinterland of self,
Backcountry, no maps, milestones or moss
Indicating direction, only loose slate
Underfoot, weary slopes up, tough slopes down.
Maybe he did want to shake her up,
To penetrate that haze of discontent
Surrounding her mildly only, and to
Reach the ferret hunter in its deep lair,
To draw out the teeth from its small furry head
And to cleanse the carcasses from her den.
Yet he couldn't say that this wasn't all him—
His own fantasy, his own sly fury
That lurked behind all his best intended acts
So that *not* doing was the best act of all.
Take that staff petition he had started—
Already he was depressed about it,
Convinced it was futile and perilous,
Too nakedly an attack on Victor.
Why is he going after his wife's analyst?
Jealousy? Envy? Shame? All of the above.
"Oh, careful, Dreyfus, careful. Keep your powder dry,
Put the fuses in your pocket," he counseled.

"Doctor Dreyfus, I'm feeling very strange—
Transported, light as a feather, agile.
You know I once wanted to be a dancer
When I was a kid. That's how I'd feel back then
In front of the mirror which was my audience—
I'd die if anyone saw me. That ended

With the big chub, periods and cup size D breasts.
When I was five I was skinny and cute,
Knew all the nursery rhymes and songs by heart—
'Little Miss Muffet sat on a tuffet
Eating her curds and whey. Along came a
Spider and sat down beside her and frightened
Miss Muffet away.' Funny, that spider
Reminds me of the snake in paradise—
Only Eve wasn't frightened away. Should've.
Think if she had been a Miss Muffet and not
A curious female falling for a con job."

Paul noted with relief the time was up.
Emily rose from the couch like a nymph.

7

He had a playful patient on his hands.
It was as if she were skipping rope throughout
Each hour, accompanying herself with ditties,
Childhood rhymes and patter, broken by musings
And chuckling.

               He felt drawn in opposite
Directions—to chastise her new silliness,
Or to join in. The latter made him anxious.
He could remember watching girls at their games
Boys were not supposed to play, or if they did,
Were not supposed to be better at. He
Never felt he could. He could never time
The jump between the double ropes two girls
Were anchoring and shaping into an
Ellipse. When he jumped in, the ellipse
Collapsed at his feet and shoulders. The girls
Giggled, starting the rope up again for
Those next in line who leaped serenely in,
Feet barely leaving the ground, the ellipse
Appearing to remain fixed around them,
That paradox of motion sustaining
Itself, becoming a picture framed in place,
Its very rhythm changing time into space
Until a misstep brought back time and chance.

So he looked on, as he always had,
As he fell into once again, as he
Listened to his patient. It came naturally.

"Tomorrow, you know, is the big, big day.
My class is putting on a play I wrote
For them—those idiot kids. A love story,
Very simple, the usual fairy tale
Dressed up in modern jive for their dumb sake.
Can you see them being kings and queens,
Princes and princesses! They'd all break up
At the first, 'Your Majesty!' So the king
Owns an apartment house, the queen runs
A beauty parlor, the princess spends all day
Filing her nails, watching the TV soaps,
And the prince is a TV repairman.
I think you can take it from there. TV breaks.
King can't fix it. Prince can. They are alone.
Queen bursts in. Jumps to conclusions. Tells king.
Prince exiled. Princess shrivels. Not even soaps
Delight her. King offers free apartment
To whoever cures ailing princess.
Prince disguised as Fuller Brush salesman
Sells her magic air freshener labeled,
'Remember Me?' One whiff and princess rushes
Into his arms. Enter queen. Enter king.
Their daughter is reclaimed and the two try
To live happily ever after in
A crowded apartment, because the king rues
His promise and the royal plighted pair
Move in with mom and pop and babes to be.
The kids love it, especially the part
About the air freshener. They screw up their noses
And go 'Phew!' screaming when the princess rushes
Into the prince's arms. Well, she doesn't
Exactly rush. She turns her head away

And sidles toward him while he stands there fixed,
Arms glued to the side, his head thrust forward
Awaiting the kiss he never quite gets.
Instead her cheek brushes against his lips
And the class erupts as if it were porno.
How do you understand kids! They get so much
Out of so little."

        With that her mood shifted.
"How can a little thing like a class skit
Set me up, stir me up, excite me! Of course,
In a different way. I made something happen.
I made something . . . or turn it around a bit—
I wasn't made . . . I wasn't made . . . I wasn't—
You know what I mean? No, don't answer that,
As if you would anyway. Don't answer."

He was caught up in the modern fairy tale,
Transposing it into the transference and her plea
Not to answer caught him by surprise. Why not
Respond? Why was she so insistent that
He not?

    "Tell me why I'm not to answer?"

"If you understood nothing would be gained.
If you didn't . . . I just couldn't stand it."

He had never heard her more serious or more
Frank. She was holding the rope at both ends,
Inviting him to jump with her, but fearful
He would fail, as he was too. He would fall
Never to be redeemed in her eyes, leaving
Her forever trapped, jump rope in hand,
The rhymes and ditties of childhood on her lips.
He was convinced of what he had to say.

"You have never felt you could take a chance
On a man. You came close a moment ago,
Then you felt you had to save me from the fate
Of all the other men in your life who
Failed you. Take that guy who wrote you letters.
You couldn't answer that last one because
He thought well of you. Had you responded
At some time he would have let you down like—"

"I'm way ahead of you, Doctor Dreyfus,
Like my father, right? You'd lay me out like a map
And trace your voyage of discovery
On my carcass."

                    "You mean like in the park?"

"What park? Like that tramp? That kite? Yes, that kite
Must be what you mean . . . Oh! *That* park! With
    Bruno . . .
The two . . . screwing. The guy screwing away
And Bruno flashing his cock at me—I fled. . . .
I hate you for this!"
                    She struck her fists hard
Against the couch, fierce tears streaking down her
    cheeks.

He was taken aback. Had he spoken
Too soon, said too much? Old uncertainties
Pinched the nerve of his resolve causing pain.
How much safer it is to watch rather
Than to play, he thought ruefully.

                              Sobbing
Now replaced the bitter tears. She breathed deeply
And when she spoke again her voice was soft.
"You didn't listen to me. You answered me

And I don't know if you are right or wrong,
Except I know what you said agonized me,
Made me want to hate you. Thrust you away,
Beat you up, trample you in the dust,
Mangle you beyond recognition. I . . .
Don't know why. I'm not sure I want to know.
Enough with men. Enough with you pricks. Enough."

He felt unjustly accused, angered, his efforts
Nullified. He knew at once that was the point.
"Strange, the way you put it—made you *want* to
Hate me, for what I said."

                              "If I couldn't hate you,
I'd give in—as I always have with men.
Maybe this is something different. I won't
Give in to you. When I've given in
Before it got me nowhere. In sex, no fun.
In work, no gain. . . . This whole thing has got me
      down.
What am I going to do now? It's all sick!
Why did I allow myself to get
Into this! It's like I said, analysis
Is for those neurotic housewives, not me.
Is this hour never going to end!
I'm on the edge and need a breather.
Ring the bell, the round's over."

                              "And who won?"
He heard himself say.
                         "It's a draw,' she said.
And she started to laugh, her laughter growing
Until she found her breath again, adding,
"But don't think the next round will be so easy!"

Startled, he discovered the hour was
In fact almost over. The clock on his desk
Seemed to have moved more quickly than their own
　　time.
And he thought of the eye of a storm, or
The wheel of a dance in which the center turns
Slowly while those on the rim must hold on tight
To keep from spinning off.

　　　　　　　　　　　　　　"Until then,"
He said, and then he thought, why "until then"?

Part Two

Frances Dreyfus
and
Victor Kleinman

8

On the opposite wall that same volcano
She had been seeing for three years. Behind,
Silence interrupted sporadically
By mind-melting words, pouring out thickly.
The picture—blue, abstract—a far-off world
In which to lose herself. Behind, a presence
Drawing her back from which she fled anew
Into that sky—clear, empty. Was it filled
Ever with geysering fireworks—red, raging,
The pale clouds hissing? Hard to imagine.
She should be saying all this, out loud to him.
Instead, "I'm thinking about my husband
And how he's sitting now as you are, not
Far from here, listening to another woman
Talk. And she must love him as I love you.
But why I should love you, God knows. You're cruel."

"In what way am I cruel to you?"

                                    "Again
We go through this. You can't love back, you can't!"
Like a dark velvet flower, silence opened.
She watered it with her quiet, spent tears.
How long could she endure this agony?

"Not the first time you have loved unrequited,"
He said, his syntax, wrongly right, teutonic,
"How you insist to love whom you cannot.
It was that way with many men going back—"

"To my father," she completed, anger
Rose again and tears. Why, why always tears
As if her solid anger had first to melt.
Only its heat remained on her wet cheeks.

"You are weeping instead of being angry
Because you must placate me for your failure
In still not being worthy of my love."

She felt a collapse inside, like a tent
Suddenly folding in the wind, or
Like a butterfly in a storm, its wings
Helpless, tossed about like a scrap of paper.
Those long walks from the Saratoga station
At night, the newsstand closed, old newspapers
Whipped up by the same wind that filled her skirt,
The centerfolds trying to fly, lifting
Off gracefully, wings spread, rising slowly
Until a gust destroyed their attempt,
Sent them flapping, twisting, protesting groundward—
A bird plucked from the sky by a lucky shot.
"You've wounded me again. I can't come back.
I can't."

       "Wounded is a strong word. Tell me
About it."

       "I feel like a bird taking off
And you shoot me down when you should applaud."

"Applaud?"

"Yes, applaud. How many would take this
Beating daily and still perfor—persist.
I mean persist. No use. I said perform."
Anger returned, self-pity tugging childlike
At its sleeve. The couch turned hard. Would it end?
When that stinking voice tripping her up would
Croak finally. But there it was—perform.
Little Frances do your thing. Against her will
She smiled, "I remember singing a song
For the company, my father beaming.
It was in Yiddish. Everybody kvelled."

"Your Yiddish is to remind me I'm German."

"You're Jewish too, but not a Yiddisher."

"You want me close only to thrust me away."

She felt a balance shift. Was there reproach
In that tone? If so, then he too felt thwarted.
"My husband speaks a radio announcer's Yiddish.
All the right pronunciations but no tam.
That's German to me. Letter perfect but dead."
She was feeling better by the minute.
Was it a cloud or the merest wisp of smoke
Lifting from the cone shape in the picture?

"You perform more often than you realize,
Using an act to make you feel better.
But underneath you feel incompetent
Unable to win my love. So you must act,
Hoping that applause will make up for it.
So with father, so with me, so with all men."

The little toy spinner once whizzed in her hand.
Amazed she watched it whirl, glittering red.

The twisted flanges blurred softly together
Appearing finally like a flower.
But when she put her finger to its edge
The flower vanished in an angry buzz.
"I'm thinking about that marvelous toy.
I could never blow hard enough to make
The flower reappear. My father could.
He would puff up his cheeks and blow and blow,
Delighting me. I'd have had him blow all day.
When he stopped I'd throw it down or at him!"

"You still envy me my interpretations."

"No, I don't think so. Admiration perhaps."
Keenly, longing and desire reappeared.
If only he were not bald, long-nosed and fat.

"How must we then account for all these thoughts
About father being able to blow the toy
And you never being so able? Also
Your anger when you could not control him?
You envied his power. What are your thoughts there?"

She was spinning downward, gathering speed.
It always ended this way—in defeat.
Always she made one last futile effort:
"The facts are on your side, the feelings on mine."

"What can you mean about facts and feelings?
You are really trying to control me,
To reject the meaning of your own words
By using other words as a smoke screen
So you can deny that I am correct
While conceding to me a small token."

"You are having trouble with my husband

Over Dr. Frank's successor, aren't you?"
She was almost shamefaced at her stratagem.
It would slow him down, not stop him, nothing would.
She knew from her husband that he was tough,
A hard infighter who hit below the belt.
Her husband feared him, hated him, admired him,
Much as she did. There was comfort in that.

"What trouble am I having. Please explain."

"You know it's hard to talk about these things.
I can't tell you about my husband's plans.
You are on the other side, his enemy."

"Again you are raising the question of trust.
You do not trust me to be your analyst.
We cannot continue on that basis.
This I've said over and over again."

Her wings became so much mangled paper.
Her will receded and yet she felt a strength
Flow quietly.

                    "I remember a dream
I had last night. I was taking a train,
Another train dream, but not the same place.
It was a glassed-in station, people staring
At me, as if I was doing something wrong.
I hid under a seat. Others were sitting.
The conductor ignored me. When the train
Left the station, I wanted to look back.
It was wet all over and I was blamed.
I protested. I never sat on the seat.
The train entered a tunnel. 'It serves them right,'
I thought for some reason. That's all there was.
Yesterday I was thinking of Europe,

The way this railroad station was glassed-in.
My husband was telling me about them.
I envy his having been to Europe
And all your trips there—gone for months.
The people staring remind me of me
Trying hard to look uninterested
When something exciting is happening.
I always found hiding exciting too.
I remember games of hide-and-go-seek
When I would get so excited I would
Start to go in my pants and have to come out,
Insisting I hadn't been caught but had
To go to the toilet. The kid who was 'it'
Would shout down my excuse and call me 'it.'
Once I cried so, it was unfair really,
I couldn't help it. But then it got dark
And our mothers called us all to come in.
That's the dream, isn't it? I'm playing
Games with you, hiding myself from you?"

"What occurs to you about looking back?"

"Did I say that? Nothing . . . except maybe
Taking a peek at you—that's all. Why?"

"Yes—what more comes to mind about that?"

"Every now and then I get the urge, that's all."

"You are even now holding something back
Because it would be too exciting."

She felt her cheeks flush. Was it with anger
Or with shame?
                    "This is silly," she announced,
"Don't all your patients want to steal a look?

I've mentioned this before. Why all the fuss?"

"You think I make a fuss?"

                              "Yes, like a parent
Catching a child at some little nothing."
What was she letting herself in for? What
New trap awaited her? She fell silent.
The office lights flickered. She felt exposed.

"You are talking about masturbation
And fearing for me to know about it."

"You know I've never masturbated."
He's wrong this time. She felt victorious.

"All these thoughts you keep to yourself. You skim
Only the surface for me. The rest you guard
For yourself, fantasies to excite you.
But you also want to see if I observe.
Will I find you out. Make you the 'it' girl."

She had to laugh at his accidental
Bon mot.
               "An 'it' girl in American slang
Is sexy—did you know that?"

                              "No, not at all,
But it fits. That's why now you thought of it.
The girl with 'it,' that's your fantasy.
You hide in a public place to be found
Before your excitement overmounts you.
You must run back to mother quickly,
End the game before the fantasy conquers
As now you hope the hour will soon end."

Right. She had been hoping the hour would end.
She felt the driving force of his insights
Excite her, unnerve her, dominate her.

"But you are silent. Hiding from me still?"

"You're right. I did want the hour to end.
I can see what you mean about the dream,
Only I never would turn to my mother."

This perplexed him. Time and again he saw
The mother-regression present but denied.
She was still fighting him, rebuffing him.
Always something held him back, contradicted.
Yet it might be true. For a moment he
Considered this alternative. But then
He said, "You reject your mother's role."

"And why not? She was never good to me."

The hour lacked a minute to its end.
He wanted so to drive this one point home.
That was the danger— his countertransference.
She evoked sadistic rage in him
He had to watch. It went back to his sister
Anna, who both adored and taunted him.
Her husband was a brilliant fool, nobody.

"We must stop now. I won't be here next Monday."

The weekend lay ahead like a desert.

9

Why was it always painful to return?
A simple thing to lie down on a couch
And talk—whatever comes to mind. Right?
Wrong, she answered herself in dialogue,
A childish lapse she indulged frequently.
He would call her late—she was sure of that.
He always did when he returned from somewhere.
Frances stiffened. Marlena had gone by.
Yes, he would likely chat with her awhile—
On her time! The bitch. Much to talk about.
After all, the poor boy had been away
All weekend and Monday. No family life. No—
Her thoughts dropped off a ledge, disappearing
As if never thought of.

                        "Mrs. Dreyfus."
She headed down the hallway, suddenly
Overcome totally by edginess
And a fluttering hopefulness she despised
In herself. A betrayal. She had a right
To be angry. Hadn't Paul hinted at that
When she mentioned Kleinman told her at the end
Of the hour about his trip? Of course
Analysts stick together, even Paul
And Victor, so Paul wouldn't come right out

And say that Victor was wrong. Damn doctors!
She saw Marlena leave Victor's office
And scurry down the hall toward her own.
Victor was already seated when she
Came in. The dread mounted as she lay down.
Why, why does she let herself in for this!
How much nicer it would be to stay at home,
Raising the kids, cooking for her husband,
Even cleaning up the house. What ambitions
Were driving her to this . . . immolation.
Exactly the way she felt on the couch.
It was a pyre. Each hour she went up in flames.
"Welcome back. I hope you enjoyed your trip.
California. Very nice. Not as
Hot as Tennessee, I'm sure."

          These civil words
Surprised her. Where did they come from? A little
Dig about California, though. Serey,
Know-it-all and say-it-all, Serey.
She always knew what the training analysts
Were up to.

        "I had lunch with Serey
Who told me. I wish she hadn't. It makes
Things so much worse . . . I got a letter
From my mother—a rare event. Complaints."
She felt sullen herself. Marlena's perfume.
She could smell it. Who needs this! she screamed
Inside herself—the feeling ricocheting
Silently like a billiard ball bouncing
Hard off the cushions.

        "Your mother wrote you?"
A chance, he thought, to hear about the mother.

"Yes." Frances was relieved to shift away
From Marlena and California. "A note
Full of reproaches. Why don't I visit
More often. She doesn't have a daughter.
Whoever heard of living in Tennessee.
It's only for Daniel Boones and Ernie Fords,
Not Jewish people. How can I raise children
There to be Jews. They'll end up being converts—
And so on. On and on and on."

        "Your own thoughts?"

"Right now I wish I were in New York City.
I feel dull, provincial and stuck for good.
I'm not capable of anything except
Having kids, looking after a house.
So what's wrong with that, you say. Well, plenty . . .
What's the use. We've been over and over this
A million times. All you say is I want—
Oh, you know—a damned penis. That's a laugh!
If you'd say I wanted long, thick hair,
Larger breasts, slimmer hips, I'd believe you.
But a penis? What would I do with it? Wave it?"

"A note from your mother makes you unhappy
With yourself."

        "My mother? Oh! Her complaints.
I don't need my mother to teach me my
Troubles. But she is Mrs. Nowhere herself.
Her idea of smart is not to be smart.
For a woman marriage and brains don't mix.
No worry for me. I'm no brain either.
But I married both in one handsome package
Except they left the heart out . . . ," she added
Under her breath, not wanting him to hear,

But he would. Why was Paul so horrible?
Something in his analysis? Who cares!
Life can't be lived taking analysis
Always into account. She wanted so
To reach out to him, touch him, move him deeply,
Beyond words, couches, hours, interpretations—
Was she thinking of Paul . . . or Victor . . . or both?
Her heart sank. It had to be Paul. Had to.

"You are silent. Your thoughts?"

                              "Did you have to
Speak to your wife in here before I came
And make me wait? It's my time after all.
There's always something else when it comes to me."
She was alarmed by the bitterness in
Her voice.

                    Victor sensed something churning in her.
Better to wait. Clearly the cancellation.
His trip. More envy! More rage! It never ends!
For a moment he heard Kurt's voice behind him:
'A phobia, Victor, you spoke of a phobia.'
And he frowned. A transference already.
He tuned in her voice, now petulant, woeful.
" . . . together. Serey knows everything. Everything,
You and Michael are close friends. She helps him
Politically. I can't do that at all.
Paul becomes so jealous!'
                              His mind had wandered.
What was she talking about? This was no good.
Always after a trip it was difficult.
The resonances were disturbed—a static
Of personal issues, fresh experiences
Interfered.

" . . . Saturday at this
Chinese place."

"Yes, what comes to mind, please."

"About the Chinese place? It's very nice,
Good food, inexpensive. And Serey hates it.
She says the food's more American than
Chinese. But her ears perked up about Paul."

She sensed something was going wrong today.
He was really not interested in her.
How could he be? All her doubts came flooding back
Dangerously.
                    "Serey can be so sweet
Though, if she wants to be. You must know that.
I admire the way she dresses. So chic.
Never gaudy, always simple, elegant.
She's European to the core. I envy that.
All her traveling, her languages.
She entertains beautifully. Always
Interesting people at her parties—
Always a surprise or two. Delicious food.
No wonder she hates that Chinese place.
Paul hates to go there. He hates Michael."

Victor heard the tattoo of hate in her words
Despite the marshmallow softness in her voice.
"You are so taken by Serey because
You think she is something special to me—
Which you are not."

                    "I don't blame you at all.
She's sophisticated and can hold her
Own with you."

"You mean were you more like she
Then of course I would not have canceled Monday,
Not gone off flying away from you, no?"

She saw scissors flying through the air.
An urge to stab possessed her momentarily
And she felt like fleeing through the door—away,
To get away, as far as possible.
She became aware that her legs were uncrossed
And quickly she crossed them.

                    "You crossed your legs?"
He wanted her to talk, supplicating
Her almost—or so it seemed to her.
She noted something softer in his tone.
Not that triphammer insistence she was
Accustomed to. She felt herself become
Responsive.
                    "Serey thinks you'd make a great
Research director. Paul disagrees
Violently. As does the research staff . . .
I'd be so tired and elated coming
Back from California, giving a paper."

"Tell me your fantasy about my trip."

"Funny I think of the social part of it,
The dinners, receptions, cocktail parties.
People congratulating you, searching
You out to engage you in discussion.
I'd never let you go off by yourself.
I'd want to be there by your side, being proud.
I don't know if I'd understand your paper.
Paul's are impossible—dull, complicated . . .
I ached to fly off with you. . . . "
                    She caught her breath—

Feeling relieved at first, then tense again,
Like a rubber band going slack, then stretched.
What would he say? Already the silence
Spoke quite loudly. She thought of Marvin—
Quiet, handsome, careful Marvin—never
Impolite, never a false move. He married
Someone else.

            Victor balanced two different views:
Was she mainly jealous of Marlena,
Or envious of him? Was the jealousy
A defense against the envy? The latter
Won out.
            "It is easier for you to be
Jealous of Marlena than envious of me,
To think that you are nicer than she
Than to be yourself the paper giver,
The large wheel, because you must then feel so
Inadequate, so incomplete."

Always the rebuff. The rubber band
Stretched tauter. *He* was the analyst
Not *me*. She started to laugh as an image
Floated past her eyes of a gorilla
Thumping his chest, booming, 'Me, analyst!
You, Fay Wray patient, small and inadequate!'
"Why are all you he-men so much alike?
Just now as you spoke I saw this King Kong
Thumping his chest. I don't envy you. Really.
But I do feel you pushing me away
As I try to draw closer, participate
In your success. My fantasy? you'll ask.
O.K. My husband is all wrapped up in
Himself—worried, angry, fretting, a real case—
Why am I saying all this to you! Of course,
You'll use it against him. . . ."

                              "You bring him in
So that you'll have a reason not to continue."

"When I was packing my suitcase Saturday
I thought of you for one wild moment.
Of you in California and me in Tennessee.
Me sick and tired of life and you flying high.
Why couldn't you take me with you or at least
Be kind about it, give me a little time,
Some forewarning when you cancel an hour.
Friday was a nightmare, Saturday worse.
Sunday I was a robot going through
The motions. A little life revived Monday
Because today you would be back . . . at least."
Her face burned, her eyes smarted, her stomach
Growled and was knotted painfully.

                              Perhaps,
Victor thought, it was mainly jealousy.
But she had said "participate" in my
Success, identifying with me
And thus possess the penis. That was right.
The oedipal triangle was brought to bear
Against the phallic urge to castrate men.
"You spoke of packing Saturday at night
To fly with me?"

                         That bitter moment
Took hold of her again. What could she say?
Paul had been so cruel that day, forcing
Her out of bed when all she wanted to do
Was cry, stare, and sleep.

                              "I was in bed all day,
Unable to do anything. Depressed,
I suppose sorry for myself, wanting

Just to hide. I felt so ugly, useless.
It was as if I were a dead lead weight.
I couldn't budge an inch or lift myself up
Until my husband read me the riot act.
I couldn't lose him too! That night in bed
I wanted so to be close to him, loved—
And . . . and . . . he couldn't do it. Nothing happened.
He felt bad. I felt worse. I wanted him so!
We lay side by side in pained silence
Until he said I make things so difficult
For him—the way I moped about when you
Were gone. I . . . I . . . couldn't take that. The nerve
Of him to blame me for his impotence!
I had to get away—I had to run.
That's when I packed the suitcase and ran
For the door, thinking for a moment of you.
The rest is . . . sordid."

"Please, the time ends."

10

Victor Kleinman awaited his patient
Nervously. An oddity for him.
Nor could he find any reason for it
Which added annoyance to his nervousness.
Vaguely his thoughts turned to Kurt and quickly
Veered off. Frances Dreyfus entered quietly
And slipped onto the couch as if intruding.
He scowled at her submissiveness, noting
That she must be excessively angry
And guilty, yearning for absolution.
For what? Her misbehavior over last weekend,
Of course—her way of reprimanding him
For his absence. He welcomed her silence
With which she started the hour. Victor leaned
Back in his chair and prepared to listen.
That special analytic calm took hold,
Dispelling the nervousness, surrounding
Himself and his patient.

                    Frances had resolved
To work today. No more useless pouting
About being left behind, about Paul.
Once and for all she must take hold of her life.
She was still young, bright, energetic.
Her children were still quite small, true, but that

Need not be too great an interference.
She had a good analyst; some said, the best.
Her husband made a good living, they led
An interesting life—perspective, that's it.
With the right perspective she could do it.
Do what? That's what was so unclear. Do what?

"I've been complaining a lot lately. I know.
But that's a waste of time. Please forgive me.
I shouldn't get so upset when you go away.
My husband's right to get angry. I know that.
I want to do something with my life. Well,
I mean I do have a lot already
To be thankful for, but . . . I had this dream
That made me feel so good about myself.
I woke up this morning feeling refreshed
With a delicious taste in my mouth as if
I had eaten a marvelous dish, but
That wasn't the dream at all. In this dream
I was a diving champion off the high board—
Me! I barely know how to swim. It was so
Exhilarating to leap into space
Knowing I could fully control my body,
Shooting into the water like a dart,
Popping up again smiling like a dolphin.
That's how I felt. A thoroughly nice dream
For a change. Earlier that day I saw
Some Olympic highlights—gymnastics actually.
This little teenager who wrapped herself
Around this bar as if she had no bones.
And I wasn't afraid of the height. And when
I came up, breaking the surface, the applause
Was like a roar waiting for me. For me!
I just recalled another part! The judges—
They were holding up cards, giving their ratings.
You were holding up a ten! Fat chance of that!

The tenth, that was the day you were away.
Also, isn't California where all
The diving stars come from? The plot thickens,
Doesn't it? Yes, I wanted to be out there with you,
Impressing you with my championship form. . . . "
She sensed uneasily an unintended
Innuendo. But she persisted gamely.

"I've told you about Richard. He was a
Great swimmer, built like a Greek god, but his face
Was pure Jewish down to the pouting lips.
You had to let Richard squeeze you or else
You felt guilty for depriving the poor boy.
I so admired his body. When he was clothed
He was like a closed pocket knife, but in a
Bathing suit he was a sprung blade, hard and smooth,
Knifing cleanly through the roughest water.
But he wasn't a diver at all. So strange.
He hated to dive. I don't see you as a
Diver either somehow. . . . "

                        Victor puckered
His lips as if at something tart. It was good,
He thought, the dream, her associations.
She was indeed working. He fell to the task
With habitual enthusiasm,
His earlier nervousness totally gone.

"Are you not poised on that high diving board
Bent on overcoming me with muscle,
Or with sex, that championship form serving
Well for both, isn't that so?"

                        "Why overcoming?
You're giving me a ten—no one ever gets a ten."

"Exactly. No one but you. Not even me.
Also the ten reminds you of my leaving,
Not so? That I will turn away in anger
At your desire to best me. Yes, you would
Even do better in California
Than I, where all the diving champions come from."

Perhaps at long last, he thought, he could tackle
This woman's deeply feared phallic wishes.
He had been right last time about her envy.
But the defense against it needed work.

"You recall your fantasy from last time
About the Wray Fay patient and the King Kong
Analyst? You fabricate it all
So that you are weak and in my power—
That power you want to possess yourself—
And by being the frail one you hide the wish."

"Pardon, but it's Fay Wray and not Wray Fay."

"Any associations?"

She started to laugh
At her own transparency.

"Turnabout
Is fair play, is it not? I'll be King Kong
And *you* be Fay Wray for a big change."

Her openness caught him off guard. She couldn't
Stop herself from continuing as if
She had taken a leap—or was it a dive?
She had launched herself into a free fall.

"No, I wouldn't mind being you at all,

At least in some ways and a while only.
I don't mind being me as much as you
Think I do, though. What I want is your brains.
That incredible way you have of making sense
Of things, of dreaming up theories, writing
Papers that people want to read and quote.
You are known to the world, you go everywhere."

Kleinman sensed the envy disappearing
In a rosy cloud of admiration.
Again she abjured her own hostility
By slipping into identification.

"You forget that in your dream you were a
World Olympic champion worthy of a ten—
The only such recipient. Not yet
Has a Fay Wray been so strong and skilled.
You want to hide that from me and yourself."

Frances felt he was taunting her, daring her
Like the boys would do at school at recess—
Daring the girls to slug it out with them.
When she was in grade school, she *would* fight
It out, kicking and scratching, making a rock fist
And trying to jab her knuckles into their
Fat, ugly faces. She hated all boys then,
But later on the fights were something else. . . .

"You know I feel you're trying to get me
Angry at you. And I don't want to be.
It would be the kind of fight in which
I would end up in your arms, quite ashamed."

"Exactly. You would need to be the Fay Wray
As a protection against the champion—
The King Kong in you."

"You're entirely wrong.
There's no King Kong in me or champion.
In any case in my dream I'm showing off—
You're missing that. Please remember the applause."

"No, I don't forget the applause. But the
Applause is for prowess not performance.
You are strongly wishing to win over all.
That's the part you cannot permit yourself
To accept openly as yours—the impulse
To triumph."

                    To triumph. Odd words, strange sound
To them, she thought.
                    "I don't know what it means
To triumph. That's for kings and gladiators
In another century. Don't you know
Nowadays no one is supposed to win
At another's expense? Only naughty boys
Triumph, sticking their tongues out, snickering,
    'Naaah!'
At you. But they're supposed to get over that."

Frances again heard hidden innuendoes
In her words but she felt a fierce propulsion
Drive her forward, surprising in the pleasure
It gave her.
                    "Sometimes this ugly research business
Strikes me that way—naughty boys all of you,
Each of you trying to be king of the hill,
Pushing one another off. Don't you know
Once it's over you'll have to work together?
How will you make up?"

                    Kleinman heard the snicker.
That was her triumph: to look down at men,

Really boys—in their fatuous combats.
She was above such silly glory-seeking.
As for being a champion, that was all
For show—a performance to earn applause,
A narcissistic display like a child
Showing off a new trick—nothing more.
Keenly he perceived the defensiveness,
Anxiety, and surrender in her stance.
How could she achieve anything for herself
As long as she had to throttle the engine
Of her ambition and practice condescension
Toward the ambitions of others? Victor's
Earlier nervousness suddenly returned.
Baffled, he followed his scattering thoughts:
Kurt, the look he gave him as he had left.
Was a shift taking place? The three women, one
Right now on the couch, eluding him.
Yes, again Bernini. In analysis
No reason to pursue. One waited. Hard
For him. That he knew. Truth and beauty.
But truth can be a false god and beauty
An ugly hoax. He did understand her,
Of that he was sure. He could help her. He
Had helped her. He felt warmly toward her now.
Was she not struggling as he was struggling?
We are never through. It is necessary
Only to think, write, make sense of it all.
Bring order out of chaos or all is lost.
With the last thought he felt a surge of strength,
A taut readiness to do battle, wage
War against a holocaust of disorder.
His patient stirred uneasily. Silence
Disturbed her.

        "You're angry at me, aren't you?"
She said. "I criticize you for what I'd do

Myself if I would let myself. Why not?
Why should you have all the fun, the headlines,
The parties and the trips? Why don't I
Let myself? That's a good question for me
To answer. I just don't have what it takes,
Period. Exclamation point. I can't write.
I'm not much of a thinker. I'm not young
So I can't start over and if I could
What would I be? I shudder at the thought."

Victor took note of the clock on the bookcase.
Time to stop. She was asking good questions
And thus she reaffirmed his strength.

                                        "We stop now."

11

There was only one thing on her mind
Today and she fervently wished it were not—
Paul. She was worried, angry, and bewildered.
On entering the office she had averted
Her eyes—she was ashamed of the last hour,
Ashamed of her cowardice after so
Strong a start. A fresh beginning and then
Life caught up with you, reminding you
That it did not stand still while you were "working
Things out." Paul. . . . She had once adored him so.
Every now and then in a stray moment
Her young love for him returned, an aroma
From the past, catching her by surprise, bringing
Tears to her eyes.

                  Kleinman observed his patient.
Yes, she was sliding back into meekness.
He could tell by her downcast eyes, bent head.
She could be truly beautiful. A strong face
Potentially. Liquid eyes, unblemished skin.
Ah! But she had her blemishes elsewhere.
Analysis was made for such people.
It even was not difficult, only
Time consuming. He thought of those astounding
Films showing seeds opening into flowers

In a matter of minutes, compressing
Hours or days into a moment or two.
If only one could compress time really
So that the film were a true record.
He was becoming impatient with himself.
These musings were pointless.

                "I guess I'm at fault
Somehow. If only I were more satisfied
With my life maybe Paul would be happier.
I know it's not so. He's always turned sour
Whenever *any* thing doesn't go right—
But I'm what's not going right—and I know it.
God! I'm all confused and it must be showing."

"What is showing is your defensive retreat
From last hour when you were readier
To examine your problems with ambition."

"Ambition? Did I see it that way? I don't know.
Maybe. I only want to do something
More with my life—nothing great or world shaking.
But when Paul is miserable, I can't
Let myself think about any of that."

"Of course, because you feel his misery
Is due to you. But ask yourself why, please. . . .
Please."

        "My hostility?"

            "Yes, go on please."

"I really get the point. I feel my own
Ambition is an attack on him, so
I'm overcome by guilt when he turns sour."

"And you come here unprepared to continue,
For success here would make you guiltier."

"The only trouble with that neat package is
You don't have Paul to deal with. He's impossible.
We do eat together, sleep in the same bed,
But that's about all. No sex. No talk. Nothin.'
At times I want to kill him, tear him apart.
A horrid fantasy of . . . of dismembering him.
I know what people really mean when they say
'I'm so angry I could tear him limb from limb!'
I am furious at him. He's an ingrate.
Look at how much he has—wife, kids, career,
Enough money, meals waiting for him at home,
A clean house, family. What's his complaint?
The world isn't turning in the right direction
To suit him. You might get to be director—
SO WHAT! It's all so ridiculous. God!
All you stupid men are the same. Little boys
Playing games with each other's lives and we
Women have to suffer the consequences."

Victor was sure that her argument had
Shifted subtly from *her* guilt to *his*
And that of all men, from her own actions
To her *re*action to those of men. Already
He could feel himself drawn in, preparing
To argue with her, to point out the flaws—
Completely futile—a reenactment
Of the problem, not a resolution.

"You wish to tear him up because he has
Everything you want and doesn't care
At all for it."

                    She tossed her head about

Angrily, sucking on her lower lip.
"Always I want what *he* has . . . I don't believe it.
I want a chance, the same chance he has had
And continues every day to have . . . . No use,
Because even if I did it wouldn't work.
I don't have his brains or yours. I'm amazed
By his research and by your total grasp
Of so much that is completely beyond me.
These are facts, not inventions. What do you
Do with an untalented blah like me?"

He knew there was no escaping the trap.
Yet if he were to point this out he would
Be falling in it again for being too smart.
Neurosis is driven by an appalling
Engine with its own powerful gyroscope.
From whatever direction you pushed it
Neurosis had a way of pushing back.
No. There was another, simpler way.

"You have, you say, a terrible fantasy
About dismembering men, isn't it so?
Tell me more still about that, please."

        "What more
Is there to say. I don't dwell on it, or
Worry about it."
        "Was there not one time
You threw at Paul's head a pair of scissors
When you were so furious?"
        "I made sure to miss.
I'm not really violent."
        "Yes and no.
Yes, you can control your impulses.
No, there *is* a violent side to you
Made even more violent by attempts

At gross inhibition. You squish—no . . . squash
Your resentment and envy so fully
That it must exaggerate itself
Hundredfold."

                    Frances was already shaking
With laughter at the "squish" instead of "squash."
"'Squish' is really much better than 'squash.'
My resentment and envy are soggy,
Limp dishrags I never hang out to dry."

At first he was puzzled by her sudden
Laughter and change of mood. What had he said
To make her laugh? Squish? What a language, English!
Of course, squish referred to something soggy,
As she had said. But what of the dishrag?
And hanging it out to dry? . . . Ah, yes, yes. It was so—
She never exposed her resentment and envy.

"You enjoy a small laugh at my expense.
Such innocent triumphs are acceptable."

"You are at it again, with your 'triumphs!'
Every time you speak I hear trumpets. I
Tell you I don't want to defeat anyone,
Just have a little something for myself."
She had surprised herself by her outspoken
Reply. In fact she had enjoyed it and
The laughter had been a tonic.
                              "Trumpets?

I do not understand quite."
                              "Marches.

Military parades. You know, your English
Should be much better for an analyst."

She startled to giggle and then felt like
Urinating. She squeezed her thighs together
And held her breath.

                         "You are angry at me,
But tell me why."

                    "Oh, I'm not angry really.
Just teasing you a little, baiting you . . .
I do find it exciting. . . . I feel you
Hovering over me . . . with your eyes . . . somehow.
I can feel it . . . I want to hide. . . . " Frances
Felt a tingle in her ear and a shudder
Passing over her. She shut her eyes tight,
Compressed her lips and adjusted her skirt.
She felt like a ship heading into a storm.

Her phrase, "hovering over me with your eyes,"
For an instant electrified Victor.
When it passed, an image clarified itself
As if the static disturbance had to end
Before he could behold the image. It was
The same three women, the same classic torso
For all three, the three heads different—
Frances, Anna, and Marlena. Kleinman
Knew he must beware his feelings, his words.
He chose silence.

                    Frances was pitching about
In a strong wind delivering repeated gusts
Of memory threatening to capsize her.
They were fearful, exciting, suggestive hints,
A vibrancy in the body, as now she felt
Above the pubis. She tightened, catching
Her breath and then felt a stifling, cramping
Narrowing as if the walls were marching

Closer in. . . . She should not. But there she was.
Downstairs, the rhythmic slide, thud, rattle
Of a game of jacks. Upstairs, she was alone.
The glossy surface was blazing with longing,
Glistening with the moisture of kisses
Where the brigand hairs spread above widening lips
Revealing bare white marches of rapine,
While the eyes were mocking whatever she felt.
From deep in some unknown locked-up place where
She had never ventured to look, Frances
Now felt a heat rise into her cheeks and
A prickle spread across the back of her neck.
With relief, she sensed how a vague memory
Was putting on a time and place, dressing
Itself in particulars and finding words:

"It's so strange to find that folded up inside
Is . . . or is it folded? . . . maybe it goes on . . .
And how connected to . . . other things that
Go on . . . down there. No one ever told me.
I didn't ask either. It came to me
Like a young kid absorbs a new language,
Only it was spoken from inside myself.
I could only hear it when I was alone.
How I yearned to be alone in those days!
I'd wait for my parents to go shopping,
Like on a Saturday. I'd say I had
Homework, or a favorite program. It worked.
The room became enchanted. The air somehow
Heavy with anticipation. . . . " She fell silent,
Reluctant to exchange the precious metal
Of secrets unspoken for the paper
Promises of another's understanding.

Kleinman watched the flower opening up.
Perhaps it was now between well-spaced clicks

Of the time-lapse camera. He would wait.

"It was just a photo. Rotogravure,
I think it's called. But to me it was like a . . .
Real person. I knew it wasn't. Yet it was
Somehow more real for me than many
I have since met in the flesh. I can't say why.
It awakened me, this black-white thing—
That's what it was, I'm ashamed to say, a photo."
Foolish as it was, she could go no further.
No, she'd rather die than say who it was.

Kleinman waited and saw the time near its end.
The hour might indeed better end this way,
The shutter closed for a day, the flower poised
On the threshold of percipience.

                              "It is
Time for us to stop," he said quietly.
Frances left not without feeling cheated.

12

Victor's mind was humming with alternatives.
Like a general studying a war map,
He was tracing the consequences of one
Or another strategy. He felt never
More alive or purposeful as when danger
Reared itself. He now knew the facts,
Not all, to be sure. That would come. Enough
To be alerted and to plan. Always
Better to know whom and what you're fighting.
When Frances arrived he focused his mind
On her with a burning concentration.

"It's been strange . . . exciting . . . frightening since last
     time.
My mind's been racing . . . all kinds of fantasies—
Even plans . . . for myself . . . filled with energy.
I must sound disconnected and I am—
Going off in all directions . . . at
The same time. But it feels good. My husband
Be damned. He's mucking around in his usual
Stew, sleeps like a stick, wakes up in a foul
Bitter mood. I think of you then . . . and . . .
Of other men— but mainly of you. . . . "
Her voice had fallen to a faint whisper.
Frances drew in a deep breath and continued:

93

"You don't look at all like him—God knows.
In fact, you couldn't be more opposite
In appearance. But in spirit you're the same.
I'm ashamed to say who I'm talking about—
You'd think me a silly schoolgirl, the last thing
I want you to think! No. In my fantasy
I am clever, shrewd, petite, and ravishing—
Everything I'm not. I so want to match
Your brilliance—no, not match it, but arouse it,
Help you bring it to a fine point, while you
Admire my grasp, intuition, knowledge
Of subjects you thought beyond me. You'd say,
'Such a slip of a girl and she knows so much!'
And I'd laugh, pleased at being called a 'slip
Of a girl'—big, clumsy me, and thrilled by your
Admiration. . . . I can't help myself. I can't
Stop wanting what I've always wanted, and
I can't say what that is—too embarrassing."
She bit into her lower lip as if
That were the only way to keep her lips
From betraying her.

                    Victor was startled
And pleased by this transformation. A bit
Soon, he thought, but welcome. A necessary
Way-station, a temporary bivouac
En route to the final battlefield of
The analysis which had to be waged
Against the defenses arrayed in depth
Of her entrenched character. But first
The weak outer ramparts had to be breached.
This, thought Victor, was now swiftly progressing.
How different it would all seem to her later.

Frances was yearning for him to say something—
To voice his approval, an invitation

To continue. Yet she knew he must be pleased.
She was opening up. She felt it. That's
What was so frightening. She felt a rush of youth—
Pleasurable, powerful, fresh, disarming—
Like a warm, moist breath of air tickling her flesh,
Playing with it, teasing it, nuzzling it
Alive. A chord sounded deep within her,
Fusing reminiscence with anticipation
So harmoniously that what Frances
Ached for and once possessed were now all one.
She *was* young again! She *was* free again!

"You won't laugh at me—I know you won't . . . will
     you?
But I was comparing you to . . . Clark Gable—
My once secret, secret love."
                                    She held her breath,
Waiting for the guffaw. Welcome silence.

"I snipped his photo out of a magazine.
Black and white. It showed him as Rhett Butler.
His dark wavy hair, rascally eyes,
A thin pencil moustache above a flashing
Smile, daring you to respond, to be
As strong, as devil-may-care as he, to
Elope with him, burn your bridges behind you.
I'd cover those lips, that moustache, those eyes,
Those glistening waves with moist kisses—
First making sure I was alone. Best of all
I'd like to sneak into my parents' room
With my photo when they were gone. I guess
Because it was a grown-up's room and I
So wanted to be grown up. Sometimes I'd
Get so carried away, I'd . . . excite myself
To a climax. It was utter ecstasy—
Something I had never ever felt before. . . .

Or since. Once in awhile I'd fall asleep
Exhausted, clutching the photo to my stomach.
My mother once discovered me this way
And awoke me. I must have thoroughly
Frightened her because I leaped from the bed
And rushed from the room headlong, locking myself
In my own room for hours, too ashamed
To face the inevitable questions.
But there were none. My mother acted as if
Nothing had happened. It was never mentioned.
For a long time I feared she would shame me,
Especially in front of my father,
So I was extra well behaved, careful
Not to cross her. Then I suppose I forgot—
And things went back to normal."

                    Victor listened.
One of the few times she mentioned her mother.
"You felt your mother sympathized, or what?"

"No, I never felt she sympathized. Rather
I suppose she was herself too embarrassed
To bring it up."
                    She was annoyed by his
Question about her mother. Why that? Always
He picked up something about her mother.
Why today, of all days? She felt that he
Had poured cold water on her ardor. Why?
He just didn't want to hear about it.
Who was she anyway, a neurotic
Female—millions like her. He's seen dozens.
But he wasn't going to get away
With that this time.
                    "Why do you grab at any
Reference to my mother? Leave her out of it.
She has nothing at all to do with what's

On my mind today." No. I won't get mad,
She told herself. Not today. Not at him.
"Please let me go on. So much is on my mind,
About you . . . and me."

                       Kleinman retreated,
Debating still whether triangular
Matters were at issue or dyadic.
Was it not that mother owned father's love?
Not so, he argued with himself. Not love
At all. Rather mother and daughter struggled
Over father's manliness. The photo was
A phallus attached to the stomach not
The true image of a male whose love was sought.
Note the ingenious mixture of traits—
Clever, shrewd, yet petite and ravishing—
Yes, ravishing with its double entendre.
She had to win through love what was not
Hers as yet, nor was she capable of love.
Men were idealized or devalued,
Clark Gable or her husband. She could not
Truly sympathize with her husband's plight
Because she envied his strength even weakened
As now it was.

                   Frances had continued:
"I want to start a business—a teashop,
A little nook of a place with a few
Small tables, quite English. Scones and tiny
Cucumber sandwiches. At first just for
Afternoon tea and then, if it succeeds,
Keep it open for lunch and continental
Breakfasts—croissants, hard rolls, homemade
Preserves. And if it really takes off—dinner,
A complete restaurant with French cuisine.
Oh! But that wouldn't be for years, if ever.

By then my kids will be grown and I can
Run the business full time. It's exciting
To even think about. Ruthie Prescott
Wants to be my partner. Eventually
She would like to add a little bookstore,
Offering the best current stuff and the classics
In paperback. Wouldn't it be a breath
Of fresh air for this stale town? I plan for it
To become a café-type place, where people
Can gather to talk, read their newspaper
Or look through the newspapers from abroad
We'd have available gratis. I see
Myself hovering in the background, making
It all work, cooking, baking, or moving
From table to table, eavesdropping
A little, or stirring up a flagging
Conversation with a tidbit of news,
Or a timely witticism or two.
And it would also make a little money.
I do want it to make a good profit
So that we'd have the means to expand it
Step by step."

          How American, he thought.
A nice sidewalk café was not enough.
It had to grow bigger and bigger, become
Perhaps eventually a chain of cafés.
He put aside his mild annoyance and
Took careful note of this more realistic,
Possibly attainable fantasy.
But where had Clark Gable gone—and he himself?
Love and ambition—the one a graceful filly,
The other a rearing stallion. How could both
Be yoked to the same wagon? And yet they must
Or the wagon moves in circles or it
Is dashed to bits.

"I must point out to you
That you have dropped the Gable fantasy
And are now describing a business fantasy.
Your thoughts?"

"I know. My mind is so scattered.
One minute I want to run off . . . with you,
The next I want a small business downtown.
Makes no sense at all. But it feels the same.
It's the same excitement, clutching the photo,
Or presiding over my little café.
But I don't know what it is, that feeling."

"It is power."

"What? I didn't quite hear you.
I thought you said power."
"I did—power."

"I'm suddenly feeling very dizzy,
As if I'm going to fall off this couch.
Power? I don't see what you mean. . . .
I once went climbing with a group of boys.
They were up ahead of me. I shouldn't
Have gone. I'm no climber. There was this narrow
Place and I froze, unable to go on.
I was helped across."

"This is the narrow place
Again, between your love and your ambition."

"You mean between Clark Gable and my teashop?!"

"No. They are both the same. Yourself you said so.
The same excitement."

"Then who? ... My husband?
You can't mean that. He's killing whatever
Love I ever had for him. I despise him.
He's throwing everything away—career,
Marriage, family—himself."

"As once you said,
If only you had his chances. . . . "

"That's right.
If only. But I haven't and I don't.
Maybe that's not so anymore. I do
Have a chance you've helped me find recently.
Yes, why can't I climb my own little hill,
One that no one else wants, but still is high
Enough. Just a little elevation
Is all I want, to lift my eyes, my pride.
If I had a husband like you, I'd have
Been there long ago—like your wife."

"You must still
Miss the point. It is not me or Gable
You much want. Not the persons in themselves
But what they represent for you—power.
The power to make your hill and climb it.
The power to have your own photo and use it
To masturbate, to have your own orgasm
In father's bed—the source for you of power—
That mother had first claim to."

Frances squinted
Her eyes as if the light had become too bright.
Her head felt charged with electric particles
Of zig-zagging thoughts she could not follow,
But which left a glowing trail of significance.
She experienced a rising tide of resolve.

Victor's crisp voice announced, "We must stop now."
The hour had unfolded predictably.
It proved to him how possible it was
To discover the shape and purpose hidden
In the heart's most chaotic impulses.

13

She was eager for her hour and alarmed
At the high voltage of her restlessness
Between sessions. Nothing else mattered
For long—kids, housework, even her fantasy
Teashop. She discovered it was surprisingly
Easy to ignore her husband, to turn
Away from him as he had turned away
From her. They lived side by side in grim
Indifference. Occasionally she would catch
A look of loneliness in his gray eyes
And a spark of tenderness, of old love
Momentarily reappearing. But he
Must be the first to speak, throw a bridge of words
Across the deepening cleft in their marriage.
In the meantime she found herself content
With things as they were between them, a new
Feeling for her. Only the extent of her
Restlessness troubled her. She felt it as
A tension of suspense and expectancy,
Puzzling because she didn't know about what—
Was it simply to be back there on the couch
Bathed in her own thoughts and in his presence?
That prospect stirred no fright or guilt as it
Once had. No. It was an opportunity—
Just that. For once she would master her life.

For once the future would follow from *her*
Decisions. No more dangling from his string.
Sex was over between them until he
Demonstrated he could *love* instead of mope.

"What a world this is! As I feel better
About myself, I feel worse about my marriage.
Maybe it won't survive. But I'm not troubled
About it. Like watching a ship disappear.
Slowly something as big as a building
In which you've lived becomes smaller than a pea
And disappears completely from your life.
You're ashore with lots to do ahead of you.
That's how I'm feeling."

                              Yes, Victor considered,
She must abandon love in order to act.
Only the stallion is hitched to the wagon.
He deserved a divorce, that piteous fool.
But he also felt the spur of her intent
Dig into his own flesh. She meant to ride him.
He could see the impending turnabout.
The disappearing boat was the lost romance
Of passive coupling, the fiction of Gable's lips
Drawing forth her kisses. He thrust his tongue
Into his cheek, stretching it, probing it.
He acquired a sudden detachment, a firm
Grasp of his current purpose. But he must wait.

"I've been feeling so restless. It's you now.
I must want to be here . . . with you, I suppose."
She could not shake her feeling of betrayal
Her words brought on. It made her defiant.
How dare Paul intrude on her analysis!
"Whatever I've said I think you're a great
Analyst. I really am feeling better

About myself. At peace. But also eager
To do something with my life. Not climb mountains,
Mind you, but sit on my own little hill
And, I suppose, build a teashop there
Where I'd love to serve you Earl Grey and scones
With double Devon cream and gooseberry jam.
And you'd pay *me*! Not as much as I pay you,
You can bet, but what it's worth—two dollars?"

She laughed, delighting in her fantasy,
Even more in the freedom to utter it.

"Or are you a coffee drinker—dark and
No sugar? Straight. No, I don't think so
Somehow. Oh, yes! Now I know—espresso!
That's it. A thimbleful of strong, thick mud,
Like that Turkish syrupy stuff. Not for me,
But in my café the menu will be long,
One of those extralength menus, listing
Choices, blends, varieties from around the world.
I'd give a free meal to anyone who asked
For a tea or coffee not on the menu."

He couldn't help thinking of Anna at her
Hopscotch, teasing him, taunting him cunningly.
That extralong list, the skeleton key.
The offer one couldn't refuse, everything
On it, everything open to it—almost.
He felt dizzy, his detachment had vanished.
A surge of violent strength pulsed through him.
His tongue made a quick circle between his
Lips and teeth, cleansing them, preparing them.

"That extralong menu, what comes to mind?"

"Penises, of course!" she joked, fearing

To him it was no joke.

"Yes . . . and . . . ?"

"Really,
Doctor Kleinman, you've got to be kidding.
Here I invite you to my café and
Hand you a menu, and you think I've put
A penis in your lap!"

"Where? In the lap?"

"Where else would you put a penis—in your
Mouth?" She blushed furiously, mad and ashamed
At the same time.

"You think I rub it off
When I talk about your wish for a penis,
As if I am looking down at you?"

Frances
Burst into laughter. "You can't mean rub it *off*!
Or maybe you do . . . maybe—." Her laughter
Rose to a new crescendo.

Kleinman frowned,
Unsure of his infraction in that fractious
Language he had long been stumbling over.
Was it "off" or "in"? It must of course be "in."
"Rub it off" must then mean to erase. Yes,
To erase, and "rub it in" to make something sore.
But then "to rub your nose *in* it" means what?
Whose nose? Hers or his? It has to do with shit,
Rubbing a dog's nose in its own shit so
It won't shit in the wrong place again. So?
How did that apply? He knew he was lost.

Her bold laughter was disconcerting him.
Her neurosis would escape him again.

"You make fun of me to change the subject
From how you wish to be the one in power,
Possessing the extralong menu, standing
Over me as I sit, I paying *you.*
Even your laughter is at my weakness.
You are the one who wishes to 'rub it off.'
But of course I should have said 'rub it in.'
Sometimes your propositions are beyond me."
Again he heard a split-second too late
Another gaff.

For Frances this was too much.
Her chest, her sides began quaking with laughter.
Kleinman looked on, vexed at his clumsiness.
Uneasily he was becoming convinced
That it was not all linguistic error.
"Propositions?" What was she proposing?
That he be her customer, admire her
Complete menu, sit in her presence. So?
Was she showing him her wished-for penis
Or her own female genitals to admire?
No. That would not unsettle him at all.
It had to be her "proposal" that he
Surrender his capacity to help her,
To use his analytic skill in her
Behalf, which she resented even as she
Praised him for it. He had to be strong enough
To win her praise, or else she would dismiss him
As she had her husband, yet ready to
Yield up his strength at her derisive assault.
Contradictory. But not in the unconscious.

Her laughter had exhausted itself, ending

With an involuntary sigh as tears,
Diamonding her eyes, lit up her merriment.

"Nothing . . . nothing I can say to that one.
It's a beauty—a rare gem! It's your turn."

"My turn to lie down on the couch, not so?"

"I know better than that. But shouldn't you
Say a little something about it, like
'You see I'm human too. I make mistakes,
I have an unconscious that trips me up
Just like yours.' That would be friendly. Too friendly?"

Kleinman felt he was losing his leverage.
She had taken the high ground, patronizing him
For his slip. She would soon devalue him
Utterly, luxuriating in his fate,
While trapping herself in high-minded triumph.

Something had slipped away. Her mood shifted.
She could not go on alone. She needed him.
Couldn't he take some spoofing, a bit of
Teasing? These uptight Germans, all so thinskinned.
She recalled a dream that brought a gasp
Of recognition. She'll not tell him. But
Shouldn't she? She had to. Otherwise it's a waste.

"I had a different kind of dream last night—
I mean—it was like something real, that could
Actually happen—not all mixed up.
I was beautifully dressed in a long gown.
It was a reception. Everyone was
Congratulating me and I was being
Gracious, glowing with excitement, standing
On this reception line as crowds pressed

Around me, shaking my hand, patting me
On the back for something great that I had done.
It didn't matter what because in the dream
The excitement was in being famous,
Popular, successful, beautiful
All rolled up together. The way kids feel
When they play. Just looking the part, acting
The part is enough to make it all be real.
As you discover later, more real than
It really can ever be. I don't want that—
A childhood fact and an adult fake.
I enjoyed the dream but didn't like it.
I didn't like myself in it."

                    Kleinman
Drew in his breath, glanced at the clock on the shelf,
Saw how little time was left, how rich the dream,
How much could be done with it. Eagerness
Flooded back like vivifying blood.
"You don't like yourself because you will not
Be real to yourself. The actuality
Of doing what you most want to do for
Yourself you deny, exclude from the dream
As from your life, as from the analysis."

She felt too much as though he were lifting her
To look out a window at an ugly world—
His world of power, ambition, and greed.
There had to be another way for her.

14

"Ruthie Prescott and I were having our coffee
When the phone rang. To my surprise it was
Paul calling from the office—he seldom does,
At least these days. He called to tell me
Serey had been put in the hospital.
At first I thought he meant something physical
Had happened to her. But it was to our
Own hospital. She'd had a psychotic break.
Donald was her doctor. I started trembling so
I couldn't put the receiver back.
Ruthie asked me what the matter was.
I couldn't talk. When I finally told her
She was thunderstruck. Donald hadn't told her.
I was stunned. We both started to cry.
How had it happened? Wasn't she in treatment,
And with Greta? Isn't that what treatment's for,
To keep you from getting sicker? Why Serey?
It could happen to any one of us—
Sometimes I worry about myself, all
Wrapped up in this analysis so that
Nothing else matters. Not my marriage. Not
My kids. It's like being in a dream
From which you want to wake up but can't—or won't,
It's scary. Maybe Serey went deeper still
Into *her* dream and it overwhelmed her.

But where was Greta? Why didn't she stop her?
Maybe you analysts don't know so much
After all. Maybe there are things you can't
Control although you act as if you can.
I'll admit that scares me. I want to feel
You know what you're doing, especially
When I am totally at sea. But then
I also wish you didn't know so much,
That what I really thought was safe from you.
I'm getting confused again—that's always
Where my thoughts end—in total confusion.
And then I need you and hope you'll care enough
To take my hand and lead me through the fog
Of my own thoughts. I sound helpless, don't I?
Shameful, isn't it? . . . And I'm not so sure
I can rely on you anymore. What of Greta?
Serey relied on her and see what happened—
I can't go crazy. I'd lose everything . . .
And I thought I was getting somewhere here
Lately. It's all a mirage. A stupid stageset.
I hear rumors too. Rumors about you.
Did you know you're leaving for Washington?
That you're not getting the directorship?
That Freeman is being considered for it?
Wild stuff, I know, but that's what's flying around.
You won't leave me in the middle of this,
Will you? That I couldn't stand, that would
Drive me over the edge. Maybe that's what
Happened to poor Serey! Maybe the Denkmans
Are leaving along with you and she found out
From Michael."
                    It was as if she heard the deep
Echoing clang of a massive steel door
Shutting. She was trapped. At the very moment
When she thought her way was opening up.
She had to be told if he were leaving—

Had to. How could she go on otherwise?
"Well, are you . . . leaving? You can't *not* tell me,
It's too important."
                    She awaited his answer,
Convinced it would not be forthcoming, yet
Painfully aware she had to have it.

Victor had listened keenly to his patient's
Struggle with the shadow-play of
Fact, fantasy, desire, and anxiety.
He profoundly enjoyed these passages
Through the narrow isthmus between pain
And despair. She must hold the rudder steady
And not let pain shatter her achievement,
Or give up prematurely and sink in sight
Of open water. There was no danger
Of a break. There was no need to tell her
Anything. In any case nothing was sure.

"You present yourself again as helpless,
Unable without me to manage yourself.
Different from before when you own your shop
And I'm the customer paying you,
And you are having a whole show of your own.
Perhaps it's not Serey at all, but your
Own anxiety over so wanting to
Do it all yourself—and without me.
You counteract your wish to be rid of me."

She had the sinking feeling he was saying
Good bye. You can get along without me now.
If you walk ahead a little you're on
Your own! A sharp pain of recognition
Accompanied an image of her parents
Hiding from her when she had run ahead,
Exploring on her own. Where was he now?

Cruelly withholding what he knew. That's for sure.

"When I was a kid out for a walk with
My parents, sometimes I'd run on ahead
And when I'd turn around they'd be gone.
I would call out for them, burst into tears
When it seemed they had totally disappeared,
As if fallen off the face of the earth.
There is just no feeling like that—completely
Gone. Then out they would pop from their hiding
   place
And through my relieved tears I wanted to
Kill them on the spot. And they were laughing,
Enjoying my helpless rage and neediness.
I never have forgiven them for that."

The memory, he thought, was quite suitable.
It fit. She had resumed her work. For him
The task was plain.
                          "It was your guilt of running
Ahead and leaving them, of wanting to
Be rid of them, that made you so frightened.
You say you wanted to kill them 'on the spot.'
Yes, but you wanted to kill them yet before—
When you ran so ahead. You can't accept
The aggression in your own ambitions.
It makes you guilty and then you run back—
Like you were doing before with me."

                                      "I can't
Understand that. I could run ahead *because*
I knew, or thought I knew, they were still there
Behind me, looking on, enjoying my success—
I mean my taking off on my own,
O.K.—but you would be here enjoying,
Taking pride in my success. But not really.

They were more interested in having fun
At my expense—and maybe you are too."

"How is it fun?"

"You sit back there hiding
From me what you know, gloating over my fright
Like my parents did."

An edge of anger
Sharpened his resolve to make it clear to her,
To bring home to her, how she crippled herself.
"See how you must make *me* into a sadist
So that you yourself can be free of guilt
Over your *own* sadistic impulses,
Your own desires, your own wishes
To strike out on your own. A good English phrase,
To strike out. I believe 'strike' also means
'To hit,' does it not?"

"But it also means to fail,
To swing and miss the ball three times—and you're
out."

"You are being aggressive with me right now
When you attack me with things in English
I cannot know. You are poking fun at me,
At my ignorance. You are the superior,
Running on ahead where I cannot follow."

"Am I? Then please don't disappear on me.
Let me have my little fun at your expense."

She was patronizing him. That was clear,
He thought, escaping thus the import of
His words. When she had accused him earlier

Of hiding he had felt uneasy, images
Of flight, the sheer swerve of motion, of wind
Through the hair tightening the scalp, possessed him
Kinesthetically. Now it was a tension
In his fingers reaching a degree of pain.
He curled his fingers toward his palm and something
Vague brought a bitter taste to his probing tongue.
A rush of vigor. His eyes trained upon her
With intensity. It was the waiting,
The patience, he knew to be his shortcoming.
He had always to fight in himself the urge
To plunge ahead through the underbrush, clearing
The way. But too often to his surprise
His patients didn't follow but veered instead
Into a thicket of their own making.
With her right now he found it particularly
Trying. He felt analysis tied his hands
Behind his back, while knowing that was false.
His hands were free; it was she who was not.
Again he felt a twist of motion, of pain
In his fingertips. The taste was of his
Last meeting with Kurt. That was over, he thought.

She was by now stubbornly entrenched in grief
That kept on growing as the hour continued.
She was hearing what he said, but somehow
Strangely it was like a pantomime, silent
On what she most wished to hear, the gestures
Dramatizing what she already knew,
The sadness in her an old recognition.

"We must stop now," she heard his voice announce
When what she most wanted was to continue.
When finally would life meet the yearning
In her heart to be both free and loved?

Part Three

Marlena Kleinman
and
Bernard Freeman

15

A flash of red past the window made Freeman
Look up—a cardinal. His eyebrows arched
Expectantly; the bird might return and feed.
Such color! He called for his next patient
And continued peering out the window,
Hoping the bird would stop at the feeder.

"May I come in, Dr. Freeman?"

                                    He turned
From the window and gestured toward the couch.
Marlena felt the gesture off-handed.
In an instant, she was angry and vengeful,
Eager to start the session on her terms:
"You were so absorbed in your bird-watching
You didn't hear me at the door. That's perfect!
My husband and analyst both ignore
My existence."

                          Freeman's eyes widened, large
Lucent eyes, that now were expressing a mild
Quizzical concern. As she lay down
He felt drawn toward the window. Now a gray
Flash and then the she-cardinal settled
At the feeder.

"Oh, by the way, some news—
My paper on children's play and analysis
Has been accepted for the winter program.
My husband writes the same paper over
And over, gives it different names, and flies
All over to read it, making a big noise.
You, you finish a paper every ten years—
Like clockwork! A very good one, I'll admit."

How quiet she once was, he mused, a mouse
Nibbling at the big cheeses. Now she roared,
A lioness bringing down huge buffalo
With a leap to the jugular. The male
Suddenly appeared at the feeder rim.
The female edged away. He turned, saying,
"It's clear your previous deference was purposeful—
It kept your bitter resentment hidden
Toward men sitting in the seats of power
Who are really unequal to their tasks."

"You are absolutely right. I think, 'Do go on,
Observe your silly birds, keep them well fed,
Don't finish your paperwork, your research—Ah!'
You are, of course, laughing at me back there."
Victor's superior smirk and Freeman's laughter,
The one remembered, the other imagined,
Together bound her spirit. Her mood changed.
"You must know that Victor is out to get
The research directorship. Your friend, Allan,
Doesn't stand a chance. The search committee
Is stacked against him. You will be alone—
With your birds!"

                    "Tell me more about these birds."

"What more? You must sit for hours watching them.

I suppose you feed them, are amused by them.
Yes, I do feel a twinge of jealousy.
I said I felt ignored when I came in.
I see where this is heading—interesting!
It does remind me of my older brother
With his incredible telescope.
Of course! A telescope is perfect. Perfect!
Voyeuristic, phallic, probing, powerful.
I did in fact wish to steal it from him
But it was much too big to drag away.
Instead, I stood around looking crestfallen
And he would pick me up and let me look.
I couldn't see a thing but I was dazzled
By his strength. He'd sweep me up like a feather.
It almost felt as if I were flying.
I leaned my head against his cheek, forgetting
My wish to peer at the heavens. He was—
Marvelous.''

   He marveled at the flight of
His patient's mind, like a homing pigeon
Let loose miles away in strange surroundings,
Circling a few times, and then heading home
Unerringly, drawn by invisible threads,
Magnetic lines of force perhaps. Is there
A paper in that? His lips pursed, annoyed
At himself for this quite unwelcome thought.
But she had stung him with her ten-year crack.
More troublesome was her husband's ambition—
Enough of that!

   "How nice of you to place
My birds among your brother's stars, yourself
At my shoulder looking out the window.
When you saw me looking up at the cardinals
You wanted me to invite you over

Not to motion you toward the couch."

                                    "Those birds!
What *do* you see in them! Just like those stars.
When I grew up and learned what stars really were—
Blazing suns, dead cinders, collapsed worlds
I felt cheated, disappointed in him
For making the world falsely wonderful. . . .
You said it was *nice* of me, didn't you?
You don't take my anger, my ambition
Seriously. You think I'm just boasting,
Don't you? Even my husband reads my papers
Just to see if I've stolen his ideas—
Some marriage! When we make love he twists
My arms around my back, pins me to the bed
And thrusts blindly, his eyes closed as if afraid
To see my expression. He's right. I detest
His passion, his grunting and snorting
And when I'm good and ready I deliver
Myself to my passion privately as he
Stokes my slumbering heat into a blaze
And I vanish into an unbounded space,
Dark, filled with rushing winds and piercing sounds.
Sometimes he becomes frightened—*he* frightened!
Imagine! Then *I* am supremely powerful!
Screaming, twisting loose, biting and scratching,
Till finally he slaps me hard. I spit
At him like a sated she cat driving off
A tom who still wants more. Then we both laugh,
Discover we have ravenous appetites,
And make ourselves huge Dagwood sandwiches.
I get excited even thinking about it!"

How she assaults him, striking back at him
Simply for his rejection of her bid
To stand beside him—a great furious cloud

Of pornography. He felt sick. His nights
Were ... quieter, shy stirrings, strokings
With balance and ritual repetitions,
The pleasure achieved as of two oarsmen
Crossing the finish line with one long stroke.
He felt his lips tighten, his throat turn dry.
For a moment he hated her. Why? He thought:
This overblown intensity upset him.
He was tempted to lampoon it—turn it
Into a Grosz cartoon of fat German
Bourgeois flesh. He smiled at the thought. But no
That would not do. *There* was the exact nerve
He had to touch: her own self-caricature.
"You've seldom talked about your love-making
In such detail and yet with such distance."

"As I was doing it I saw your face
And I wondered how you were taking it.
'That will drive the birds out of his fuzzy brain,'
I thought. 'That will stir his languid hormones.
Maybe even get him furious at me.'
Enough being a mouse, Miss Politeness
Nineteen six oh. But it's all quite true
Nonetheless."

        A picture formed in his mind.

Paunchy Victor glued like a mating frog
To Marlena as she bucked and tore at him.
He smiled at the humor in that odd scene,
The turnabout. Something was echoing
In his mind. The meeting yesterday. Victor,
Haranguing as usual. Marlena smiling
Quietly, egging him on. This she was
Doing right now with him—but differently—
Not with a smile but with a leer. She set up

Her brother too—gawking at him lovingly
While unmasking his heaven as a fake.
Why? Because she hated the love men stirred,
The passion and the need they made her feel.
He was ready!

                    "You are still at the window,
Wanting to look out with me and hating me
For it, as you hate Victor for making
Passionate love, stirring a response
Which you must then enjoy only by yourself,
Just as you came to reject your brother's
Stars because his strength excited you."

"At the meeting last night you were so silent.
I admired you for it. Victor was grim.
He always gets that way when he's smelling
Victory. Your silence puzzled him—cool,
Seemingly indifferent, reserved, and calm.
He's convinced the research position's his
And he awaits some signal of defeat
From you and Allan. He flies off tonight
For California. It makes him uneasy
To leave the field before the white flag's raised.
You might have a trick or two up your sleeve."

"In my comment I called your attention
To how you reject your own tender feelings
By hating those who arouse them in you."

"All right. But *you* must also be troubled
By Victor, only you can't talk about that.
Is that too much reality for me?
Or for you? . . . All this fighting bothers me!
Why can't I have my own analysis
Without my husband's business butting in!

I know I raised it first. I know it matters
But somehow I wish it were otherwise—
That I wasn't a psychiatrist, that you
Were not at odds with my husband, that he
Was working someplace else. And yet I know
It really doesn't matter. There's still me
And there's still you—and this analysis."

There was a sensible core to the woman,
He thought. Thank God for that small voice of reason.

"But one last comment on things political.
Dreyfus is causing trouble in Research
Against Victor and Allan both. Does he
Himself want it? He's so obsessive,
Has such trouble with his hostility.
You'd never guess he had any ambitions.
I suppose you'd know. . . . Oh! Could you be using
Him against Victor? That would be clever!"

She was causing him uneasiness again.
Paul Dreyfus was a puzzle in all this.
He felt the thread of the hour slip from his grasp.
It was time to stop. The birds were long gone.
It had turned dark outside. She bounded up,
Exited quickly without looking back.

16

"When Victor returns I'm a three-year-old,
Eager to see him, too angry to show it,
And spoiling for a fight. I manage indifference
While he is fussing to tell me everything—
Nearly. After awhile in my own sweet time,
I'll offer him a drink, sit down at his feet,
And listen to him. . . . How often I've done that—
With my father, brother, a few boy friends.
I feel like the RCA Victor dog
Gazing into that large trumpet speaker
On those old Victrolas. How tiresome you
All are! You are the first man who *listens*
For a change, but I am still at your feet.
You do listen and you do understand.
I think of this room, this couch, you back there
As an island of sanity for the insane.
At times I think I am totally mad
Trying to do so much, so earnestly—
Papers, presentations, patients, teaching,
Supervision, meetings, house, children, husband—
Madness. At night I lie down in my bed
And everything starts to spin as if
All day long I have suppressed the spinning
And now when I am at last motionless
The pent-up spinning like a spring leaps out,

A crazy jack-in-the-box. Or like when
You've been swimming all day and then at night
In your bed your body feels lifted up and down.
It's good to lie down here and rest up.
Strange how safe I feel. It's the only place . . .
I thought of you today. You can be so
Deeply quiet as if your silence were
An ocean. . . . How I long for a vacation!
Sunbathing, swimming, just nothing to do. . . .
It is! It is! It is like a vacation
In here. I really have hit upon it,
Haven't I? The couch is my beach and you
The ocean itself—deeply, deeply quiet.
And for fifty minutes I can breathe easy,
Gaze across my inner horizon—for birds!
That was a bit nasty! I can't help it.
Put me with a man and I must twit him
Sooner or later."
                    The lightness in her voice
Did not betray the sudden anguish she felt
At committing an old mistake again.
Tears started in her eyes and the silence
Punished. Freeman waited, mused, and smiled
Faintly. Her own feelings would do the job.
No need for words for now. A patient sea,
Analysis, moving with its own tides,
The storms only at the surface, noisemakers,
The leviathan depths unaffected
Where the ocean's life truly exists and breathes
Imperturbably. Or, its calm
May hide profound upheavals, continents
Separating, merging, islands being born,
As the rim of land shakes and men totter.
Freeman, in his oversized leather chair,
His feet stretched onto the matching hassock,
Felt the voluptuous tickle of power—

And thus the smile. But his gaze turned outward.
The birds were always there and the squirrels
Robbing the poor birds blind. So they could fly!
But wings, as the New York cab driver says,
Don't bake bread. You can starve with fancy wings.
It was always necessary to be practical—
Squirrel-practical. He checked his thoughts
And he wondered. Had he joined his patient
In her sharp jibes about his bird-watching?
No. The birds were for him parables only.
He could not see himself traipse through the woods
On cold dark mornings to await the arrival
Of some rare twit of a bird. Not for him.

Marlena waited for a blast of coldness
To blow her off the couch and out of the room.
Already a crystalline brittleness
Shimmered in the frozen air of his silence.
At first a vague memory of illness
Cast a fleeting shadow and then it began—
An uncontrollable shivering.
Where was the blanket she could pull over her?
Where was the warm hand on her forehead,
The voice telling her she could stay at home
That day? She would hunker down, snuggling
Under the blanket, breathing in the wool
Fuzziness and feel so safe, suspended
In her wool, warm, cocoon. Shivers
Ran the length of her body, shaking the couch.
Her voice trembled as she tried to speak.

"Heavens!
What's happening to me! I can't stop it.
Someone is shaking me like a rattle."
A sudden gloominess took hold of her.
The shivering ceased. She closed her eyes, waited

For him to speak. But he did not. Silence—
Bitter, condemning, mind-altering
Silence. She circled over herself, cocking
An eye at the puny form far below.
What a piece of earthbound baggage is the self.
Only the intellect can soar and sing.

"I know your birds now, dear Dr. Freeman.
They are your ideas of me, or my ideas
Of you. Your bird-watching is all in the head."

"So I'm all figured out. How about you?
You were so distraught a moment ago,
Feeling like a rattle in a baby's hand."

What good did it really do to attack.
The weight of her own assault was turned
Against her. He would not fight back like Victor.
"I can't help being me! Can't you see that?
Me, me, me, me, me—a one-note aria.
How awful and screechy. My intellect
Is my passport to peaceful me-lessness,
Or it's a winged horse for me to mount and ride—
To steer and to spur, finally to cage it.
If you like, my intellect is my falcon.
Oh, I wish I could send it up this moment
To hover above the couch and poke your eyes out!"

"Clearly you want to turn my birds against me
Rather than against yourself. Something happened
Awhile back. Your voice trembled. What was it?"

"Who knows. I get so disheartened with myself.
Always the same mistakes. I felt peaceful,
Relaxed, sensing you back there as a friendly
Presence. And then the claws, the petty claws. . . . "

"Tell me about that shift."

                      Marlena tensed,
Felt herself become annoyed. He was probing.
Well, wasn't that part of analysis?
Grudgingly she cooperated, saying:
"When I was about six, I hated school.
Hard to imagine that, I suppose. But
True enough. My first grade teacher frightened me.
She'd take attendance, then look under your nails,
How I feared that inspection! I'd hang back
As long as I could. But my turn would come.
I would panic and start to cry. She'd take
Both hands firmly in hers and say grimly,
'What nasty things have you been doing with them
Lately, Marlena? Why! They are perfect!
What a strange girl you are. You may sit down.'
I wanted desperately to hide. 'Nasty things!'
'Nasty things!' kept shouting loud in my head
So that I thought everyone could hear it.
What horrid humiliation. Often
I'd play sick in the morning and mother
Would let me stay in bed."

                      Freeman listened,
Puzzled. What had all this to do with the shift?
With whom was she snuggling in bed? Always
A bed with her, like the last hour. Masturbation
Certainly was in the picture somewhere.
Freeman did not enjoy being puzzled.
He frowned and his thick eyebrows bruised each other.

"When mother would come in to visit me
I'd let her feel my forehead. I'd pout
As if expecting that she'd see through me
And I was already reproaching her

In advance. She'd smile knowingly
And announce I had a raging fever.
Her baby was desperately ill. Only
An emergency treatment of love could
Bring me round. She'd climb into bed with me
And we'd hug and snuggle, giggle and gossip—
So much better than that ugly teacher . . .
My mother close to me. Can you imagine
What that was like! I can feel it now.
Nothing else existed. . . . My 'bon-bon' mother.
I'd call her that—'Bon-Bon,' and she'd call me
'Cher-Cherie'—silly, sweet, and delicious.
No one would be at home. Father working,
Brother at school. At first she'd scold me gently
For being naughty and getting sick. I'd make
A long face, looking so woebegone she'd
Cover it with her hand, exclaiming, 'Horrible!
Don't make yourself so ugly. It might stick,
Then where would you be? An ugly girl
Wanted by no one, no one at all! Smile!
That's much, much better. You'll marry some day
After all.' I'd say teasingly, knowing
Her answer, 'Bon-Bon, why must I marry?'
She'd reply, 'What else is a woman to do?'
'Why can't I stay with you, Bon-Bon, forever?'
'Cher-Cheri, how marvelous that would be!'
And she'd sing a song in her beautiful voice.
I would take her hand in mine and place it
Against my cheek and fall soundly asleep."
Marlena crossed her hands over her bosom
And stared at the ceiling. "It's all school now,"
She said, her voice flat and sad.

                                        Freeman
Had listened intently, deciding now
It was time to speak. "Yes, the birds are ideas,

The unhappy ideas of brother and father
Which take me from you, as does the part I play
In the research directorship matter.
You do not want to see me at those meetings.
You want me here, waiting for the sick child."

Marlena's thoughts were racing toward the evening.
A few people would be over: Kurt, Greta,
Michael, Donald, and old Rupenthal, always
Falling asleep. But he was necessary. . . .
She knew she was waiting out the hour's end.
And soon it came. She left as though released.

17

"Last night I made you sit invisible
In a corner taking in the fun and
It was fun. Victor wanted a gathering
For a few intimates. Old Rupenthal
Was actually on his mind. He can be
Crusty and unpredictable but he craves
Admiration especially from the young.
That's why Michael and Donald were there. And I
Was not to be backward in friendliness.
Victor, you know, is suspicious of my . . .
Involvement with you, what I do or don't
Tell you. Occasionally he will pump me
Quite discreetly. Of course, I tell him what
I think I know. But he knows far more than I.
What can I learn here? Except what you're like
And that he already knows well enough.
At times, like now, I can step back and see
It all for what it really is—a crazy
Chess game with people as pieces like that scene
In Alice—the real and unreal confused.
At times I feel that only this experience
Is real—The chess game come alive, while life
Out there is the game, or dream from which we wake.
Crazy for Victor, Kurt, Greta, and myself
To embroil our careers in this toy kingdom

Where grown analysts play at tin soldiers,
Beat their little drums and plot quaint stratagems—
That's what I gave you to think in that corner.
Then I could wear a distant amused smile
All evening, noting to myself those things
I'd report to you today for us to
Chuckle over—of course, not aloud from you."

Freeman was made uneasy by all this
Camaraderie until he recalled the
Previous hour. He was the corrupting
Mother joining her in her war against
That masculine world, that fake toy kingdom.
Only mother and she were real and mattered
As they cuddled together in her bed
Escaping school and father and brother.
He felt as if he could foresee the flight
Of her mind from the moment of its launching.
There was a profound satisfaction in that.

"It's so strange to feel relaxed for a change.
I don't know what's come over me. But I
Like it very much. I concede you've helped.
And why not? I've had worse patients than myself.
But I shouldn't belittle your achievement.
At the very least because it's my own
As well. Last time I spoke of analysis
As a vacation. I'm on it still, but
Now I know it and so much the better.
Oh, I wish I could enter your mind and
Fish in it for those elusive gourmet
Interpretations—all filleted but for
One bone—shall I call it the sticking point?"

Freeman was impressed with her playfulness,
Or was coltishness an apter word for it?

The quiet mouse, the roaring Amazon
Were both gone. Here was an entertaining child—
"Cher—Cherie." How analysis made time
Into a backward walking clown wearing
It's face on the back of its head so that
It walked backward into the present and
Always faced forward toward the past.

                                                Marlena
Was remembering: "One time we took
A trip, 'Bon-Bon,' and myself, on a train
To visit my grandmother. I marveled
At how I could see at the very same time
My face in the window and the fields beyond.
Was I really in the fields or were the fields
In the train with me, or were we both
In the windowpane like mounted butterflies?
I decided on the last. I would blow breath
On the window and draw butterfly
Outlines, while 'Bon-Bon' smiled at everyone passing
As if they were on promenade. My 'Bon-Bon'
Was of another century, ignorant
Although she was of it. And I was there with her.
How wrenching growing up was, one big shock
After another. . . . But I'm on vacation—
'Bon-Bon' and I—Oh! I just recalled a dream!
I was swirling, swirling like on a huge
Carousel. I had to keep my balance.
Everyone else was riding a horse or lion.
I was trying to find mine but couldn't.
Then as I almost fell off I lurched backward
Into a seat and there were you, knitting!
I was so angry at you for knitting
That I started to push you off the seat
And you turned into a post! Which I grabbed.
Poor Victor wakened me because I was

Choking him."
               The telling of the dream had
Sobered her. She felt vaguely uneasy.

"I'm full of childish things today—carousels!
I can see what I am doing. Can't you?
I'm making you into my mother, 'Bon-Bon.'
I need you so to be a sanctuary,
I am so divided and perplexed, proud of Victor
Really, knowing that success in this tough world
Is not delivered on silver platters.
You have to work for it, yes, even plot,
Politic, and wheedle for it. Virtue
Seldom triumphs without a bit of a boost
From the right person at the right time. But
It can all get so tiresome. That party
Is a case in point. Rupenthal wheezes
Like an old tea kettle and when he laughs, he
Coughs, breathing out salvos of spittle.
The man for all that is urbane and witty,
Charming, even sly. He knew why he was there
And was enjoying it. Victor could relax
Because he knew that the best policy
Was for all to have a good time. Soon enough
Curiosity would bring the talk around
To politics. Michael, always a bit
Off the subject, was talking paperweights,
While Donald listened politely. Rupenthal
Was almost dozing off, stiff drink in hand.
I brightly raised a toast to paperweights
Which baffled Michael, amused Donald, and
Stirred Rupenthal awake, who joined the toast,
Downing his scotch neat in one drowning gulp.
Kurt observed that other toasts might soon be
In order on much weightier subjects.
Old Rupenthal broke into an infectious

Grin and granted that he knew what about.
Turning serious, he looked toward Greta
Seated on the couch near Victor and said,
'We must be absolutely certain that
Victor becomes the next research director.
He is too good a man to waste, you know.'
Then as if noticing Victor for the first time,
He exclaimed, 'And there he is, quiet
As a church mouse!' Victor smiled not knowing
If Rupenthal were joking or serious.
Woodenly he said, 'I am here and ready.'
'Of course you are,' Rupenthal added, smiling.
Kurt read the byplay and raised another toast,
'To Hans Rupenthal, a man who sees all,
Knows much, and says little.' Old Rupenthal
Beamed. Michael, sensing nothing as usual,
Stroked his chin sagely and sententiously
Proffered the opinion that Fabrikant
Was not to be dismissed so lightly.
Kurt fixed Michael with a raised eyebrow stare
And a sly gentle smile as if saying,
'Dear Michael I know you, and you know I
Know you. Please don't show your foolish self
To all this company.' Only your former
Analyst can say so much with a smile.
You could sense the transference tug Michael
Felt as he fell silent and, lowering his eyes,
He picked up a paperweight from the table
And began inspecting it for hidden flaws.
Donald was suggesting that Fabrikant
Was not that seriously interested
In the position. He was too deeply
Involved in his research. Kurt was nodding
In agreement not so much with the truth
Of Donald's point but with its smooth bridging
Over of Michael's boorish seriousness.

The party was meant to stay light-hearted.
Greta asked Victor to put on some lieder.
Victor obliged and as Schubert sang Goethe
We all grew silent in homage to success.
I could still see you in the corner, smirking."

Freeman was following raptly. He
Was reading the map of her past as it
Lay superimposed on her present life—
An overlay revealing the real
Features and their original names. But more
Important still you could now trace her route
Through life which otherwise would be obscure.
The snake in her maternal paradise
Was mother's ignorance of this century—
That was the way she put it before.
Mother did not equip her with a horse,
Or lion, but offered a flat bystander's
Seat and busywork—that's why the knitting,
The anger in the dream. But why the clutching?
"Bon-Bon" was too good to give up and too
Weak to rely on. Vacations can't last.
The world of lions and horses, victor
And vanquished, was still turning and she
Could not get off. He had to give her a lion
Or at least a horse to ride or the game
Would be over. All clear but he would wait.

"That dream I must say troubles me greatly,
Although I can't say altogether why.
But with it went my good vacation feeling.
Oh! I always had to go back to school,
You know. I learned to like it eventually,
Even do well. But I always felt as if
I had to keep my hands behind my back
So no one would check my fingernails.

That's why I'm shy in public. Real silly.
I wonder if you're laughing back there—with me
Or at me? No comment on the party?
Nothing useful there for you or Fabrikant?
Your friend is dead, believe me, and you too
Will not get anywhere. And why should you?"

Freeman felt the wave gathering its force.

"Just kibitzing on the sidelines gets you
Nothing but a few derisive glances.
You can't steer events while sitting on your hands,
You know. At least I hoped this analysis
Would make it possible for me to play
Myself a more active part in all this.
Victor treats me like the little woman.
Make a party, smile for old Rupenthal—
Shit! I'm on the staff. I have a say.
Neither of you thinks I really count.
No doubt about it this analysis
Weakens me, draws my teeth and nails right out.
I should quit. What do I have to show for it?"

Freeman felt the wave crashing about him.
These were the experiences so vital
To the treatment. To feel and profoundly
The inner prick of one's wildest being.
Only then was it time to give it a name
And a habitat.
                    "We must stop for now."

18

She knew it had to be a difficult hour
For her. Caught. She was caught. Sooner or later
It had to happen. Loyalty to herself
Versus loyalty to Victor—and the Cause.
The Cause! No doubt it was important.
She herself was more practical. And Victor?
Practical with a difference. He perceived
The present as a vector only, poised and
Aimed at the future—the immediate
Moment of no intrinsic importance
Or value. It only mattered when it fit
Into the smooth trajectory toward the future.
And now there was something wrong with Serey.
Donald had told her about the phone call.
Where on the curve was that likely to fit?
She hadn't told Victor yet. This was her
Own private moment to relish in secret.
And not even tell Freeman? Not yet.
She had a score to settle with both of them.

"Ambition, I'm thinking of ambition.
It took me awhile to find it in myself
And now it is a welcome fever, a new
Kind of heat that boils up with an odor
Of ozone and electricity. With me it

Comes on with a rush and I must mobilize
My energies immediately, putting
Them to work because the fever soon passes,
Leaving me feeling limp and even used.
But take Victor. Ambition is for him
A natural condition—a pleasure
Of mind and heart to be enjoyed and savored.
No one should misunderstand Victor on
That point: He is not wracked or tortured
By ambition because he lacks all guilt
About it. His mind tells him what to do
And how to pursue it and his heart says:
Do it. Those who oppose him are respected
If equally ambitious, or considered fools
If they insist they act only on principle.
You, he respects although he doesn't share
Your goals. Fabrikant still mystifies him:
Naked ambition lacking all purpose.
Dreyfus is the quintessential naïf,
An oversized babe in the woods, hoping
He'll be discovered to be a great savant
And unanimously crowned as king
Of no matter what land—in the meantime
No one else must be king and anyone
Who tries is evil, evil, evil."

Freeman wondered where last hour's rage had gone.
This talk about ambition was simply
An intermezzo, a span of bridge music.
(He liked the simile and the faint pun.)
Comparing hers and Victor's ambition
Was a thin screen for comparing his and hers.
Was she putting herself down, or putting
Him down? Or was it to be heard either way?

"These different ambitions, are they separate

But equal?"

"That's naughty, Doctor Freeman."

Startled by her reply, he asked, "Naughty?"

"'Separate but equal,' that's what they say about
Segregated schools for black and white kids!"

Freeman went blank for a moment and then
Flushed from the base of his neck to his bald pate.
Blood throbbed in his temples. Had he said that?
Yes, he could hear himself saying it. A slip.
He had spoken in the midst of thinking—
A totally bad business. Freeman smiled,
For he now saw the aptness of his slip.
"Isn't the point that they can't be equal
If separate? And that's the rub?"

                              "Not at all,
Marlena pounced on his effort to ease past
His flub. "That's *your* point not mine. Your mistake,
Not mine for a change. For Victor, ambition
Is full-time, lifelong. For me it's . . . a fever,
Like I said. . . . I mean, it comes over me."
When she heard herself say "fever" again
It's other meaning hit her—illness, disease.
She felt like throwing something at his head.
Had he tricked her with his slip? He's too shrewd
By far!
                "You were calling me a nigger
Who does a frenetic tapdance and then
Sinks into the background, saying, 'Yes, suh.'
You couldn't hear me taking pride in my way
As opposed to Victor's. No. His way, of course,
Had to be better. Superior. The white hope."

No doubt, Freeman concluded, he had been
Nettled. But her anger was expected.
The wave frozen in motion at the end
Of the last hour was now riding into shore.
Yes, let her feel it, taste it swirling over her.
He settled comfortably into silence.

Marlena grit her teeth and folded her arms
Across her chest. She could be as silent
As he. Let the damn hour go down the drain.
Let them all go to hell, every man-jack
Of them. Her thoughts turned to Serey's phone call.
Yes, she would dwell on that. Donald told her
How strange she sounded. Secretly, Marlena
Wondered if Serey were coming unwound.
A bad time for it. But she dismissed
The possibility. Serey was too shrewd,
Too capable, her ego too strong for that.
Yet, stranger things have happened. In her way,
Serey played a key role. She rallied the wives,
Especially the younger ones, behind
Victor and Kurt, lauding them to the skies
As their husbands' saviors—in their strong hands
The future was safe for psychoanalysis
And so were their husbands' jobs. No small thing
Given the huge debts incurred for training
In the Institute and for those treatments
For wives and children. Like an Escher drawing
In which fish turn into birds and back again—
Patient becomes analyst, analyst patient.
And who knew what about whom, where, and how
Provided a cloaked background of uncertainty.
First, Donald knew, he told Paula, of course,
In confidence—professional confidence—
Then he told her, again in confidence.
She had not told anyone yet. But wait!

Greta must know and if she knows so must Kurt.
Has he told Victor? Damn! Victor must know
And had not told her! That bastard, just like him!
Now that she had found a target, Marlena
Opened fire all down the line:
                                        "I am fed up
With all of you and with this half-baked hellhole.
I could just divorce Victor, quit training
And this useless treatment, take the kids and head
For New York. I was offered a job at Sinai—
Not a great job—but it's New York, continue
My training and make a new life for myself.
Who says the director of research needs
To be married? Have kids? Who says that you
Need to have me as a patient, or I you?
More fish in the sea, more birds in the sky.
My mother would be overcome with joy
To have me back East. She'd help with the kids
And I'd bless my lucky stars to be through
With the pack of you." Fiercely, Marlena
Bit off the last words. Her knuckles were white
From clenching her fists. She drew her arms closer
To her trunk as if intending to present
A smaller target for the counterattack.

"It seems I have offended you. Tell me how?"

"Not just you. All of you. Don't ask me why—
I'll get even more furious at you."
She started laughing. It was a hollow laugh.
"I had this absolutely crazy dream.
'Bon-Bon' and I lived inside this cannon,
Like mice. At the peace bell in Hiroshima,
We discovered a bird's nest on top of it—
A bird's nest with nestlings in it—imagine.
Everyone was supposed to ring the bell

For peace—whack it with a big attached log.
That's this goddamned place—a giant peace bell,
Supposedly. Ha! With all us birds inside
And you guys whacking it with your giant logs.
This is too good to be true." And she broke out
In loud laughter from the pit of her belly
Unstoppably. Tears came to her eyes—
Fresh, cool tears brimming over like beads
Of liquid on the lip of a full cup. Freeman
Was startled by the sudden turn in her mood.
The dream was of interest. In a cannon?
But that could wait.
                    "You're enjoying a joke
At my expense, I guess at all men's expense."

"But you know I don't see the humor in it
At all. I could as easily cry and I am.
I grow sad when I think of poor 'Bon-Bon'
And me in the cannon. Once at the circus
I saw a man with goggles get shot out from
A cannon into a net. I started
Crying because I thought he was dead but
He got up and took a bow. Those birds survive,
Don't they."

          Freeman wondered, "Why sad in there,
In the cannon, I mean?"

                    "Sad because me
And 'Bon-Bon' are making do together
As we often did at home until father
Came home and then it all changed completely.
When I was young mother just abandoned me
To look after father. I sulked about that.
Later I joined in. That worked much better.
Father would sit me in his lap and in

His deep voice he'd ask me about my day.
But I never thought he really meant it
Because he was always looking at his
Newspaper. Every now and then I'd snatch
It from him and put it behind my back,
Grinning fiercely all the while. It was
No game for father or for me. He'd scowl
And take it back, wagging a finger at me.
Then I'd slide from his lap and join 'Bon-Bon'
In the kitchen. I'd ask her what made papers
So important. And she'd say in her high voice,
'That's how men find out what they're up to
In the world.' I asked her if she read them
And she'd reply, 'Oh yes, mostly the comics
And the woman's page.' 'Cher-Cherie,' it's much,
Much more exciting to learn about whose
Marrying, getting engaged, or having babies,
Than all that boring stuff about wars and taxes.'
But I wasn't fooled."

                    "So home was transformed
From the peace bell for mother and her nestling
Into the cannon's mouth once father returned.'

"You are too neat by far, Doctor Freeman."

"I see there is little I can say that
Will please you today. Perhaps another time."
He indicated that the hour was up.

Marlena felt a sudden urge to stay put,
Not get off the couch. Let him push her off.
The thought was enough to bring a fleeting smile
To her thin lips. She rose slowly, fixing
Her skirt, sitting a moment at the edge,
And then, standing up, she took her time exiting.

19

She was the mouse again, Freeman noted.
Bending over, making herself small, slipping
Onto the couch with a diffident smile.
Too much, too much anger last time, he supposed.
It was not worrisome to him. One waits
Out the storms, the becalmed days, the returning
Calendar of old selves. Each time a deepening
Occurred, a change in the infrastructure
That took time to shift the visible and felt
Surface. Freeman was only mildly troubled
By his patient's struggle with reality—
The politics, her husband's role in it,
Her own part—and his. Always there had to be
Reality—a foil against which neurosis
Stood out more clearly, a stage for the true
Drama to unfold—the playing out of forces
Within the person. Always tragedy
Was intrinsic, the tragic flaw. Comedy
Always turned on coincidence, accident.
Analysis was the fine clinical art
Of tragedy—to correct the tragic flaw.
With psychoanalysis no real
Hamlets, or Oedipuses—only fantasies
We could all afford. As for Victor, well—
His uncorrected flaw might be his undoing.

151

All the while he mused his patient was silent,
Looking pale, contrite, fidgeting with a
Kleenex, with which she dabbed her nose.

                                   "I've a cold,
A drippy cold, the worst kind. My head's stuffed.
I feel like a lead balloon. I'll try my best.
Bear with me. With a stuffed head it's hard to think.
I don't know why, but last night after supper,
The kids in bed, Victor in his study,
I started to cry. I was going to read
Something or other—nothing professional—
I wasn't up to that. I just felt . . . inept
And terribly sad . . . fearful . . . like a dark cloud
Was settling overhead . . . and as I cried
One thought kept returning—I wanted only
The best for Victor, the very best. When
The children stirred, I rushed to quiet them
So that Victor would not be disturbed. His work,
I must confess, makes my efforts appear
Trivial. His scope and depth are breathtaking.
Mine . . . like painstaking needlework.
When I first met Victor . . . I've told you that
Already, haven't I, several times . . .
He explained things to me, affectionately.
He loved to have me understand as he
Understood things. . . . It was a revelation—
A man who told me what the headlines meant,
Not like my father, or like my mother.
And he was so involved . . . in everything—
Politics, literature, theater, dance—
Just plain having fun—and fun meant good sex,
Which was another revelation to me.
Sex and more sex! I felt surrounded by him,
Invaded by him, totally possessed by him,
As if an army had stationed itself

In every orifice of my body—
And nothing human was alien to Victor,
Of that I can assure you . . . God, how great
I felt then! My body, my *being* came
Fully alive for the first time. I was
Like a countryside, ignored and neglected—
Mainly by myself—suddenly blossoming
Because Victor knew how to cherish its
Most forsaken, shameful places and make
Them seem attractive, even beautiful. . . .
I was crying last night I suppose because
I miss those times, I miss that love, I miss . . .
Him. . . . " And Marlena shut her eyes tightly
As if trying not to see what was plainly
Already there to see.

                    Freeman leaned back,
Stretched his legs out on the hassock, laid
His slender hands on his stomach, and waited. . . .
His sad patient, although still out at sea,
Was heading into port. Not yet time
For the pilot to take the helm and guide it
Into its berth.

                    Marlena sneezed and blew
Her nose while shaking her head dolefully.
"My what a terrible cold. It keeps on dripping!
I hope I don't give it to you."

                    Freeman's
Ears perked up—was this the pilot's cue?
"You keep calling attention to your cold,
And it does sound bad. Perhaps you should be
Home taking care of it."

                    "And miss my hour,

Especially after last night?"

                                   "But you're
Worried about giving me your cold, stuffing
Me up as you are stuffed."

                                 Marlena's mind
Veered suddenly as if it were on a curve
When just before it was on so straight a course,
Although the way was petering out. . . . She was tired,
She had not slept well. Victor came to bed late
And wanted to talk. Had she heard anything?
For no good reason things were slowing down
On the research front. She wanted him just
To hold her, stroke her, maybe have sex, but not
Badger her about politics. Anyway
Whatever she could tell him, he must already
Know. She told him about Serey. Victor
Became frightfully alarmed, which surprised her,
And she awakened fully, insisting
All she knew was about the strange phone call.
As quickly as he had become alarmed,
Victor turned calm, and as she had often
Seen him do, he performed that odd gesture
Of pushing his tongue into his inner cheek
So that the cheek swelled out. After a moment
He abruptly declared, "We shall see." And
Came to bed, drew her to him, and after
A perfunctory kiss penetrated
His erect penis into her vagina
And at last he embraced her. By morning
Her head was throbbing.

                                 "You are taking aim
At my cold, aren't you, and what it might mean?"

"Taking aim?"

            "Yes, I do see it as hostile.
Can't I have a cold in peace?"

                "Of course you can—
That's the whole point—in peace, not intruded on."

"I suppose I should tell you too—about . . .
Well . . . about Serey. I so didn't want to—
Not to tell you or Victor. . . . Keep it to myself.
Instead of a cold I'll give you a secret.
Isn't that better?"

            "You are tiptoeing
Today, fearful of—"

           "My hostility,
I suppose, always that. But I'm sick of it.
All of it. And yet I want Victor so much
To succeed . . . so much . . . I didn't want sex
At all last night—only a cuddle but
He's always so ready. A chastity belt
Would have been the thing!" And Marlena laughed
Out loud, her mood changing for the first time.
"Wouldn't that have been something! Victor, lance
At the ready, and bang! Right into solid
Tight shut steel! You know, ordinarily
I'm quite ready too, and get off in my
Own way. But this time I felt different.
I wanted the good old days back, I suppose,
When he devoted himself to me in bed—"

"Like an invading army?"

           "Yes, that too

And more beside. But then I wanted to be
Possessed, no, reclaimed—my body reclaimed
For me, softened and polished by love so
Everyone could see how cultivated
And well-tended it was. A beloved jewel.
I felt that way, shamelessly. I was his.
And in a deeper subterranean way
He was mine. And then I started to hate him
As much as I loved him and needed him.
How I filled George's ear with tales of Victor's
Unsavory doings as we lay together.
Always that was the prelude to fucking—
Good, hot fucking, not lovemaking. Not with
George who was totally out of it all—
An engineer who built bridges and screwed
Whatever moved. Just the right man for me—
Uncomplicated, uninvolved in my life
Or Victor's."

        She was not heading into port
But veering out to sea. He had better
Carefully step back and let her steer the craft,
Although he was tempted to keep one finger
Lightly on the helm.
        "Your stuffed head, it seems,
Is another safer way of closing up
As you so much wanted to do last night."

"You may be right. It came on in the morning."

"And also to keep me out of your head—
Another man who wanted in on his
Own terms."

        "But exactly what are your terms?
I still don't know for sure. What will you end up

Really giving me . . . for good? A better life
With Victor, a life without Victor, or . . . what?"

"Yes, what? Note how Victor always figures in."

"Of course he must. I don't know what you're after."

Freeman felt that his one finger had proved
Too much for the helm. Better to have put
Both hands behind his back and waited, waited.
Now he must wait for another time.
As for Serey, Paul had told him the news.
Puzzling, but likely of little consequence.

20

Freeman was mightily annoyed. Dreyfus!
He had almost ejected him bodily
From his office before. Idiot!
Rarely was Freeman upset. His approach:
Reflect, anticipate, and thus avoid
Disagreeable surprises. But not
With Dreyfus, who always jumped the wrong way,
Counter to his own interests certainly,
But often messing up the board for others.
Now he wanted a staff petition sent
To the president demanding an end
To the search and a new committee formed.
What nonsense! How could the president avoid
Naming Victor, given the circumstances.
And Freeman had already established
In his own mind his place in the new scheme,
And a fallback position if anything
Went wrong. But ruefully he thought nothing would,
Not with Victor at the controls. He felt
Himself to be in an odd yet privileged
Position, dealing with Victor on many
Issues, large and small, winning some, losing most,
Pained by the tumultuous nature
Of his theories, more broadsides of conceptual
Grapeshot than pin-pointed, articulated

Marksmanship. One simply stepped aside
And let the rush of sound and fury pass by.
No sense in standing one's ground against such
Wind and shrapnel. And what of Marlena—
Victor's wife and his own patient? In that
The rare privilege of his position
As analyst—to see the skein of events
Playing out through another's eyes, aware
Increasingly of how those eyes refracted
Some events, bending, magnifying, shrinking
Them, and reflecting others with purest
Exactitude. For a moment a thought
Troubled Freeman. How does one tell the difference?
But the thought vanished in the ease of settled
Conviction. One knows as the optician knows
Which way the letters face and which they are.
He called for Marlena and readied himself
For the privileges of what he had called
In an old oft-quoted paper, *alter-sight:*
The view from the other, distinguishable
From *in* sight, which was the view limited
To one's *own* ability to discover
The other's experience. He pondered
The previous hour—her stuffed head into which
He was not to intrude unless he cure her
Fully, the growing conflict in her loyalties
Between Victor and her analysis.
Marlena hurried toward the couch, furtive
Almost, a quick glance at Freeman he read
As reproachful.

        "I want this analysis
For myself. I want you to . . . to devote yourself
To me—at least for this time, my time, which
I pay for. But you don't, do you? You're off
Somewhere high and mighty in your peerless mind.

No. I don't care about that. No. As long
As that peerless mind is mine, mine right now."
She froze suddenly into brittle silence,
Sensing that the wrong word could shatter her.
This, she thought, was the transference neurosis.
It was crazy what she had just uttered.
Where could it have come from?

                              Freeman wondered
Too about this sudden squall of affect.
It had a place in the long-range forecast
He was sure, although its exact occasion
Could not be anticipated. A local, transient
Blip on the radar screen but worth a look.

"My mind is to be yours?"

                         "I misspoke. I meant
That your mind for *this time* should be for me,
Only for me." And as she spoke the same
Force of feeling stunned her into silence.

He let his mind float back to images
Of ocean currents, navigating instruments.
Again she was heading out to sea—further,
Deeper. This time no mother along. No father.
No brother. No husband. Except she summon
These ancient shadows from within herself.
Yes, like the Flying Dutchman her ship sailed on,
Steered by a long dead crew, real only
In the narrow straits between him and the couch,
Which could broaden into an ocean's width,
Shifted by the plate tectonics of treatment.
Slowly over the years continents merged
Of vastly different topographies.
Green Asian highlands loomed above African

Rain forests. Or easing gradually
Apart, substantial stretches of assured
Regularities could let in a fresh
Stream of surprise.

　　　　　　　　Marlena was a soft slide
Away from panic, which was entirely
New for her. Where had the certainties gone?
Everything had contracted to a pinpoint
Like those medieval tricksters who scratched out
The bible—was it on the head of a pin?
She could not allow this. Her life was there,
On the other side of the threshold. Not here
With this gargoyle—this stone carving, unchanging
Monster of certainty, looking forever
Down at her perplexities. And yet she knew
In some small diminished square of being
That monster or not he *was* there for her.
She struggled to hold onto that belief
While the once stable ground trembled forebodingly.

"A strange image keeps coming before my mind
Of straight sheer walls on either side—narrow,
Dark, a wind blowing through it, a cold
Nervous wind—I meant a swirling wind not
Knowing which way to blow. At my feet a
Rattle of loose pebbles making it hard
For me to walk. Like a nightmare about
To happen. Only I can make it come
And go. And when it goes it is all bright,
Pure, incandescent, limitless—only
I distrust it somehow, as if it were
Pure sham, a come-on . . . I'm . . . I feel confused."

Marlena was breathing as if asleep,
Deeply, her body filling at each breath

As if it had been emptied. She had an odd
Impossible thought—that with each breath in
She was pregnant and with each breath out
She gave birth. She started to laugh.
                                        "I'm having
A regressive experience. Very interesting!"
Hatred. A red coal. A loud bell stabbed through
The patchwork of consciousness she had just
Swatched together. It quickly unraveled,
Leaving her naked. The towering walls loomed
Taller, piles of jutting stone. She'd be crushed.
"It's all rock walls and . . . breathing . . . just breathing.
And light, shameless light . . . and breathing . . . just
   breathing."

"*Shameless* light?"

            "Sham . . . I meant sham—not . . . not pure
As it looks. . . . Nothing is ever as pure
As it looks," knowing at the same time that
She was wrong. She fought off a dangerous
Wave of fury.
                  "Take psychoanalysis
For instance. All devoted to the patient,
Pure as driven snow. But is it really?"
Her heart wasn't in the attack. She went on
Unable to bring back the launched arrow
To the bow. "We all know that no analyst
Is exempt from countertransference and
What is that but an impurity although
My husband and countless others insist
It can be useful—like the grain of sand
That starts a pearl."

                  Freeman's thin lips drew down
At the corners. A mistake his asking

About the shameless light—a bad mistake.
She was floating in a dimensionless world,
No x, y, or z axis—and his voice,
Let alone what he said, erected planes
Of external reference. The pure psychic
Stuff of which dreams are made and the wandering
Shadowy selves inhabiting them exist
In a groundless recurrent evanescence,
Changing form at a speed greater than light.
He could feel the lodestar pull of her psyche,
That permanent part of her buried beneath
Circumstantiality, and he knew
His own thoughts were pulling against its power
Into excesses of intellect. And thus
The mistake. Silence, the celestial
Remedy for geocentric clamor.

Marlena waited, poised like a diver
At the lip of the board, her back turned toward
The water, her face toward the steps leading
Yet again away from the necessary leap.
She could see herself, her back curved, arching
Like yearning itself toward the descent.

"I'm blocked . . . I can't think of anything at all.
Just a blank, a miserable blank like
That blast of light. That's what it must really be—
An emptiness parading as something
Great and luminous. I'm furious at myself
And at you. Why can't I be a huge wind—
A tornado twisting you all up
In my insides and spitting you all out in .
Splinters!"
          She started laughing, enjoying
Immensely the churning in her bowels
And the drawing sensation of saliva

Pooling under her tongue. "I might just do it!
Suck you all up through my asshole, crush your
Bones in my gut, and then crack and crunch them
Into little bits in my mouth and spit—
SPIT YOU ALL OUT OF MY DREARY LIFE,
EVERY LAST MOTHERFUCKING ONE OF YOU!"

Her voice clattered against the walls. Freeman's eyes
Opened wide as the merest smile floated
Across his lips. It was in fact time to stop,
A good time. Marlena lurched from the couch,
Unsteady on her feet, glared at Freeman,
Swung the door wide as she left and slammed it.

21

Freeman was awaiting Marlena's hour
In a state of special calm created
By a perfectly balanced cat's cradle
of conflicting obligations, the tensions
Themselves guaranteeing equilibrium.
The president had called him in private
To solicit his opinion on the search.
Was Victor really the best candidate?
Should it really be a psychoanalyst?
After all it was research. Very few
Analysts *did* research, except maybe
Dreyfus who wasn't yet an analyst.
He reminded the president of Victor's
Achievements, nationally recognized.
The president confided a worrisome
Doubt to Freeman: Does analysis work,
Or is it all *theory*? Furthermore, should
Psychoanalysts run all departments
For their own good and the good of the place?
He could talk to Freeman because Freeman
He knew had perspective, he wasn't caught up
In that intense European frenzy
That mixes up conviction with ambition
("Don't quote me on that!"). A cool American
Head was what was needed. Freeman took a while

Before responding. Was there a chance for him?
He set the thought aside like a chess move
Best postponed until nearer the end game.
He said that if Victor didn't get it
He would likely leave and with him others.
It would be a substantial loss for the place.
The president sputtered in anger, declaring
It would be just like those people to leave!
Play it my way or I take my marbles
And go home. No American sense of
Fair play, compromise, working things out.
It was wearing him down. He was sick of it.
Freeman saw his opening. Perhaps he should
Postpone his decision for a time, let
The dust settle. No need to rush into
Something he wasn't sure of. Perhaps in time
After mulling it over with a few friends—
He was always ready to be of help—
The issues would sort themselves out and he
Would feel readier to decide the matter.
The president was quite relieved and said so,
Assuring Freeman that he was his most
Valued consultant and a good dear friend.
But Jackson would be stepping down in two weeks.
Whom should he appoint as acting head?
Dreyfus? That would antagonize Victor.
Of course, why doesn't Freeman take it now?
He was an analyst fully acceptable
To Victor and the others. Would he do it?
Freeman said he very much wanted to help.
He would need to give it some thought and then
He would suggest they meet to discuss details.
The president was grateful. Freeman pondered
On life, its interesting twists and turns.
He felt sure-footed in a slippery world.
Dance and weave deftly, escaping punches

From whatever side, keeping your balance,
Counterpunching just enough to score
On points, no brutal knockout blow needed.
Both combatants on their feet at the end,
Unmarred, shaking hands with mutual respect,
But each knowing who the better man was.

He was ready to attend to his patient
To whom he felt as strong an obligation
As to the president and to the place.
He could see his duty in both directions
Clearly. Yes, they could conflict but they needn't.
It wasn't as if he had campaigned for the job.
He had been carefully correct and abstemious.
The patient had once described him
As on the sidelines. He was still there but
In another entirely temporary role.
The cat's cradle could slip from one set of hands
To another, its form intricately changing
Without the string ending in a tangle.

His patient looked drawn and pale, her lips trembled.
"I haven't been sleeping well. Either I feel
Like kicking Victor out of bed or like
Gathering him in my arms and hugging him.
He's so calm and *untalkative*! He—
Of all people—untalkative . . . I'm furious . . .
I'm frightened too. . . . Something is happening to
    me . . .
It's not just this damn analysis . . . well,
A good deal of it *is* this analysis—
The rest . . . is Victor."
                            As if an oven door
Had suddenly swung open, a blast of rage
Rushed outward, igniting her too-cautious words
Into torches of accusatory flame.

"I want out! I want out of this analysis!
I want out of my marriage! He's . . . you're
Using me! That's right, using me. All right—
I've used him. Maybe I've used you. What else
Could I do when neither of you will let me
Stand by your side, confide in me, trust me—
Treat me like a grown-up. *You* sit back there
Measuring your precious words in spoonfuls.
He screws the living daylights out of me
At will, and goes off to his fucking wars
Dropping off a dram of his precious come
To keep me for awhile. I've had enough!
Basta! Genug, in his ass-backwards language.
If this is acting out make the most of it!"
And the oven door swung shut, her words settling
Downwards like crisp tatters of scorched paper.
She felt chilly, very small and abandoned.
And she hugged herself, her hands on either side
Reaching under her as if to encircle herself.

How completely she was confounding him
And Victor, Freeman marveled. What she wanted
Of him—trust, confiding—she could expect
From her husband or father, but not from
Him. From him she could expect help and insight.
How powerful her feelings must be to fault
Her judgment so completely. How profound
Her craving for parity, once beyond
Her means, but now within reach, justifiable.
"Remember those times you wanted so to look
Through your brother's telescope and felt father's
Indifference to mother's interest in the world?
How much you feel the same now toward me
And Victor, as if I too were withholding
The universe from you, keeping the world
Entirely to myself—and other men.

You are enraged, although now it's all there
Within your own reach."

"Is it now! Says who?
Suppose I told Victor I was just plain sick
Of this whole place and wanted to leave, period,
Whether or not he got his damn directorship?
Or I told you I wanted another analyst
Because I don't feel I'm getting anywhere,
And I told the Education Committee
That you're too cold, distant, and fancy for me
And not a very good analyst at that?
How would all that go over with you both?
Of course, Victor would pack his grip and say,
'Yes, dear.' And you would make an appointment
        for me
With the Education Committee. Fat chance! Victor
        would
Tell me to deal with it in my analysis,
And so would you. I'd just be an acting out,
Castrating bitch, right? So much for the world,
The universe, now being within my reach."

Freeman could not help being shaken by
His patient's violent assault on his skill.
Whatever modicum of truth there was
In it, however, was far overshadowed
By an old score she felt she had to settle
Once and for all—and he could help her with that—
To show her that the game was long over and that
It did not pay to tilt at those old windmills.
Her lance was better used for other targets
And that she had a lance as good as anyone's.
"Yes, you *can* leave. And yes, you can complain
About me. But then what—"

"Then what?! Revenge!
The salt taste of someone else's blood—yours
And his—on my tongue. And both of *you*
Left behind, wounded and bewildered—hurt
Beyond comprehension—that's what!

"And then what?"

"That's enough. Or are you now hinting in
Your usual sneaky way that I'd be guilty,
Need to punish myself or whatever.
No. Then the slate would really be wiped clean
For a fresh start on all new terms—my terms.
And they'd be a damn sight fairer than yours."

Freeman found his thoughts drifting back to his talk
With the president and wondered what that meant.
His own deal? His own terms? Was he, like her,
Seeking his own revenge, his reason the same?
No. He had been ready to accept Victor
As director. Only when the president
Called and demonstrated his ambivalence
Did he offer himself as a way out—
And temporarily at that. No, not the same.

Marlena felt she was high on a trapeze
And when she looked down they were rolling up
The safety net. She was tumbling through the air,
But whose strong arms would catch her now? Freeman
Was sitting astride the opposite bar,
Arms folded. And Victor was down below
Rolling up the net. 'Don't worry, Cher-Cherie,'
She heard an old sweet voice whisper in her ear,
'In the circus it's all in fun. They all
Stand up and take a bow when it's over.'
'No, mother, she heard herself say half out loud,

'Some don't.' And the sweet voice went dead. Marlena
Struggled for breath as if she were in a void,
An emptiness, silent and enveloping
In all directions. There was no way out.
As Marlena left the hour, Freeman
Observed the birds and the squirrels feeding.

Part Four

Serey Potmose
and
Greta Denkman

22

"I have so much to talk about today.
The plot is thickening, but we shall prevail."
After saying "we" she became uneasy—
Was it presumptuous? Or nicely loyal?
For Michael's sake she had to be careful.
"I worry about Michael. So quiet—
Who would guess he is a prize-winning poet,
A biographer of Keats—all in Spanish.
He is so pleased by yours and Kurt's interest."

Greta Denkman stirred heavily in her chair,
Grimacing, compressing her lips, angry.
"Are you so uncertain of yourself that
You must always be selling me Michael?"

Serey suddenly felt grim and resolute.
Always, always one has to be on one's guard,
Especially with analysts who can't
At all understand their own politics.

"You sound so angry. I suppose it's me.
You're right. Michael, Michael—my weaker self.
With him I feel like the potter at the wheel—
Such good moist clay, such total absence of form.
Men lack definition for all their muscle.

My uncertainty is solely about you.
I sense a void at times, a no-thing-ness,
Le néant—vous savez? I feel drawn—drawn
Into a dark vortex. . . . "
                                        Serey silenced
Herself. She *had* felt drawn. What was happening?

"I . . . I . . . don't know what made me say that just
    now.
Dark vortex? . . . Of course, tornados—nighttime.
Nightmares . . . I would laugh at my own night
    terrors—
Pavor nocturnus . . . even as a child.
How silly of me I would say next morning
When my parents told me how I had wakened
Screaming, sweating, clutching the bedpost.
They would join me in laughing. It was over.
I had headed off their worrisome questions.
Clutching a bedpost? Screaming? Sweating? Not I!
Another child but not this child!"

                                        Greta
Saw the point, knew how difficult her task,
Felt a twinge of pity for this woman—
Young, handsome—married to a bedpost!
The word had leaped into her mind unbidden.
How had it come? The potter's wheel, a lathe
Turning a wooden block into a post—
Fashioned, sculpted. Greta often pondered
On how her thoughts turned elastic. She said,
"Isn't it that you also desire
That I too stop asking worrisome questions
About taboo subjects?"
                                        Too too clumsy,
Thought Serey, *gross* was the word occurring
To her. "You are right, so right, absolutely."

"Repetition, as they say, 'Protests too much.'"

"Again you are right. What am I saying!
But that was a hard thought for me to say—
I felt your interpretation was . . . obvious.
Who does want to be grilled on taboo subjects—
Not I, not anyone. But there's more to it,
Isn't there? You're too experienced to give
So banal an interpretation.
Michael has often said that novelty
Is at the heart of interpretation.
I must be fending off something."
                                        "Go on."

"The vortex draws me back." She started to laugh.
"Seriously, she caught herself, "the vortex—
That vortex. . . ." Madness, such madness, she thought.
This hour was dragging on. When would it end?
Silent Michael. She had to talk about
His future. "I must talk about Michael
And if I must, I must. How silent he is.
My father was a lively, witty man,
Certainly not as smart as Michael—no.
But quick, charming, his eyes always twinkling.
It was my mother who was silent—mute!
Yes—mute! Always something black about her.
Mourning, always mourning. He had to have them,
His affairs, my father. . . . What an intriguer
He was! I think he enjoyed the politics
Of love more than love itself. Once I helped him.
I was already older—sixteen, seventeen.
He could be so bored, my poor, bored father—
So bored. I just remembered—oh, my! Phoebe!
She must be picked up at school and I can't.
Michael must do it—Damn! He will object,
He's in such a cloud, a fog."

                                    "Tell me, please,
About your forgetting." Greta Denkman
Jumped at the rare opportunity
This patient provided by making slips.

Serey was annoyed. It was all nonsense.
How did she get herself into all this?
Michael, always Michael. He had finished
His training analysis with Kurt, dear Kurt,
And insisted that it had upset her.
He could tell that she was not herself, in bed
Especially. So distant, so detached.
She had really not felt that way at all.
Quite otherwise. She was eager to launch
Them into the senior analysts' circles.
Kurt delighted her—so European,
A truly gifted conversationalist
On art, literature, wines, politics,
His way of leading you with a question
To which you had to know the answer or
Fail to receive that secret entre-nous smile
Reserved for the cognoscenti. Serey
Said, "I'm thinking, would your husband go fetch
Your child in the middle of the working day?"
She knew Greta had no children. "Would he
Grumble, protest, or just raise his eyebrows?"
Serey felt tired suddenly. "That gray is back—
Like a switch. . . . Why do I keep on trying?
Michael was right. I become detached
But only when it all turns gray, so gray."

Greta knew that Serey was now depressed.
It was good that the symptom has entered
The analytic conversation. She waited.

Serey moved her head slowly back and forth.

The word *no* formed on her lips. Not again.
Oh, God! Not again.
                  "What made it turn gray
Just then? I must . . . I must associate.
I was mean to you just then, of course.
You are so mute or saying such obvious things
That I learn nothing from them. You must know
How much I respect and admire you for
Your intelligence, your quiet certainty
About yourself. I feel that way myself."

The gray was lifting, dispersing like a fog.
She must do something about Phoebe. The child
Would not wait long, not Phoebe, she would take off
For home, the shortest way, over fences,
Down alleys, running across streets, not looking
Out for cars. Where did that child come from?

"Phoebe's a problem. She's always getting hurt,
Not minding, not like either of us at all.
Wild. Wild!"
                She must go to pick her up soon.
How close to the end of the hour? Suddenly,
Inexplicably, she began to cry,
Sobbing, angry, lost. "Why do you keep me here?
My child may get run over by a car,
Or ripped by barbed wire on a jagged fence!
You are so mute! So indifferent! So German!"

"You are not being stopped."

                            "True, but then I'd
Be acting out—leaving an hour! Michael
Would be disgraced."

                    "Always Michael," said Greta,

"He is the bedpost of your life. Holding on
To him when the nightmares of your feelings
Threaten to darken your life. And I am mother,
That mute figure, rejected by father.
How hard to be a woman with a child."

"How do you know? You have no children—none!"

She caught herself. She felt bitterly betrayed
By Michael, who had led her into this.

"I am not myself today. I'm so on edge
About Victor, you know. So important
For him to become Research Director—
Important for all of us, for the place.
I've heard such unsettling news today."

She waited for the expected effect.
Greta was torn between anxiety
And the knowledge of what Serey was doing.
She thought of a compromise solution.

"Since you must tell me, tell me—but you must
Know what you are doing."

                              Serey agreed,
"Of course, I know and I must deal with it."
She felt penance had been granted.
"Today at lunch I learned from Frances Dreyfus
That Paul will fight Victor's designation.
He'll go to the president and argue
That since Victor had never done research
It would be wrong for him to be the chief.
The research staff would rebel. So would he.
They'd say the clinicians were taking over
And that they would put an end to their research.

They'd find it hard to get government grants.
Paul said the staff wants Allan Fabrikant.
He himself is not too sure." She waited
For Greta's response.

"Intrigue interests you.
How did you say it before? The politics
Of love he enjoyed more than the love itself,
Your father?"

That was unfair, thought Serey.
She got what she wanted and not even
Thank you. Instead this analytic riposte.
But she would play her father's game.

"Of course
It does. In Maupassant's little love tales
The fun is all in the game of love not
In its consummation. Les petites belles dames
Talk, talk, talk about bristly mustaches
But its the maneuvering that really counts—
Who takes whom from whom, where and when.
I suppose I'm more nineteenth than twentieth
Century."

Greta said, "Our time is up."
As Serey rose she suddenly thought, "Phoebe!"
Greta pondered the fate of Serey's treatment
As Serey fled, her square-jawed face stricken.

23

"That minx was sitting and waiting
For me, would you believe it, my one
Totally unpredictable child—an elf
Brought her in the middle of the night."

"So many strange happenings go on for you
In the night—elves bringing babies, nightmares."
Greta felt she had to move quickly or
Serey would shift into her unflappable
Self, the Maupassant demimondaine.

Serey winced and gathered her wits about her
Which were like well-trained actors on stage, ready
To recite their lines, making sure to occupy
The spotlight that kept the darkness at bay.
She sensed Greta's bulk behind her casting
A lengthening shadow over her on the couch.
The gloom had to be dispelled, quickly, or
She would suffocate.

                              "Yesterday I saw
Donald Prescott downtown. We had coffee.
I learned that he will be terminating.
Interesting. He's so unhappy at home—
That wife of his with her fake English teas

Attended by those colorless biddies
Who talk only about uplifting subjects—
Who will bake cookies for the art show,
Or collect the rummage for the grateful poor,
What novel should be 'reported on' at length.
Donald is an interesting man. I
Love the twinkle in his crafty blue eyes.
And since his analysis his face is more relaxed
And he smiles more often. Ruthie will never
Hold onto him unless she too is
Analyzed and her superego relaxed.
It happens often, doesn't it—the wives
Following the husbands into treatment?
It's pure self-defense. Your husband falls in love
You don't know with whom or what except
He stares at you with blank eyes, eats too little
Or too much, loses interest in sex,
Or suddenly becomes a Marquis de Sade
Arranging imaginary tableaux with you
As centerpiece. One day deciding to give up
Everything and the next smirking smugly
At how marvelously well things are going.
Unsettling. Inscrutable. Insufferable.
Where is the fresh bright boy you married? Gone!
Yes, he was a bit of a bore, childish,
Self-important, caught up in business quite
Beyond you, but secretly you were convinced
That really didn't matter. Grown-up toys.
No more. You bore the babies, rocked the cradle,
Ran the house, looked after his career so that
He met the right people who liked him
Because they liked you, your cooking, and
Your way of leaning on their arm. And then?
All that thrown into confusion. The rules
Changed. And no one forewarns you or cares how
It affects you, least of all your husband.

He must be in love with someone else, you think,
But his analyst is a man. No matter,
They say he thinks of him as a woman
And loves him, or her. Perhaps there is a rival—
A female colleague, snippy, twice-divorced,
Eager for a man who is her equal,
Who plays tough tennis and bests him
At case conferences. And he feels delighted
That he can let a woman show him up
And he loves her for how good she makes him feel
And you grow tired and frightened of these games."

"'You'?—Who is this 'you' behind whom you hide?"

"The 'you' is Ruthie Prescott, Frances Dreyfus,
Even Marlena Kleinman, and perhaps you too—
Who knows what you were like before Kurt's
      training."
Serey was aware of an unwonted
Bitterness in her voice—a desire to beat
The shadow back and give it a human face
As vulnerable as hers, as womanly.
Greta felt the bile and subtle appeal
To close ranks. Underneath, she wondered, was there
Sympathy for the mute mother—a bond
Forged by suffering at the hands of males?

"The 'you' then refers to all put-upon wives."

"Put-upon? No! No wife need be put-upon.
The unfairness is in the exclusion.
You can't be in the club of those who count,
Although you suffer for it. I am here
Because of Michael. I don't really need it."

"You don't need to stay."

"Oh! And if I quit?
How would it look for Michael. His wife quits
Treatment. Acting out. Unfit for analysis.
I have not worked hard all these years for him
In order to have it all elude me now."
Serey felt she had gone too far, shown her hand
Too openly, and yet she felt she must
Go on, knowing that she would take it back,
Or try to.
            "You said Michael was my bedpost.
No. He's really my ticket of admission
To the club. But all this is so much talk
That changes little. Now Victor—there's a man
Who makes things happen. You'll laugh when I say
He's like my carefree father, but he is.
Not in appearance. Not at all. My father
Was tall and slender, thick dark hair, and a smile
That could light up all of Tennessee. He cried
Easily you know. When I would hurt myself
I'd go to him because I was stunned by
His tears which would flow when he saw my bruise
Or scrape. He'd cry and grow angry, shouting,
'Who dared to hurt my little darling!' shaking
His fist quite dramatically. I'd giggle
At the show, so pleased by his heroics.
Then he'd take me for a stroll and a treat.
There were advantages to getting hurt,
Believe me. Victor can feel and show it.
So hard for most men. Michael is a sphinx
Who doesn't pose any riddle. I know him
Like a book. Victor electrifies
But he's also shrewd and knows how to plan
Ahead. I was surprised to learn he played
Poor chess. A fault. I could go to sleep with him."
Serey discovered that her thoughts had run out.

Greta found her own thoughts moving warily.
Yes, she had escaped back to the gossip,
But there was something shrill, frightened about
Her cattiness. Was it only envy
Of men, mainly of her own lumpish husband
Whom she had in fact successfully
Steered through medical school and residency
And now through analytic training? Greta
Admired her for that and felt sorry for her.
Serey had been wrong about her. She had
Married late, after her training Serey
Was bright, able—and yet even so . . .
Greta mused, even so. . . . How depressed she was
When she saw her first in consultation.
Pale, grim, yet her eyes sparkled like a
Fountain frozen in winter. No tears or
Complaints, only 'Michael thought I should see you.'
It took three interviews for her finally
To cry as she smiled, thin-lipped and angry.
She confessed her bafflement at herself—
Her insomnia, loss of appetite,
Disinterest in sex, the gray mood,
All starting suddenly—or so it seemed,
Just when everything was bright—Michael
Terminating his analysis, soon
To be graduating from the Institute.
Greta had concluded that Serey suffered
From a depression in an hysterical
Character structure brought on by Michael's
Success. Analysis should help. It wasn't.
At least not after two years. Greta
Worried and waited. So much reality
Continually got in the way—all this Research
Director business—Victor, Kurt, Fabrikant.
But it was also true that Serey used it
Like Scheherazade and her thousand and one tales.

For only a moment Greta paused after
Making this analogy, for Serey
Was crying. Her mood had changed during
The long silence.

                    "It's Michael's fault, isn't it?
I know it is. I was once very happy.
What am I saying! I am still happy—
Very happy. It's only a mood . . . a passing
Mood. If father were here he'd shake his fist
At it. . . . Make it go away."
                              Serey's voice faltered
And though her lips remained parted as if
To utter speech no sound emerged. She lay
Breathing unevenly, immobile, cold.

"You wish I could make it go away too
By getting angry at Michael for you."

"No! No! Don't blame Michael. That would ruin
Everything, everything. He's innocent.
That can't be said, look how much he helped me.
Brought me to you. Really forced me to come.
And I'm glad I did. It's been so helpful
To both of us. And such an eye-opener.
How much one recalls one doesn't think one knew!
Like some thoughts today about father. Really!
Marvelous!"
                    Serey began to chuckle
And then to laugh, covering her mouth politely.

Greta said, "Our time is up" and sighed softly.

24

"Oh! I could kill that Michael for his silence!
He comes home from the Kleinmans' and doesn't
Say a word! And if I sit him down and
Question him he grows restive and angry.
All he wanted to talk about were weights—
Paperweights! He utterly baffles me
Sometimes. I guess the party was for Rupie—
A good idea. Victor knows how to play
His hand. C'est fini. All but the shouting.
Fabrikant is finished. No one supports him.
What will be the next excitement, do you think?"
Greta chose to remain silent, as Serey
Felt an inward flow of words, a slow seeping
As of blood from a hidden, unhealed wound.
As she talked on she felt herself weaken,
Almost perceptibly.

                    "One has to realize
How much Victor's appointment means to us,
All of us. At long last research is ours.
Now it can be redirected, redefined
So that real psychoanalytic research
Can be done by the right people. Of course
There is the matter of the research budget—
A half-million dollars! Imagine that!

Victor, Kurt, and you, with help, of course,
From Marlena and Michael can produce
That large-scale study of psychotherapy
I've heard Victor talk so intently about—
A thorough detailed study of carefully
Selected cases to answer once and for all
That preposterous question—does it work.
Psychoanalysis? We see it working
All around us. The changes I've witnessed
In people in just a few years—Mon Dieu!"

Greta recalled the bitter words of last hour,
Of wives following in their husbands' footsteps,
Baffled by the impact of analysis
On their spouses and seeking the same remedy
Solely to keep their marriages from failing.

"Of course there are other feelings you have
About analysis, judging from what you said
Last hour."

                    Serey felt the bandage rip off
And a sudden welling up, a gushing
That had to be staunched at any cost. But
She felt inert, frozen as if she were
Watching herself die and was welcoming it.
She heard herself say out loud, "This is nonsense!
Nothing but nonsense. I must get out. I must!"
She started to lift her head and couldn't.
Again she heard herself saying out loud, "Nonsense!
Nonsense! Why are you keeping me here against
My will? Why are you torturing me? Why?!"
The effort to talk sapped whatever strength
Serey had left. She closed her eyes and lay
Immobile, feeling nothing.

And Greta
Was alarmed for a moment. Serey had
Responded to her interpretion.
Indeed she did have other feelings about
Analysis. She did feel trapped, tortured.
These were true feelings emerging in an
Hysterical fashion. Nothing more serious.
At least one could find out, Greta thought, pursing
Her pale, thin lips for one doubting moment.
"Trapped and tortured—exactly your feelings.
But how has it come to be this way?
Because you must follow in Michael's footsteps
No matter what your own wishes might be.
To save Michael from your wrath you must blame me.
It must make the analysis very hard."

Serey echoed Greta's last words, "Very hard . . .
Very hard. . . . " but with no strength of feeling.
Greta prompted Serey, "Yes, please go on."
"Go on. Yes, please go on," Serey echoed.
As she heard her own voice say, "Go on,"
The phrase took on a deep significance
And a queer, troubling equivocality.
She heard herself think in her schoolgirl French,
"Va t'en! Va t'en!" and then in English, "Get lost"—
And the word *lost* suddenly brought with it
A rush of tears like a wave breaking into
A thousand bits of foam, fragmented, short-lived.
Her tears quickly ceased, drying up, leaving
Behind a cool taut feeling on her cheeks.

Greta noted the cloudburst of tears. She said,
"You are so distressed, so very unhappy
And yet you can't give your feelings full rein
For fear of hurting Michael, his career."

Serey was remembering an incident
Which took hold of her as if it were happening
Again. Going swimming with a friend, both twelve.
The friend jumps in, Serey after. The friend
Screams out, "I can't swim!" starts to go under.
Serey grabs for her under the chin. Her friend,
Wild-eyed, grasping, closes her hands tightly
Around Serey's throat. Serey struggles for breath.
She feels herself begin to go under.
Suddenly a blind white rage possesses her.
She digs her fingers into her friend's throat,
Clamps them viselike, vowing never to let go.
Her friend's eyes bulge, horror-stricken, disbelieving.
And then her friend lets go, her eyes roll up.
Serey pulls her the few feet to the shore.
Moments later they are both laughing madly.
Serey could hear that wild, nervous laughter
Interspersed with soblike gasping for breath.
It was much later that she noticed blood
On her hands and a long gash on her friend's throat
From which blood oozed, half congealed, glistening
     darkly
Alongside the pearl-like gleam of seawater.
The feeling then was like that feeling before:
Of vague, disquieting significance,
Of a fascination almost dreamlike,
Of a deep unsettling uneasiness
Which rose upward from the belly to the mouth
Becoming a mild nausea remembering
Some past revulsion. "She's ugly," thought Serey,
"So ugly, old, obese, and slow-witted."
She summoned up Greta's face which floated
Balloonlike in front of her and disappeared.
She felt utterly alone, engulfed in silence
As if suspended in the seamless reaches
Of outermost space—and she was benumbed.

Greta waited and wondered. No response
To her previous words, except this distance
She felt growing between them. Never before
Had this happened. She had to be angry
And this an extreme defense against it—
But why so extreme? Greta was worried.
She must first deal with this defense and not
Venture to touch the rage beneath. So much
Was clear. But how? This poor young woman was
Perhaps sicker than she appeared—much sicker.
The thought alarmed Greta. Had she been wrong
Initially? Serey was no hysteric.
If not, what was she? Was analysis
The treatment of choice? Greta's keen intellect—
Annealed by the fiery years of her
Long apprenticeship in a different practice
Treating borderlines and schizophrenics,
Addressed the unforeseen as if expected,
The manner of all seasoned clinicians.
Right now, she reasoned, she must reestablish
Contact with her patient, gain time to think,
While providing Serey with some relief:

"No matter where you must take yourself, know
I am still here. We are still together."

Serey heard the difference in Greta's voice—
Again the two mad friends at the seashore.
It was when she threw her head back laughing
That Serey noted the gash. For a moment
She thought her friend had snapped her head back
    too hard,
Tearing her throat by the sudden strong jerk.
But why the blood trickling on her own hands?
Serey started to laugh and found herself
Staring at her hands which she held poised like snakes

In front of her eyes. Greta was mystified
And knew her patient was experiencing
Things she could not share.

She said, "I am still here."

Serey clenched her hands together, saying
Loudly, "On the beach where ignorant armies
Clash by night, we two, too true together,
Too true, too true . . . together."

Greta relaxed.
Her patient was returning.

Serey went on:
"*Dover Beach* by Matthew Arnold. I read it
When I was twelve. All I remember of it—
'Ignorant armies clash by night.' That's good.
All armies are ignorant. Tolstoy said that.
I remember that from *War and Peace*. You know
I used to read a lot as a teenager.
Good books, literature—Maupassant, Flaubert—
Even tried to read them in French—that was hard.
My father knew French well. He was so pleased
At my interest."

Greta witnessed how Serey
Was knitting herself together around father
And his flirtatious love. Not around mother
Who remained an abstract presence—powerfully
Mute, her outline indicated by contours
Formed by other presences.
"Your father was good
To you and loved you very much," Greta said.

"Not too much, I hope!" Serey said lightly.
Greta knew it was safe to end the hour.

25

Greta Denkman approached the hour with Serey
In a sullen mood. At breakfast she had
Groused at Kurt for his carefully manicured
Rage at her—it was precisely that—
For mismanaging Serey's analysis.
How had he put it? "The simplest cases
Sometimes pose the greatest difficulty
Because we prepare ourselves for obstacles;
Then like a man who pushes too hard at
An open door, we fall through unexpectedly."
She had retorted, "And you didn't open
At all that locked door of a husband of hers."
She then put aside her pique and asked his help.
After she had described the hour, he paled,
Turned his head aside and drew in his lips
Like a child rejecting distasteful food.
He had not liked what he had heard. Greta
Smiled, lowering her brows as a mother
Might in mild reproof. No, she knew her task—
To treat a rapidly worsening case:
First she must isolate the case from all
Contaminants, as a surgeon prepared
A sterile field before operating.
She had to sterilize herself as well,
Which meant an utter detachment from all

Politics—which were sheer psychic pollutants—
No matter if her husband were offended.
Her first and last responsibility was to
Her patient, whose life might well be in her hands.
As Greta summoned her resolve to act,
Her thin lips were drawn in a harsh grimace
And her nostrils flared, while her eyes narrowed.
It was a face set to oppose the most
Baleful enemy.

When Serey arrived
She handed Greta a folded sheet of paper
And sat down in a chair, avoiding the couch.

"What have you given me?" Greta wondered.
Serey turned her head aside, her chin raised.
Greta unfolded the paper and said:
"It would be better if you read it to me.
That way you could tell me all about it
As you read."

Serey snatched the sheet abruptly
From Greta's hand. She stuffed it in her purse,
Not bothering to fold it, and burst into tears.
She shrugged, walked over and lay down on the couch.
Greta's eyes narrowed further.

"It's no use.
No one will listen to me. It's a joke."
Serey burst out laughing, a peal of laughter
Ending in a soft whine like an afterthought.

"I am ready to hear what you have to say,"
Greta said, her voice steady, resolute.

"Then why didn't you read my list?"

                                        "Was it
A list? Why don't you tell me about it?"

"Oh, no you don't. It will be recorded
And then you will play it for Kurt and Victor . . .
Maybe even Michael."

                        "I'm glad you wanted
Me to see it."

                    "Of course, you're my analyst."
And Serey once again burst out laughing.

"Yes I am and I want more than anything
To be of help to you. No matter about
Kurt, Victor, even Michael. You matter."
Greta felt relieved to have made that statement.

A tidal wave of anguish rose up and
Swept Serey far beyond Greta's office,
Far into the hinterland of her being,
Covering the deep valleys in an ocean depth
Of unbounded, unnamable feelings—
An ocean that was now effacing all
Familiar landmarks.
                        Serey whistled,
More an involuntary escape of breath,
Then whimpered as if at a painful thought.
"I do not see why I cannot have him."
She half rose from the couch. Greta

Immediately said, "It's not yet time.
Please continue. Who can't you have?"

                                    Serey
Lay back down. "He's on the list. Read it."

Greta replied, "But the list is in your purse."
Serey nodded her head as a dull child might.
The swift motions of her thoughts were becalmed
As if the forces moving them had ceased.
She lay on the couch staring aimlessly,
Her eyes turned opaque, saliva gathering
In a corner of her mouth, dribbling down
Onto her chin. The exquisite vitality
Of mental being was ebbing away.
Serey began stroking her forehead, pressing
Her fingertips down hard as if to crank
Her brain to life. It sprang into livid rage.

"You're dead! You breathe and laugh, but you're dead—
      fini!
You didn't ever used to laugh—always
So quiet. But you laughed that time—no lip-laugh
But a wide-open red-throat laugh. . . . Listen,
No, please, listen to me—a soundless laugh."
And Serey's voice dropped to a whisper.
"With a little, bitty gurgle at the end."
Her voice resumed its loudness and intensity.
"Yes, mother had such a lovely carriage
Before I was born. Then I got the carriage,
You know, and the nursemaid. Like a column,
An alabaster Grecian column—beheaded.
YOU ARE DEAD and I'll not cozy with you—
Ever. DO YOU HEAR ME! No more stroking."
Serey clamped a hand over her mouth and gagged.

Greta's fingertips had turned cold as she
Struggled to fathom her patient's meaning.
On another track her mind was racing
Toward a painful conclusion she was still
Trying to avoid.
                    "Sometimes things get confused.

But we can work together to straighten
Them out." She then waited for a reply.

"No you don't. No 'togetherness.' Not again.
Ever." Serey leaped from the couch, backed up
Against the door and gripped the knob tightly
But did not turn it.

                She was frightened but
Wanted to stay, Greta noted. Some hope
In that.
       "Why don't you sit down and we'll talk
About the list." Greta realized that
The list was Serey's slim hold on sanity.
Serey suddenly flitted toward the chair
And sank into it as if she wished to
Disappear. She stared vacuously at Greta
Who cleared her throat nervously, waiting
For Serey to speak. But she soon took note
That Serey was lost deep within herself
And was no longer apprehending her.

"Perhaps you can tell me about the list."

Serey automatically retrieved the list
From the purse and began to weep as she
Smoothed out the crumpled paper on her lap.
"Look what happened to my list! It's all smudged.
Everybody on it is mixed up with
Everybody else. I can't make sense of it
Anymore." And she crushed the paper between
Her palms and flung it to the floor. She sobbed
Fitfully although her eyes were now dry.

Greta feared that with the list rejected
Serey would plunge into madness again.

"It was such an important list. Let me
See what I can do for it."

                              Greta leaned
Forward to pick up the list. Serey drew back,
Lifting herself in the chair, her face strained
With fright and revulsion as Greta moved
Closer in her effort to retrieve the list.
Greta placed the list on the desk, carefully
Smoothing it out and noting that it was damp
And indeed the ink was smudged but not badly.
"There. It is all right now. Not too smudged at all.
Shall I read it and then you can tell me
About it?"

                    Serey shook her head and formed
A voiceless no with her lips that Greta
Chose to ignore. She read the list silently.
It was prefaced by a brief paragraph:

     "To Whom It May Very Specially Concern:
     I being of sound mind and body do
     Declare that what I shall list below
     Is the whole Truth and nothing but the Truth,
     So help me God. Amen."

                              The list followed
In hand-printed letters most in lower case,
But some in upper case haphazardly:

     "President: Herr Doktor VICTOR KleinMAN.
     VICE-President: Herr Doktor Kurt DENKman.
     General-in-Charge: Frau Doktor JOLLY LEAD.
     Saint-for-a-day: Mon aiMABle Michel
     Secretary-of-ALL-SECRET-Affairs:
     Sir Donal Prescott, Lord of Fife and Drum.

Maids-in-Waiting-foreverEVErmore:
Dame Ruthie, Dame Francie, Dame La Seriosa.
Lords of the Unloyal Opposition:
Bernardo FREEmon, Brother Fabricious,
Sister Paula B. ROUGH, Sir No-Account
APAULing Dreyfus."

                    Greta was frowning
Deeply by the end of the list. She looked
Directly at Serey. "I am the one
Very specially to be concerned with this
Important list. You are right to let me
Read it. We will study it together."

Again Serey bolted for the door, pushing
Against it with the force of her momentum
While struggling to open it with her hands,
Gripping and twisting the bronze knob. Greta rose
Quickly from her seat. Serey gasped and slid
To the floor, her back flat up against the door,
Both hands limply falling to the side, her
Head rolling loosely onto her shoulder, her
Hair clotted damply on her pale forehead.
Greta froze in her stride toward her, noting
The terror in Serey's wildly upturned eyes.
She herself was breathing hard and trembling.
A bond, not unlike that of enemies
Who know each other well, each respecting
The other's prowess, sprang up between them.
Greta felt her patient's raw furious pain.
Serey felt her physician's stubborn resolve.
She picked herself off the floor, retrieved her purse,
Preparing it seemed to leave. Greta looked on,
Narrowing her eyes as if cigarette smoke
Was arching past them. Serey hesitated.
Greta said, "You are certainly free to leave

But I think you should rest a little first."
Serey obediently lay down on the couch,
Clutching her purse to her breast, breathing deeply.

"You are absolutely right. I'm exhausted.
Enormement fatiguée." With these words
Serey's voice assumed its normal light
Sarcastic pitch as if expressing mild
Disbelief at what she herself were saying.

"Yes, do rest awhile. Where are you going next?"

"Home. The kids will be back from school at three.
And then there's supper to prepare. C'est la vie."

Greta was reassured. Perhaps it could
All be contained within the treatment hours.
Perhaps it was a transference psychosis,
Transient and curable. And yet
There was no longer any doubt that Serey
Was much too fragile for analysis.

"I'm feeling rested now. I must go, you know,
Duty calls. Shall I return tomorrow
As usual?"

                    "As usual," Greta confirmed.
Serey smiled wickedly as she left, stirring
In Greta renewed anxiety for her.

26

As soon as Serey entered Greta noticed
The spit curls like inverted question marks
On both temples. Her mascara was darker,
Thicker, making her eyes larger, luminous.
Was there also too much powder on her face,
And redder lipstick than customary?
Yet otherwise Serey seemed her old self.
She lay down on the couch unhesitatingly.

"The children were so difficult today,
Fighting over breakfast, which Michael can't stand.
I tried of course to settle things down—but
Phoebe, who else, that little firecracker,
Refused to eat anything. She announced
She was on a *hunger* strike! She had heard
Something about hunger strikes in her class.
When Michael asked her why she was striking,
She looked hilariously puzzled. Mon Dieu!
She didn't know what a strike really was!
But she went off without eating, while Michael
Mumbled something about females starting young.
For that remark I insisted that he eat
What Phoebe had left untouched. He glared at me,
Called me crazy, and left for the office.
Hilarious. My little lost angel.

Michael. Saintly, atmospheric Michael.
Atmospheric is a good word for him.
Elevated, vague, only partly there,
But essential, yes essential, for me.
Without him I cannot breathe, I suffocate,
The way I sometimes feel in here." And she
Broke off. She wet her fingertips and fixed
The two spit curls further in position,
A wicked smile playing on her lips.

Greta balanced two approaches in her mind:
One, to take what she said at face value,
As if the analysis were resuming
After a brief detour, as it were; or
To treat today as a sealing over,
A mending of the seam so badly ripped
Last time. The former approach was seductive,
But she knew it would be foolhardy. Wait,
Yes, wait until the seam mends. Yet how strong
Would it be then? Strong enough for analysis?
Her doubts had grown deeper since last session.
Even though Kurt was insisting that it was
Transferential, a phase of the treatment,
A regressive shift. She was not so sure.
Kurt, she knew, had reason to push that view,
But she had stubbornly purified herself
Of all political motives—a patient's life
Might be at stake. So might her own marriage,
At least its hard-won equanimity.
After so many years of pitched battles
Over territory, sexual freedom—
He had to have his young girls now and again
And she her private vacation abroad
With her lifelong friend and confidante.
Hers she felt was a substantial tie,
Nothing sexual. A lasting, warm personal

Relationship in which much had been shared,
Good times and bad. Frieda, long divorced,
Had a grown daughter whom Greta adored.
There were times when she felt that Serey could
Evoke that affection. Wait, wait, Greta
Continued to counsel herself and thus
She husbanded her patience.
                  "It's hard to
Look after a husband and children too,"
She acknowledged, carefully steering clear
Of any comment on Serey's "suffocation"
In the hours.

              In the meantime Serey
Had grown grim, her jaw jutting forward, her
Lips compressed so that the red was smudging.
"I'll not drown in all this. No matter what.
I'll know how to save myself. I'll not sink
Like a stone."

           "Tell me, please, what you are meaning?"

"I'm sure I've told you, n'est-ce pas? About Pia?"

"Perhaps I've forgotten but I don't recall."

"She was—is—my best friend . . . from childhood on.
But one thing you must know about Pia,
She couldn't swim a stroke. And I, of course,
Was a furious swimmer. Once we forgot
Ourselves on a hot, hot summer day.
Pia jumped into the water and before
My very eyes began to—go under, drown.
I plunged into the water . . . to . . . save her.
The bitch began to pull me under, climbing
Over me, holding me down. I clutched at her throat,

Digging my fingers in deep to choke her.
She let go of me . . . and . . . I pulled her to shore.
We laughed and laughed at our stupidity.
It isn't difficult to murder someone."

How beleaguered this young woman was feeling,
Greta noted. "It's good to have the strength
Needed to protect oneself." Still careful,
Greta would not risk anything further.

"I took on a name for myself then, a name
To match my victory over death. There was
A tough, silent character in Hemingway—
For Whom the Bell Tolls—a hard, older woman
Whom I called La Seriosa. That's the name
I took, La Seriosa. That's who I am."

"Yes, that's what you must be now for a time,
Until the struggle is over." Oddly,
Greta could hear a resonance in that
Phrase provoking an angry uneasiness.
Whose struggle over what? This young woman's?
Her own with Kurt? Kurt's with Victor? And all three
With Freeman and Fabrikant? She had vowed,
No more for her. No way to do analysis
In this fishbowl of a place. She yearned to leave,
To be in New York or Chicago, where
Size alone guaranteed anonymity.

"Now Phoebe will know how to breathe on her own.
That child flew from my womb, a butterfly
Already winged and beautiful. She never
Crawled. Stood up one day and walked. That's Phoebe.
Never let me cuddle her. She'd arch her back
And make a face. Mon Dieu! Admirable!"

Greta felt as if the anchor of the hour
Had been weighed. The session was adrift.
It needed steering and she lacked a crew.
She had to take a chance.

> "Too bad that Phoebe
Had to do it only by herself since
I'm sure you wanted to assist."

> "Did I?
I did? But what use is there in going back.
Phoebe is an arrow who will find her mark."

"An arrow is launched from a bow and aimed."

"No, no. She's a self-propelled arrow—a missile
Then."

> "Like Phoebe you must make it hard for me
Right now to help you because you fear drowning
In that help." Greta held her breath, unsure,
So unsure of her grip on the case, on
Her own life.

> Serey began to hum a song
Unfamiliar to Greta. But at one point
She heard Serey voicing under her breath,
"It ain't necessarily so." Greta knew
She had lost the gamble. They were adrift.
Serey once again patted her spit curls
And rubbed her lips together making even
More of a red smudge. Her mascara had run
Where a few cornered tears hung shimmering.
Serey fidgeted and then announced:
"Well, Mon General, I have sent the list
To the former president so he will know
Who is to succeed him." With that she rose
From the couch, bowed her head toward Greta and

Strode from the office.

                                Greta was stunned and sat
In a benumbed silence for several minutes.
She realized her patient was deluded.

27

Serey had missed two sessions without calling.
Greta had not hesitated to call
Herself but Serey was not at home. She left
Messages that were not returned. Greta
Frowned as her dismay deepened. Kurt was
Relentless. A dry smile on his lips, he
Teased her for her earnestness, her worry—
Too involved, too thin-skinned. It had to hamper
Her objectivity and thus her skill.
Her patient needed her detachment not
Her motherly fretting over her "madness"—
And he always said it with quotes around it
That at first bewildered Greta and then
Infuriated her. She saw through him.
Serey had to be treatable for his sake
And Victor's, of course. That famous letter of hers?
An acting out of rivalry with Greta.
She too could be a kingmaker. Greta
Listened with disbelief although she pondered
Kurt's analysis. She hoped he was right.
Strange things can happen in analysis.
Perhaps she was being too motherly.
Had she not enjoyed fleeting fantasies
Of having Serey for a daughter?
Had she not thought of protecting her

From the politics—from Kurt and Victor?
Let Michael be the sacrificial lamb
If necessary. He was bound and muzzled
By nature anyway. But Serey lived
Powerfully by her wits and impulse—
A grown-up Phoebe. Greta winced at the thought.
She was pitting herself against her husband,
Her patient against his. That way lay disaster.
No matter how barren their marriage had been
Otherwise, it had borne that rarest of fruits—
A twin, self-same career, carefully tended,
Demanding disciplined pruning, forbearance.
Their labors had been crowned with a rich bloom.
Now the fruit was ripe. Victor's directorship
Would be the setting for their enjoyment
Of all that they had nurtured and foregone.
Kurt would be director of the Institute,
She would head a child analytic program,
With Marlena as her heir apparent.
The rich mantle of psychoanalysis
Would enfold the institution, warming
Its cold psychiatric heart. Her thoughts worked.
She had indeed lost her perspective as Kurt
Had said. She was readier for Serey
Now whether she came or not to the hour.

Greta had called the front desk. No Serey.
The phone rang. On the other end was Michael.
"Well, what's to be done? I cannot make it out."
The line seemed to go dead. Greta said,
"Hello? Hello?" Michael answered, "Hello.
Have you hung up? I cannot make it out."
And resumed his silence. Greta inquired,
"What can't you make out?" Michael seemed to hum,
His way of musing over an answer.
"You know, it's the nights. More than anything else."

Again the silence like a deadening void.
"The nights, Michael? Whose nights?" "Your patient's,
 of course."
Greta's impulse was to hang up hard, annoyed
At this puzzling, piecemeal way of talking,
Like signals from a distant galaxy.
"Michael, what is it that you want to tell me?"
"You know what it is. She can't sleep for long
Without waking up screaming, clutching her throat.
Well, she . . . you must know this . . . about last night—
About her wanting to cut herself, her throat,
I suppose? It must all be in the treatment.
I kept . . . I stopped her and she . . . attacked me . . .
Mon General? Who is that? She called me that.
Her crazy father called. He speaks French to her.
She makes believe she understands it. Smiles
As she talks to him. . . . It's guilt." And his voice
Ceased as if he had thrown a switch—abrupt,
Empty, disjunctive silence. For Greta
The pieces, for all that was missing, cohered.
"Can Serey come to the phone?" "Where is she?
Last night she left . . . toward morning . . . nothing
 said."
"Are *you* all right, Michael?" "They are at school,
The children. It's fine . . . fine." Greta was alarmed.
Where had she gone? She was suicidal.
Kurt was entirely wrong. She was plainly
Psychotic. She had to be hospitalized.
"Michael, let me know if Serey returns,
And if I learn where she is I'll call you."
"It's still very early. I'll be at work."
With that he hung up.
                              Again the phone rang.
"Greta, so glad I reached you. Hope things are well."
Greta went blank, unable to place the voice.
"There's someone here who I think should talk to you.

I wasn't quite sure what to do with her.
She's talking French half the time and telling me
My term is over—completement fini,
Is how I think she says it. That's right, I think.
I had only high-school French matter of fact.
Oh, well. . . . Is it all right to put her on the phone,
It won't mess up her psychoanalysis?"
The mild, apologetic voice was now
Unmistakable. "Please, Chuck, put her on."

As the phone changed hands there was a roaring
Exaggerated sound drowning Serey's voice
For a moment.

          "C'est fini, Mon General.
La guerre est terminé. A nous la victoire,"
Serey's shaky, hoarse voice cantilated,
As if she were reciting verse.

             Greta
Considered her response. Should she ask Serey
To come to the office? No. She'd refuse.
Or ask the president to take Serey
To admissions where Greta would join them?
He was a psychiatrist. He could see
For himself. But was she really psychotic
And a danger to herself?
             "I would like
To see *your* victory, Serey. We must meet
As soon as possible to ensure it."

The loud amplified roaring sound reappeared
As Serey dropped the phone.

           "This is Chuck speaking.
I'm prepared to take her to your office.

She said she had an hour. I suppose
That would be all right, quite proper, you think,
I mean from an analytic . . . perspective?
I'm not an analyst, you know. Just a
Doctor who hasn't practiced in a long time.
I might say (his voice lowered) she's in bad shape.
Never seen her this way. Treatment must be
Tough for her. Sad to see."

                    "Please, Chuck, call Michael
And tell him to bring her to my office.
He's still at home. A bit of a crisis
In her treatment. I'm sure it will soon pass."

"Of course, Greta, of course. I've no doubt at all.
She's too solid a person and you yourself
Too sound an analyst. Look, already
She's chatting away with Betty in the kitchen
As if nothing at all were wrong. You're right.
I'll call Michael and she'll be over there
In no time. Great talking to you."

                       Would they,
In fact, be "over in no time?" How
American he was! "Great talking to you,"
As if it were a social occasion.
She had to be prepared for them if they came
And ready with something else if they didn't.
But what? Hospital? So difficult with staff
And family. She became aware how
Much she wanted to believe Kurt and how
Little she did. He was wrong. The clock showed
Half of Serey's hour had passed. Soon her—
With alarm she realized her next patient
Had to be canceled. She hated to do that.
The smooth progression of hours was so

Vital to analysis. It was its
Form, shaping the limitless time
Of neurosis into inescapable units,
Doses of reality for both
Analyst and patient. She had to cancel
Doctor Flores with whom she had just begun,
A new Chilean candidate in training.

Twenty minutes passed before they showed up.
A faint knock on the door and then Michael
Gently pushing it open, a big smile
On his face.

              "May we come in," he asked.
Serey was clutching his arm while clasping
Her coat collar tightly around her neck.
As Michael entered the office she clung
To him, moving almost in lock step with him.

"Well, a little late for her hour, but
Here she is." Michael was summoning up his most
Tactful manner, a great effort for him.
Serey was now trying to hide behind him,
Away from Greta. Michael withdrew his arm,
"I want to read a certain magazine
In the waiting room. Tell me when you're through."
With these words he swiftly left the office,
Leaving Serey without a place to hide.
She burst into tears, began to sway
Back and forth, moaning softly as she did so.
Her face was drawn and pale, no trace of makeup
Or the spit-curls. When her hand dropped to her side,
Greta noted that under her coat she still wore
Her pajamas. So this is how she paid
A visit to the president? To her
Surprise, Serey lay down on the couch and turned

Her entire body toward the wall, away
From Greta, still wearing her coat.
                                    Greta waited.
She felt as if she were with a sick child,
A quiet, troubled vigil, waiting for
The child to wake, open its eyes and be well
Again. But she knew it was not to be.
Not without some time in the hospital.
But who would doctor her there? Perhaps Prescott.
Yes. A fine, reliable person. Discreet.
And now how to get her there.
                                    "You're so tired,
So much has wearied you the last few weeks.
I can see how you need a rest from everything—
Children, home, Michael. You have tried to do
So much for all of us. And now you need
Something for yourself—" Greta drew in her breath.
"I would like you to go into the hospital
For a short time so you can come to yourself.
And then we shall see what more's to be done."

Serey sat up on the edge of the couch,
Gathered her coat about her and stood up,
Like a soldier awaiting the next order.
At first surprised, Greta quickly perceived
What she had to do.
                                    "Let me call Michael
And all three of us will walk over there.
First let me make a call." She dialed Prescott.
"Is Doctor Prescott available? Fine.
Hello? No time to go into detail.
Serey, Michael, and I are on our way
To hospital admissions. Can you join
Us there? . . . Yes, that's right . . . You're not surprised.
    Good."

Serey had stationed herself in a corner
Where Michael found her. Greta drew on her coat
And the three left through the rear door, walking
Slowly across the campus toward the squat,
Brick hospital building made up of several
Additions in different styles, depending
On who the donor was and when the gift
Was given. It stood directly opposite
The smaller, wooden research building once
An antebellum mansion. The three
Disappeared into a side entrance
Of the hospital's mock-Tudor addition.

28

An attendant brought Serey to her hour.
Greta greeted her in the waiting room
Where she found her quietly sitting, staring
Ahead of her. When she saw Greta, she arose
And waited for Greta to bid her follow.
In the office she peered about as if
Unsure of where she was. Greta bade her sit
Across from the desk. Serey glanced
At the couch, then out the window. To Greta
She seemed distant, composed.

                              "How have you been
Since I saw you last?" Greta asked, her tone
Matter of fact, acknowledging the gap
In their contact.

                    "As well as can be expected,"
Serey replied, "Why did you want to see me?"
The question caught Greta by surprise.

                                        "Why?
Doctor Prescott tells me you're ready to
Resume. You've made great progress in hospital.
I am glad for that. He said you also
Wanted to see me. Is that not right?"

Serey for the first time looked directly
At Greta, her eyes sunken as if in retreat
From all that she had seen, the mascara gone,
The spit curls vanished, her hair neatly
Tied in a bun at her neck. Greta observed
In Serey that sleepwalker calm produced
By medication whose chemical powers
Defuse the explosive bursts of manic
Energy and refill the sinkholes of
Depression. But does the calm provide a place
From which the patient can survey herself,
Absorb the shock of psychosis, reflect
On the inner disaster as another
Weaker, more dangerous way for reaching
The same ends as neurosis? All this Greta
Pondered as she returned Serey's direct,
Impassive look.

        "Yes, I did . . . I suppose I did.
It's all one to me, who I see. I want
To leave the hospital as soon as possible.
My kids need me. Michael needs me."

                  Greta was
Not reassured by Serey's response.
              "I see
What you mean. Of course you should leave as soon
As you are ready. Your kids do need you,
As does Michael. How might I be of help?'

"Tell Don—Doctor Prescott I am ready
To be discharged. You see I am myself
Again. No more nonsense."
            The last she said
With a hint of a wry smile. So far the
Only touch, Greta thought, of her old self.

"Is that what it all was—nonsense? I didn't
Think so."
                    Greta knew she was venturing far
Beyond where her patient might be. She waited.
Serey broke off their direct visual exchange
And studiously looked out the window.
She pursed her lips, lifted her chin and stroked
Her neck dreamily.
                    "It's all over now,
Isn't it? The nonsense, I mean. All over.
What is there to talk about? To understand?"

Good, good, thought Greta, she does pick up the
    thread.
"Maybe now it's over, it would be good
For you to know what happened to you."

                                    "To me?
Why to me? I am nothing in all this.
Better ask what has happened to all of you."
When she said this last, Serey's eyes moved back
To Greta's and a flash of accusation,
Of bold challenge reappeared.
                                    "I must go now.
They are waiting for me." With this
She stood up and moved toward the door.

                                        Greta
Raised her voice as if its loudness would halt
Serey's departure.

                    "But you *are* something in
All this. Everyone knows that. I know it."

Serey turned toward her.
                    "No, I am nothing."

And she slumped back in the chair, staring at
The floor, lost in querulous thoughts, her lips
Twitching in some mute colloquy with herself.

She stayed, Greta thought. She does want to find
Something out for herself. But troubling Greta
Was Serey's accusation: "Better ask
What's happened to all of you." Was it not
Beside the point, Greta reasoned. True or not,
What mattered most was Serey's own well-being
And how Greta could help her to restore it.
The politics were over. They had lost,
Although Kurt insisted that Bernard Freeman's
Appointment as director was temporary—
Until the dust would settle that Serey raised.
She herself was not too sure. And Victor's
Attitude supported her belief. He had
Seemingly lost all interest in the position
And was talking up a move to California.
Kurt again insisted it was a tactic—
Shrewd and calculated. And then Kurt hinted
If Victor were to leave why not consider
Him a candidate for the job? Alarmed
At this loss of judgment on her husband's part—
He could claim no real qualifications
For the position—she decided to
Hold her tongue and let events take their course.
And there before her was that strange catalyst—
No, not catalyst, more like a fuse
That itself disappears in the explosion.
And she, Greta, was trying to reassemble
The tattered shreds of this poor demented
Creature who, she was convinced, would never
Be the same. A mistake, a big mistake
To have taken her into analysis.
The tests had raised some question. They always do.

But she had seemed like such a classic case—
Hysterical, intelligent, living
Entirely through her husband whose career
Was more her creation than his. Maybe,
Maybe had there been no complications—
Michael and Kurt, Kurt and she, Victor—
No, pure adventitious coincidence.
Her ego was not strong enough for analysis,
Pure and simple.
     "You want me to say you're
Better?"

    Serey immediately looked up
From the floor and with a plaintive glance of
Disbelief, said, "Yes, please. I am, I am
Better. Will you say so?"

      "There's no doubt at all
You're better than I saw you last. You must
Know that yourself."

      "Yes, but they need your say-so.
You're the analyst. You know my case best.
You are all so powerful. Aren't you?"
This last was said with the merest hint of
Irony that was not lost on Greta.

"No, it's really Doctor Prescott who decides
With you. I can give him my impressions.
But he and you decide. I am not so
Powerful as you believe. I can only
Offer my help so you can understand
What all has happened to you."

"Your impressions? But they are important.

He'll depend on them. Maybe you all want
To keep me in the hospital for awhile
Longer—keep me from interfering—No,
I didn't mean that. I take that back. Please
Give him the best impressions of me, please.
All I want is to be back with my kids,
My husband, and my home. Maybe I can
Continue to see you then—once in awhile,
That is, to keep in touch. Yes, keep in touch."

Greta sighed deeply, disconsolately.
"Yes, we should stay in touch. I think you've
Come a long way since I saw you last. Perhaps
You still have a little way to go, but
You must discuss that with Doctor Prescott.
Shall we see each other again next week?"

Serey rose hesitantly. "Will I be
Leaving . . . soon? Next week?"

                                    "I'm sure your doctor
And you will work it out. I'll see you then."
With that Greta rose and escorted Serey
Out the door and to the waiting room
Where other patients looked on curiously,
Several wondering where they had seen her before,
The tall, young, smiling attendant rose
To take Serey back to the hospital.

Part Five

Victor Kleinman
and
Kurt Denkman

29

It was a narrow office, the large desk
Against one wall pushing Kurt's swivel chair
Almost against the opposite wall. Kurt
Could barely tilt back. He preferred sitting
In his analytic chair near the window,
Looking toward the door. The couch extended
Almost as far as the brown swivel chair.
In a corner alongside the door was
Another chair, small but comfortable.
Here Victor was sitting, laughing gleefully
As Kurt looked on, a thin smile on his lips.
They spoke to each other in German.

                         "Now,"
Said Victor, "it is ours for the asking.
Your committee report will nominate me
And disrecommend Fabrikant. Marvelous!
You will admit that my idea is sound—
To *disrecommend* Fabrikant—coup de grace!
You have a draft for me to see? I leave
Tomorrow. It will give me some relief
To know it is settled."

                    "It is not settled
Yet," Kurt spoke softly, smoothly, gutturals

227

Almost sibilants, his tone slyly taunting.
His friend need not be so relieved, he thought.
Let him fly to California worried,
A little reminder that he needed friends.
Victor's glee changed quickly to alarm.

"What can you mean? Is there some new trouble?"

"Not really, but—," he was enjoying Victor's
Lability, his adolescent eagerness.
One could play on his moods and ambitions
As on a harpsichord—first the lower
Keys, then the upper—flip the lever—
And one could play both together loudly.

"You know the president decides on this.
Others have his ear as well as we do,
If not more so."

                    "Not at all! His is ours.
Make no mistake about that. He is ours!"

"What makes you so certain?"

                              "Because he knows
Without us—you, me, Greta—he cannot
Run this place. Fabrikant cannot do it."

Victor knew what he was doing. Dear Kurt,
He thought, was jealous over his promotion,
So he reminded him of their common cause
Which would be advanced by his promotion.

"What am I to do with Marlena, Kurt?
She is utterly impossible these days—
Envious, vindictive—she may upset things.

She is remarkably silent. I fear
Her silence, though, and I fear her analyst.
Freeman is a subtle man—a stiletto
Behind a cloak. She has to be with him
To some extent as well as be against me.
I must be careful what I say to her.
It goes right back to Freeman who uses it.
What can we give her? She is ambitious.
Training analyst as soon as she can
Meet the criteria?"

         "Why not. Marlena
Is a bright and able clinician."

Kurt's face had lost its thin-lipped smile.
If only he could be sure of his friend,
What he was really thinking, wanting, feeling.
Director of Research? Was that all? No.
Hardly. A decent budget, some prestige,
But on the periphery of the place—
Not at the clinical heart.

         "Dear Victor,
You have Marlena and I have Greta.
At least Marlena is still young, vibrant.
Greta grows more manly as she grows older.
I expect to find a penis there someday.
And I have such a weakness for young women
Despite my physical difficulties.
This back of mine keeps me from enjoying
The fruits of my own analysis."
         Kurt
Stood up, tried to straighten his back, and then
Lay down on the couch.

         "There was Naomi—

Dark, thin, moody—so easy to impress.
American women are all unopened
Flowers—morning glories in need of light.
A smile, a touch, a sparkle in the eye."

Victor became restless. His friend was off.
This rehearsal of sensuous delights
Annoyed him. Was Kurt toying with him?

"Kurt, please! I leave tomorrow. You know that."

"Her husband with his bashed nose—always busy
Adding up his numbers in his little room.
Some men pursue nature relentlessly
Armed with shotgun and shell, each shell
Filled with hard, round numbers which, as they hit
Their mark, turn to shit. . . . Her behind, Victor.
Was small, flat. It's virtue was in the motor
That drove it. Sheer paroxysms of lust!"

"Kurt, you are wanting me to know something.
You are interested in Marlena, hah?
She has spoken to you about us, no?
Our lovemaking?"

                    Kurt had struck home better
Than he had hoped. He had been teasing only.
In fact, half lost in his own neurosis,
The couch summoning associations,
He had almost forgotten Victor's presence—
Not quite—oh, the unconscious could be sweet.
Marlena! A squat piece, saggy-breasted,
Always slouching as if afraid to stand straight,
Sliding by, a half-smile on parted lips.
Youth! That was in her favor, precious youth!
Kurt grew surly and depressed, suddenly

Feeling hurt, aggrieved by Victor's suspicions.
For the first time he raised his head from the couch
And looked toward Victor seated at the edge
Of his chair at the foot of the couch.

"You are mad! Paranoid and mad! Marlena?"

Victor felt his friend's disdain and he sulked.
"She is impossible these days. Terrible!
We grapple with each other in and out
Of bed. My success infuriates her.
She so reminds me of my sister, Anna,
Adoring, taunting, cutting me to the quick
For every triumph, every achievement.
There is something about myself I have not
Understood. My analysis failed me
When it came to my sister and myself.
Self-analysis hasn't helped either.
I am a lion with a thorn in his paw,
Kurt, I feel such power, productivity—
I can write a paper over a weekend.
I am developing a new synthesis,
A totally new theory! And yet
I must limp instead of leap. I must grovel
Instead of roar. Other women don't help.
I can roll them over with one paw."

Victor squinted, his eyes glistened hotly.
Kurt knew that Victor had been carried away.
He often was by his own violence,
A force that swept facts, ideas, theories
Before it like a juggernaut. Awesome
Yet pitiful, like a tidal wave ending
In a harmless ripple. His sister? Perhaps.
Kurt's back hurt. Psychosomatic? Maybe.

"Victor, we are old friends. Isn't that so?"

Victor turned abruptly toward the couch where
Kurt lay turned to one side, clearly in pain.
"Of course. What makes you stress the obvious?"

"For different reasons. We are both suffering,
Each with an obstacle in his path,
Each having been well analyzed. Correct?"

"Yes, yes . . . go on. I'm listening." Victor squinted
Again, this time as he resumed his gaze
He saw that Kurt was looking at the ceiling.

"As you say, self-analysis doesn't work.
I have found the same to be true—For years.
I have often thought of reentering
Analysis. But with whom? There's no one
Trustworthy. The place is too small. And yet—"

"Again you are driving at something, Kurt.
Out with it!"

                    Victor, as usual, was impatient.
Kurt was offended by Victor's urging—
So lower-middle-class.
                    "Conversation
Of a certain high-minded sort, intimate
And insightful, isn't that analysis?
A relationship of trust. Experience,
Knowledge of the theory, an empathic ear—
Isn't that what makes a good analyst?
Hold off! I'm getting to the point. Victor,
Let's analyze each other, free ourselves
From these last obstacles. Agree we are
The two best analysts here, and as patients

We are better off than most. We could
Cure each other in a matter of months."

Victor's laugh was often loud and shrill.
This time it came out a baritone chuckle.
He was astonished and impressed by Kurt's
Unique idea. Of course their talk often
Traded interpretations, lapsing at times
Into associations just as before.

"Kurt, an incredible idea! A first!
It will break new ground. We will have to take notes!"

He stirred uneasily on the couch. Always
The notes, the discoveries, the new ground.
How Victor could weary him.
                                    "Listen,
Victor, we must this do for ourselves only.
It must remain between us. No one else
Would understand."

                    "You are right, of course, Kurt.
It is always that way with new attempts.
And I so want to get rid of Anna."

"And I of my cursed back," Kurt added.

"But what of the transferences, Kurt,
How can we deal with them?"

                              "As always, Victor.
Don't we always see them in the other—
Use them sometimes?" he added wickedly.

"Yes, yes . . . I do confess we do," said Victor.
We should begin when I return from the West."

30

"Good. Good. I'm glad we could get together
Early today. Much to talk about. My trip—
Exceptional, my paper well received,
Aside from a few egoistic diehards.
But—any news here? Any developments?"
Victor had barely settled in the small chair,
While Kurt glanced out the window pondering.
Victor was back and his bad back was back,
Excruciating.
                    "The Research Department
Doesn't want you, the staff is up in arms
Demanding that Fabrikant be appointed."
Kurt knew he had gone beyond the facts—well,
Victor deserved it—"Paper well received!
Aside from a few egoistic diehards!"
He would soon enough find out the real truth.
Victor exaggerated, especially
His successes.

                    Victor became quiet.
He had a sense that something was afoot.
All that could not have happened in two days,
A weekend at that. Kurt knew that Victor
Quiet meant Victor thinking and suspicious.

"Greta learned this from Serey who had lunch
With Frances Dreyfus. It is cooking but
Not yet boiling over. We have some time."

Victor grew angry. "You were exaggerating,
I believe, isn't that so? A bit of envy,
My friend, a nice welcome back present?"

"Yes. Yes. You are right old friend. Envious
And quite worried for our sakes. Perhaps
We have overreached ourselves. Perhaps
The Research Department is not for you.
Could it be the wrong war at the wrong time?"

Victor was not quite believing his ears.
Kurt had been the one to urge him on.
Kurt had laid out the strategy. He had
Picked the search committee single-handed.
No. It was envy. He had been too brash—
A fault of his. Too enthusiastic—
As usual reaching out for that embrace
Belonging to the victor. Of a sudden
An image came of Bernini's statue—
Apollo reaching for Daphne already
Changing into the laurel. . . . He felt sad
And desired a different kind of talk.

"Kurt, I need you very much to help me.
Remember our resolve to analyze
Each other. I want to begin now."

                                        Kurt
Was startled. He had been preparing himself
To respond to Victor's assault on his
Assessment. But this sudden change of tone
Baffled him. Had something happened out West?

An affair? A blow to his career? Perhaps.

"Victor, of course I remember our resolve.
I myself suggested it. Please, lie down
On the couch."

                "This time me, Kurt, next time, you.
Agreed?" Victor said as he laid himself down.

Incredible! Years suddenly dropped away.
The couch had a familiar comfort to it,
Like an old embrace. He even felt lips
Brush against his cheek—a little gust of memory
Without time or place.
              "As I flew over
The Rockies I became phobic—I mean
I had an anxiety attack—a real one.
My first one in years and years. My teeth chattered.
I broke out in a sweat. I felt like jumping
Out—I mean, rather, I felt I could fly,
A delusion. Not a dream. Not a fantasy—
A conviction—an utter conviction.
I had to fight it off. To fly, to fly
Over those mountains, rising on updrafts,
Banking into canyons and screaming
Into the wind furious against me, its
Strength created by my own speed—"

                        "You talked
Of fear, Victor, a phobia."

                    "Yes, yes, I know—
It was the temptation to fly I feared."
The Bernini statue appeared again,
An image suddenly blotting out all thought.
He saw the formed space between the figures—

Like a negative hallucination.
The figures disappeared. The space dissolved
Into infinity.
                    "I met this woman
In Los Angeles who pestered me
All night at this reception. Pimply, ugly—
A candidate. I told myself she must
Be had that night. Later I asked myself why.
Can you guess?"

                    "With whom was she in analysis?"

"Brilliant. Katz, who hates me with a passion.
I smiled to myself. I would like to shove it
Up his ass, and make him bray like the ass
He is. You saw his stupid attack on me
In the *Quarterly*? It must be answered
Quickly before it seems to have hit home."

Kurt had slouched in his great chair enjoying
The pungent aroma of his friend's associations.
His trips were always good for one wild story.
But he caught himself listening in another way—
The "phobia," the flying—what was that about?

As if responding to his question Victor
Said, "Too much. Too much. I overwhelm myself.
Before the anxiety attack came on
I had been going over my paper.
It was like an engine revving up—whoosh!
My thoughts took off. A half a dozen things
Became clear. What precisely is the self?
How is it related to our impulse life?
The ego? Early object-relations?
Primitive defenses? Our affect life?"

Kurt felt his role take hold. "And now what's happening?"

As if caught by a springe in midair, Victor's
Flight was arrested. He felt angry, hurt.
"What do you mean, now? I'm associating."

"Of course, but are you not flying high, right now?
Lecturing me on those things I know
So well." Kurt was a little offended,
Revolted even by his friend's boorishness.
A woman he had to have. An analyst,
He had to screw. An intractable issue,
He had to solve. Where will it end? And when?
And how would he and Greta fare in this
Whirlwind? "Victor, you are afraid of yourself.
You fear the strength of your will." I fear it
Too, he thought.

　　　　　　"No, Kurt, not my *will*, not that."

"The great engines of life are greed and rage.
They work well below the water line
Powering this luxury liner we are on.
How is all that primal, physical
Even mechanical energy transformed
Into those smooth elegant voyages
We take through life to dance music, waltzing
In salons with Picassos on the wall,
Our greed satisfied with hors d'oeuvres,
Our rage smiling in our teeth, while our lips sing
Schubert, recite Goethe. No, not the will,
Unless the will is only the visible
Propeller churning the water. Kohut is wrong.
Grandiosity is an open mouth, sucking
In all sustenance and spitting out hate.

The idealized parent he makes so much of
Is a mood of satisfaction—that's all,
A state of the purified pleasure ego."

"Note, Victor, how you have shifted from air
To ocean, from high to low—like *Icarus*."

"Icarus! Watch your envy, Kurt. Recall
That you are *analyzing* me. Icarus!"
One myth brought another back, only now
The god stood alone, a laurel wreath on
His brow. "No, Kurt, think of Apollo instead—
And Daphne, she who changed into a tree
Rather than fall into his arms."

                              "Victor,
We are jousting, not analyzing. It's hard."

As usual, Victor sensed his friend's fatigue.
It was a moral fatigue, a weariness
Of spirit. One does not give up. Never.
Especially when difficulties abound.
One flies in the teeth of circumstance
For there is where the prize must be. Always
From the nettles we pluck the flower. From
Hatred, love. From chaos, order. Always.
"Kurt, of course it is hard. But necessary.
Please be patient with me. I am in need.
There is more, much much more that I must relate."

"Listen, Victor, I will try. You be patient
Too. But we must stop for now."

                              The two friends
Had left much business unattended.

31

When Victor entered Kurt was already
Seated behind the couch awaiting him.
For a moment Victor hesitated,
Perhaps he should sit down first. But Kurt
Inclined his head toward the couch and Victor
Lay down. Troubled by second thoughts, Victor
Also had business to conduct with Kurt.

"Paula is back. I'm sure she will support me.
She admires me greatly because I can think
And write, talents she does not possess at all.
But I also know that she despises *you*.
What goes on between you? Some past history
I know nothing of? My judgment tells me
That her good sense will prevail. Who else is there?
Fabrikant? She has no regard for him.
Dreyfus? Out of the question. Freeman?
She would vote for an iceberg first. So that
Would leave the full-time researchers. My God!
That crew of cockroaches are best left to crawl
About their research grants. She can have no
Sympathy for any of them. And that
Leaves the field to me. I must speak to her
Soon and be sure to enlist her support."
Ordinarily, he would expect that Kurt

Would have something to say. Victor waited,
But Kurt remained silent. Victor shifted
Uneasily on the couch. He drummed his fingers
On his jaw, thrust his tongue against his cheek—
And waited.

        Kurt surveyed his friend, sensing

His growing unease and waited.
                        Victor
Shut his eyes and a burst of images
Like fireworks lit up the cerebral darkness.
Familiar faces on unfamiliar bodies.
The bodies were all female and sculpted
To perfection, arranged in classic poses.
The faces were painfully real and trite,
Caught up in commonplace expressions, ugly
In their unflattering banality.
Yet they were no less than themselves, faces
Well known to him, one loved, another treated,
A third there from his earliest remembrances.
But their immortal part was their liquid
Universal forms. All had the same body
In different postures, like studies for
A formal portrait. But more than rough sketches,
They were molded, three-dimensional
And utterly fixed in their arrangement
So that each face seemed caught in a stone vice.
His mind immediately went to work
As the explosion quickly disintegrated.
He had to capture it in a photo frame
Of instant, candid intellect so that
At leisure he could cross-examine it
With his magnifying analytic lens.
But there was no time for that now, Kurt was
Waiting and this was analysis.

"You can't imagine how staggering it is
To rediscover the power of the couch—
What lies behind one's eyelids once closed
Against the daylight trivialities.
Somehow even the directorship
Falls under that humdrum pall—vanity,
Yes, it is all vanity. Even
My images cannot escape that tension
Of opposites. Just now three images
Rose up behind my eyelids, strange hybrids
Of faces well known to me and bodies
Of unsurpassed perfection. One and the same
Body for each—the idealized forms
Making the familiar drab and pointless
Marlena, Frances Dreyfus, and Anna.
Marlena's face wears a sly, impatient smile
As it sits on top of this graceful figure
Stretching away from me; Frances Dreyfus
Is crying, of course, reproachfully, her
Eyelids lowered, her lips pouting. Ah, but
That same graceful figure draws the eye away
And Anna's face with that knowing, raised-eyebrow
     look
Unaware of the fabulous riches
Of that self-same form beneath her."
                                   Victor paused,
Then warmed to the task his images posed:
"Ah Kurt, my friend, how truly unaware
Hysterical women are of the beauty
They possess and how neurosis tarnishes
This treasure. That is what my images mean.
A *furor therapeuticus* possesses me.
I could cure them all so that their true worth
Could shine forth unblemished. I know
There is a hatred in me of their sickness.
Do you know that Hawthorne tale of a great

Alchemist who weds this beautiful girl
And on their wedding night he discovers
A blemish on her cheek. He cannot touch her
Until he has removed it. But none of his
Potions or salves works, in fact they make it worse.
The blemish spreads with each application
Until her beauty is utterly destroyed.
Our work is like that sometimes, Kurt—wasted
And defeated by stubborn resistance,
Negative therapeutic reactions.
That's the meaning of Hawthorne's tale.
The seeming blemish is a defiant warning—
Unknown as such to the possessor, but
Clear in its hostile message nonetheless:
'My beauty beckons you to follow close
But you must accept this fatal error
Or you will be happy with none of it.'
But the blemish is only the surface sign
Of a deeper rottenness and rejection.
If only *they* would accept our love of *them*
Then the blemish and the rottenness would
Disappear. It sounds as if I am saying
That all women are Loreleis—drawing
Us upon the rocks. But we, Kurt, unlike
Those frightened sailors will not stuff our ears
Against their song; rather we strive to save them
From their own hostility, to turn these
Loreleis into . . . flowering laurels. . . . "

Victor frowned at the appearance of "laurels."
It did not quite fit and somehow echoed
Other previous thoughts. He stopped talking
In the midst seemingly of eloquent ideas.

Kurt had grown more aware and more puzzled
By Victor's flood of images. He sensed

A dark vitality like an underground
River flowing underneath his friend's excitement.
He too was surprised by the word *laurel*.
It was a point at which to start:

                         "Tell me,
Victor, what comes to mind about 'laurel'?"

"Laurel? You're right to ask. A good question.
It seems I was telling you about it
Last time, wasn't I?"

                     "No, Victor, not so.
I have no memory of hearing that
Last time."

                "Ah, yes! Right! Right! Of course!
The image of Bernini's statues drifted
Into my thoughts last time but I must not
Have mentioned it. A resistance. But why?"

Kurt began to see some sense to it.
"Victor, last time you had just returned from
California. What triumph has escaped you
That you wished to hide from me—and yourself?"

Victor's frown hardened. He should not be angry
At Kurt. He was right, at least it made sense,
But it was all tangled. To be honest
And thus to be helped might mean his defeat,
Or at least to feed Kurt great ammunition,
But what must he be thinking! He had no real
Idea! His anxiety and suspicion
Were like clouds in a bright summer sky, floating
Harmlessly because no storm was brewing—
Soon a breeze would tuck them away behind

A hill and lay them to rest.
                    "I don't know, Kurt.
And yet I feel you must be right somehow.
It's all up in the air—just before I saw
Clouds floating in a serene sky, harmless
Perhaps—Yes! Yes! of course, my phobia—
The flying. You must recall my account
Of my anxiety attack on the plane,
And yet now it all seems utterly pointless—
It has all turned pale and flat. Why go on?
Shall I get up, Kurt?"

                    "Hold on, Victor, please.
Clearly you are even now resisting
Strongly. Therefore something must very much be
     there.
We have a few more minutes left to go.
Shall we not observe all the proper rules
If this is to work for you—and then for me?"

Victor's impatience to end grew stronger
Still. He felt that his friend was after something.
Would this nonsense jeopardize his plan,
Or could he benefit from it and rise
Above these complications? Even so
He had felt that strong undertow in him
Of troublesome remembrance, wordless still.
It could work and free him—but from what
Exactly? How strange it was and thrilling.

"Kurt, you are right. I want to continue
But I am at a dead end. Perhaps tomorrow
We continue with more courage on my part."

Kurt pondered on this new reality
Taking shape before his wondering eyes.
Both he and Victor stood up. As Victor left,
Kurt looked down, letting him pass, unobserved.

32

It was already late when his patient arrived.
Victor stumbled on the threshold, caught himself
And quickly stretched out on the couch, his belly
Shaking from the effort.
                                    "Stumbling, am I,
Already? Let's see what one can make of that.
I am worried, Kurt. About you. About
Everyone involved in our business.
What could be holding up the president's call
To me? The committee has acted. So—
What more is there to do? Or is there something
Going on I don't know about, Kurt. Is there?"

Kurt enjoyed the silence he was imposing
On his friend. Victor had not as yet grasped
The obvious his own unconscious had
Clearly revealed. Here he was an eager
Candidate for the research position,
Qualified in every way for it,
Who becomes symptomatic, frightened
Of his own ambition. What else could he make
Of his "high flying" anxiety, his manic
Sweep carrying all before it—right over
A cliff. Kurt was alarmed at his conclusion.
Was he too going over that cliff? Was Victor

Warning him unconsciously of his intent?
That Hawthorne story about the blemished bride
Ending with the maiden's beauty destroyed—
Was that further evidence? Kurt considered
His alternatives, shifting his weight uneasily
In his chair, a spasm gripping his back.
Too soon to draw attention to all that.
First one must deal with Victor's projections,
His blaming others for standing in his way,
Including himself. And then one must attack
The symptom. Attack? Why attack, he wondered.
Unlike himself to think that way. Was he
Already so identified with Victor
That he is himself attacking? Dangerous.
His expression turned sour. There was Greta's news.
Serey may be much sicker than supposed.
That has to affect Michael and through Michael
Himself. Not his greatest success, Michael.
But serviceable. If Serey went to pieces
Now it had to undermine their position
With the president who was always
Fed horror stories about analysis
By the research and family people
Who either claimed it didn't work at all
Or worked too well.

                    Victor was fidgeting,
Tolerating the long silence poorly.
He was torn between the urge to push on
And an unwelcome feeling of sadness
Which started as a dull ache in his stomach
And grew like an orchestral swell, a chord
Absorbing one by one all the instruments.
At first he fought against it.
                              "Kurt, it's hard
For me to leave our business unattended.

Perhaps we should have another time
For our work. The decision has to be near.
It means a great deal to me—and to you.
If anything is happening I need
To know. Likely nothing. The president
Is up to his old obsessive tricks.
A man like that should not have two ears, or two
Anything. It only gives him choices—
Who to listen to with which ear. Yesterday
I heard that Dreyfus had a meeting with him.
The halt leading the blind. What's wrong with him—
That Dreyfus? I have nothing against him.
His work is innocuous. But he hates me—
A pure projection of his own repressed
Ambition. All these cautious obsessives
Who cannot deal with their own aggression
Give me a pain in the ass. Then there's Fouchault.
A well-matched pair, he and Dreyfus. Nothing
Fazes him! Imagine! An imperturbable
Frenchman! Impossible. But underneath
It all the same mired-down hesitation,
The same aversion to mixing-it up,
The same overblown concern with fairness.
Always they are confounding ideas
With realities. Because reality
Often has an ugly side, they reject it
Out of hand in favor of the impossible,
Instead of transforming what is ugly
Through the empirics of action. How can
They do clinical work with that attitude?
Why does talking about Fouchault sadden me?
I feel lessened by his indifference
To me, to the research issue. He lives
Analysis twenty-four hours a day.
He thinks of time as if it were a glacier
Slowly inching forward. No need to rush,

No crisis, no catastrophes. Only
A curtain slowly descending on our lives.
I cannot stand such defeatism! Never—"

Kurt saw an opportunity.
                              "Why so shrill?
Why so irritated by poor old Fouchault
Whose youth was shattered by the Vichy French—
As you well know? I wonder if you
Yourself might not have some second thoughts
About research that you ascribe to Fouchault?"

Victor's sadness deepened. Kurt was weakening,
His one most important ally. Why now?
But he knew the sadness went beyond that.
It brought with it a familiar ache and longing—
Of something, someone eluding him still.
Bernini knew it. All artists know it,
Artists of fictional creations and
Artists like himself who created facts—
Necessary, mutative realities.
Analysts are artists in that same sense.

"You fear my ambitions, Kurt, because you fear
It would destroy you. And I fear your fear
Because it nullifies our one great chance
To redirect this place in the service
Of analytic science—its rich resources
In money, people, space are ours
Like paints on an artist's palette, the canvas
Stretched before us, blank and waiting. Tomorrow
It will be too late."

                              "Why, Victor, too late?"

"Tomorrow is always too late, dear friend,

Because others will take today for themselves."

"What of this analysis? Are you prepared
To continue even now with it,
Tomorrow and the day after tomorrow
As well as today no matter what else
Happens? We ask as much of our patients.
And what of me and my turn on the couch?"

"I see, I see what you are reproaching
Me for. You cannot believe me, I know,
That beyond what I desire for myself—
And I admit I want much for myself—
Exists a greater, selfless ambition
For a cause—for psychoanalysis
To survive and grow. We need a research base
Badly and it is within our grasp right now.
Kurt, let us not stand in the way ourselves."

For a moment Kurt was stirred by Victor.
They *had* worked hard and brilliantly together
And were close to achieving the prize. True.
What then? Or better still, would they in fact
Achieve it? And despite their close teamwork
He saw that he could not be sure of Victor.

"How are we to understand your symptom?
Your anxiety, your fear of killing yourself?"
Kurt felt he might have gone too far, too fast.

"Exactly, Kurt. How? Was it to kill myself
Really, or to conquer my own restraint
By imagining an impossible feat
As absolutely possible?"

                    "No, Victor,

It was a manic mask hiding depression."
There was no going back now, Kurt realized.
"If it were exuberance of spirit
There would have been no anxiety, no fear,
Only pleasure."

Victor steeled himself. He knew
The battle was underway in himself,
With Kurt, and with that always elusive world.

33

Victor did not need urging. He lay down
Spryly on the couch, readjusted his jacket
And folded his small hands over his belly.
Kurt keenly eyed his friend with surprise. Why so
Lively with so much happening out there?

"I had this incredible dream last night.
It brought a sudden dawn right at midnight
When I dreamt it. I had written myself
Into bleariness and fallen sound asleep
Without Marlena who was reading something
Downstairs. I plummeted asleep, so quickly
Did I enter into the deepest of sleeps.
And there was my Anna playing hopscotch,
Her raven pigtails flying, her skinny legs
Dancing from square to square, her face set grimly
As I remembered it from our childhood games.
She could be ferocious in pursuit of
Her pleasures—my little Anna. And then
I noticed that each time her foot landed
In a square it vanished and in its place
Was a springtime flower—a daffodil,
Yellow, nodding gently in a soft breeze.
My heart filled with exquisite sadness, Kurt!
A truer feeling I have never had.

My eyes brimmed with tears. There was my Anna.
She was dancing away from me—and toward me,
Yes, toward me at the same time. As her back
Receded, her little figure dancing
Toward the last square, her pinched little face
Loomed larger and larger in front of me.
I was reaching toward her when suddenly
There was a flood of bright sunlight. I was stunned
By the miraculous change, overawed,
So much so that my sadness lifted and
Instead I felt rapture, exaltation.
I opened my eyes fully expecting it
To be morning. But the clock said midnight
And Marlena was not yet in bed—Ach!
It was a sickening let-down! Sickening!
You must help me discover what it means.
Kurt, it holds the key, the key to Anna—
The key! It just occurred to me. A key
Was what she was using to land on the squares!
What do you call them in English—Ah, yes!
A skeleton key. She threw it and where it
Landed a flower sprung up. Dragon's teeth,
Kurt, do you remember? For every tooth
A giant sprung from the earth. And her face,
Kurt, was like a heavy full moon—pock-marked,
Yes, like Anna's face—just a few small pocks—
Growing closer and closer, fuller and fuller.
And I felt such warmth, such joy. I could taste it!
And like a montage, I could still see that
Little figure dancing away, one foot
To the left, next to the right . . . and then that
Magnificence of light, golden and pure,
Blanching out utterly the sweet moonlight.
With a dream like that one is tempted to
Take it whole, treat it as one rich metaphor.
But you won't let me get away with that.

So—let me get on with it. Anna, Anna, . . .
Did you notice, Kurt, how often I said,
'My Anna' and 'little Anna'? Unusual.
You see, Kurt, how in the dream I was treating
Her as my child, not my older sister.
Interesting!" And for the first time, Victor
Grew silent, his thoughts changing track abruptly.
His mind filled with phrases from his paper
He had been writing before falling asleep.
He could feel the fluent energy of
His pen racing across the page in a small
Economical script, the ink flowing
Swiftly, obediently, forming
Compressed ovals, short strokes and loops like eyelets.
He was proud of his unique, legible script,
Immediately identifiable.

"Victor—"

"Yes, yes . . . I know I've stopped talking. Just now
My thoughts turned to the paper I was writing
Before falling asleep, the one on the self,
The origins of the self. How absorbed
I had been until suddenly, bleary-eyed
From fatigue I dropped asleep. How strange it was.
One moment working at full tilt and the next
Sound asleep—and soon dreaming incredibly.
What a fantastic three-ring circus, Kurt.
And who by God is the ringmaster? Really.
The self. Not always with success. But the show
Can't go on without him—even in sleep,
And certainly not in the center ring—
That's good! That's good! The center ring, that's where
The main action is, whether awake or dreaming,
Conscious or unconscious. The self, Kurt, may plan,
Organize, and direct, but to execute

He must draw on resources outside himself.
Talents, skills, knowledge, even memories,
Especially peopled memories, approving,
Criticizing, understanding, cautioning.
Within those peopled memories are also
The affects and the drives themselves—the tigers,
Lions, leopards that must be made to jump
Through fiery hoops. And let's not forget
The powerful, amiable elephants
With their emblematic sequined mannequins
Perched between their ears—purest libido.
But where, where did this ringmaster come from?
There is the infernal rub. The metaphor
Collapses, horse and rider swallowed up.
Freud put the ego aslant the mind like a
Supernumerary cockade. That ditty,
How does it go? Stuck a feather in his cap
And called it macaroni?—"

                    "Victor,
You are delivering a paper right now
And using it to escape dealing with your dream—"

"Don't stop me, Kurt. The meaning is on the way
Through the paper. The self is there from the start
Like a supersaturated solution,
Not yet visible, or separately
Operative, but there nevertheless.
Only the minutest of changes is
Needed for it to appear suddenly
Fully crystallized and stable. But what,
Kurt, is that change? That's when I fell asleep
At the very edge of discovery.
So the dream has to provide the answer
To the paper and to my own meaning."

To Kurt, this all sounded preposterous,
Febrile, even manic, a furious
Effort at denying some ordinary
Unappetizing reality, like
Losing the fight for the directorship,
Now very possible in view of Serey's
Unfortunate reversal.
                              "Listen, Victor,
You are trying to swallow the dream whole
In order to be rid of it. Please, attend
To the parts—the meaning has to be there."

"The key, you mean—might be the key?" and Victor
Chuckled, enjoying his pun.

                              Kurt pondered
This new mood, suspecting now that Victor
Might be aware of more than he was saying.
Victor would not let himself surrender
Totally to his neurosis, that was plain.

"Why was it a *skeleton* key? Phallic,
I suppose, generative—once it hits
The ground, a flower springs up. Anna, you know,
Always deeply resented my maleness.
The square disappears . . . boundaries vanish.
Undoubtedly again a reference to
Phallic power. But I make sure it's hers
Only in a game—a child's game. . . . But now
The sadness at her receding form . . . what . . .
To make of that. . . . My liveliest feelings
For Anna were always hate, fear, and desire.
Yes, a yearning for her approval.
She made it hard to like her. Even now
She dismisses my career as based on myth—
That's what psychoanalysis is to her—

A myth masquerading as a science.
I suppose I remain the child to her,
As I was from the start. So in the dream
I make *her* the child. . . . Her face like the moon—
Of course! The Isakower phenomenon.
Quite amazing! Even my words—'I could taste it!'
It was a breast about to enter my mouth.
Who else could it be but my own mother.
Indeed she had a round pale face unlike
Anna's narrow pinched face. . . . Imagine!
Reviving such an early memory.
And then the sunlight—a golden, gorgeous coin
Obliterating the moon. Where am I
In all this? Passively looking on, feeling—
How different from my waking self. . . . "

                                        Kurt
Was still impressed with Victor's defensiveness.
The associations were largely self-serving,
Bringing no news from the unconscious.
He was still "discovering" this and that,
Amazed now by his dreams as he can be
By his papers. Yet he might have a point
About his passivity in the dream.

"Tell me more about the daffodils, Victor,
So specific a choice."

                    "A springtime flower,
Nothing more. You see them sometimes in the snow.
Brave things. You are not picking up my point
About passivity. It bears directly
On the self—what my paper was about.
Let me continue. But first a bit of news.
I saw the president and pushed him hard
To make a decision, indicating

We might all leave if he did not act soon
To approve me director as the committee
Recommended. He agreed to decide
After one more meeting with the committee.
What was this, I wondered. I asked him why.
To tie up a few loose ends. Always loose ends—
His life is one loose end—classic obsessive!"

Kurt was alarmed at Victor's threat—all leave?
Including himself and Greta? Had he
Presumed that much? Some passivity!
But that was the point. Exactly when he
Started to consider his passivity
He recalls the visit to the president.
Precisely when he is on the couch, he
Creates this fantastic marvel of a dream.
But there is no escaping the brute fact
Of his symptom—his great anxiety.
He goes too far with the president so that
He runs the risk of destroying his chances.
What does the president really have in mind?
Or should he himself visit with him first?
He must certainly protect Greta and himself.

"Notice your shift to an active self when
You were about to consider another view—
Your passivity in the dream. Also
You experienced your phobia when again
You were passive, borne aloft in a plane.
You suddenly had the urge to fly *yourself*.
In the dream you abruptly waken yourself
With a vision of dawn, its golden sun
Surpassing the moon. The sun is always male,
Victor. You turn from the full breast of the moon,
Fearing passivity, and rise with the sun."

For the first time Victor listened, astonished,
A vague uneasy sense of possibility
Possessing him. For a brief instant, anguish.
He'll offer Kurt a gift to close the hour with.
"It occurs to me, Kurt, the daffodil
Is in the narcissus family and
Thus we have the link to my paper,
On the self—very nice."

                      Very nice indeed,
Thought Kurt. So nice of him to tie it up.
No place for loose ends with Victor at work.
He realized that as the analysis
Progressed, as it had, their friendship had cooled.

34

Victor's face gleamed with anticipation
Of his meeting with Kurt. He had used the word
Session in his own mind, he felt so eager
To continue where he had left off. Kurt,
Quite otherwise, was perturbed, suspicious,
Convinced some plot was afoot—too much was
Happening at once to be mere coincidence.
He viewed his colleague's disregard
Of recent events with equal suspicion.
Perhaps he knew more than he was letting on.
Or perhaps, as he had warned the president,
He was prepared to leave along with Greta
And himself—again his bold presumptions!
But Kurt had decided to play along.
He could always dissociate himself
From Victor's threat simply by saying that
He had not spoken for them. In the meantime
He would see what came of Victor's tactic.
Victor amazingly enough decided
To continue with the analysis.
He had hurried into his office at the
Appointed time and stretched out on the couch
Immediately, but then had grown silent.
Yes, Kurt thought, why not play out this tactic
Too. But whose tactic was it? His or Victor's?

Or was it a tactic at all—this display
Of virtuoso analytic hubris,
For such he knew it to be. A queer smile,
Ironic and bewildered, skirted Kurt's lips
For he also knew that something was happening
Between them in these hours—an analysis.
True, with strange parameters, but only look
At Victor on the couch and he himself
Prepared to work. Wasn't there Victor's symptom
And his own? The irony was in the ends
Not in the means. And for a moment Kurt
Stiffened. Were all the ends foreseeable?
A thought he then dismissed. If not foreseeable
In all particulars, at least expectable
In a general sense? What more could one ask?
And here was his friend and ally reclined
On the couch—a man of talent and strength,
Shrewd, vigorous, a master of strategies
Whose mind had absorbed a dozen theories
And was now in the throes of creating
A new one—No, he had to be admired.
Yes, and also feared. But neither had he
Escaped the brand of neurosis, the mark
Of our exodus from Eden, the murder
Attempted of our past natural pleasures
At our mother's breast, at our father's knee.
Poor Victor had reached new heights only
Dreamt of by that little boy and he had swooned
At the prospect. And now the tightrope hung
Across an abyss, stretched from past to present.
Would he negotiate it and if he fell
Who else would he take with him? To his credit,
Thought Kurt, he was there stepping out on the rope.
It was he, Kurt Denkman, who was terrified,
Knowing the odds and the world's frailties.

Victor's silence had been an act of restraint.
He had been struggling to banish the humdrum,
For such he now viewed all that had been happening—
Serey's mad letter to the president,
His puzzled, inquisitorial response
In a private meeting Victor had with him.
"Has her analysis been helping her?
Is this some transient slip in the transference?
Or is it something more serious—a breakdown?
Why is she telling so many people
About it? Very distressing, isn't it?"
Not once did he touch on the sorest spot—
Serey's mad appointment of him as president.
He had brought it up. "She made me president.
Quite something, isn't it?" "Oh yes," he said.
"I noticed that. Very strange, wouldn't you say?"
Victor dropped the subject. The damage was done,
He felt. This cowardly, doubt-ridden man
Would never act now unless he forced his hand.
And then there was that Dreyfus petition.
A fool, a holy fool in some strange way,
A fool inspired by abstract principles.
He tries to sail with the word *Wind* tacked on
His sail, while disregarding any real
Wind as untrustworthy. Out of touch,
Totally out of touch with his aggression,
His ambition. And thus very dangerous.
Like a loose cannon on a deck, its weight
Now a weapon in its own right. A mistake,
His past dismissal of this righteous fool. . . .
If only he were less impulsive. Enough
Of this, he chastised himself. One has only
To act when the time is ripe and to act
Forcefully with facts in hand. They cannot
Triumph because they do not cherish victory,
But wish only to stave off their defeat.

Now he must turn to other things. Victor
Tried to quell an agonizing sadness,
More ruefulness than melancholy.

"Two things keep melding in my mind: Anna
Dancing away from me in my dream,
The god Apollo pursuing the nymph
Who'd rather turn to laurel than be his.
You recall how daffodils sprang up
Behind her each place she dropped the key—Anna
I mean, not the nymph. They both swirl through my
     brain
And a question possesses me—Why, why, why
Would they do this? Very painful. Mysterious.
You see, Anna in the dream disappearing
And approaching at the same time. So clear!
Exactly as she was—is—with me now.
Always I was frightened and enthralled by her.
Of course she was older, bigger, smarter—
The usual—but something else. . . . Something else.
Hopscotch is a girl's game. That's partly it.
She flaunted her girlishness. No doubt a
Reaction formation against her penislessness.
But more, or something else . . . I can't—don't know
     what."
Victor bit into his lower lip, seeking pain.

"And what of the daffodils—your gift to me
Last time?"

                    "Oh yes, the link to narcissism.
Narkos, the sleep of death. That nymph, you see,
Prefers to surrender her human form,
To sink lower into a living death
As a rooted, unresponsive thing—a tree.
My sister in the dream strews the same death

In life behind her.... Yes, yes, I begin to see!
The same with all these people who turn away
From a higher, better path in . . . vengeance.
That's what it is, Kurt—vengeance at the gods
For being gods. And if they cannot accept
The higher, they take the lower. Anna too.
I was the one son and the younger at that."

"But just before you felt it was something else."

"When? Oh, before . . . perhaps." He made a fist
And dug it hard into his other hand.
An exquisite longing spread upward from
His navel, settling in his chest like a bird.
He could see it preening its feathers, the curve
Of its neck superbly graceful. The bird
Could not pass into air. Its claws piercing
The branch it perched on held the bird earthbound.
Its wings beat the air vainly.

                        "I want so much . . .
But what do I want? I can taste it . . . feel it.
Such desire, Kurt, I first felt in adolescence.
Pure, pure blind wanting, unaware at first
Of its object, even of its aim—of what
It really seeks and why. Only a delicious,
Excruciating rising up. As yet
It cannot find its true release, but it is
Glorious in itself, a rich sunrise
Before the sun appears . . . How good it would be
To feel that way again! To live in blind
Expectation . . . waiting for the world to dawn!"
And Victor grew inconsolably sad,
On the verge of bitter, reproachful tears.
His hands dropped from his chest limply to his side.

Kurt was listening watchfully, never sure
If what he heard was shrewd perception or
Raw spoken feeling. He had been impressed,
Alarmed, and yet for all that reassured
By the counterpoint in Victor's recital
Between a princely certainty of purpose,
A lèse majesté, so provocative,
So admirable, suddenly giving way
To a turning inward, a turning toward
The pure pleasure of the autoerotic.
Is this then what the flying means? And why
It was so feared?
                    "What you want, Victor, is
Also what you apparently fear."

                              "Just so.
I was thinking the same. The directorship?
No. That is politics and policy—
Neutral, objective, outside myself. No.
It is something much closer to the bone
Of my very being. Tied up with Anna,
Marlena too, and in some annoying way
With Frances Dreyfus. I cannot tell you why
Except I keep getting put out with her
Unwillingness to deal with her mother,
Although she is doing very well recently.
Marlena has grown quite grumpy lately,
Something to do with her analysis.
But I think it all has to do with Anna."

As if on a bare field marked by thin white lines
Stretching to a point on the horizon,
The three statues reappeared to Victor—
Beautiful replicas of a Roman goddess.
Generous breasts, widehipped, palpable round bellies
With deep navels and a gently rising mons.

Each as if made by the same hand, exactly
Identical except for the heads, which were
Those of Anna, Marlena, and Frances.
The expression on each face was distant,
As if indifferent to the wealth of beauty
With which each was similarly endowed.
The image was clearer now than it had
Ever been, freighted with even greater
Significance. It took his breath away,
Rendering him entirely inarticulate
As if it existed in a wordless world.

How Victor wanted to continue. But time
Was passing. The next patient was waiting,
Kurt caught himself thinking, as Victor got up.

35

The two friends had met on the way over
To Victor's hour. They walked in silence,
Victor lost in thought, Kurt stealing glances
At his old friend, trying to gauge his mood.
Once in the office, Victor lay down stiffly
On the couch. Kurt settled uneasily
Into his deep leather chair, prepared to wait.
The silence was a palpable presence,
A third party, like an uninvited guest
Neither wished for, but both had to entertain.

The image in Victor's mind was of a sea,
A long white cuff of waves turning over
Into a loose unraveled surf spreading thinly
Until only the sand's lingering wetness
Recalled the sea's deep element. *His* silence
Leaned like an oppressive sky heavy with clouds,
Bulking hugely, illuminated from within
By lightning, like giant jack-o-lanterns.

"Those twilight storms arriving like express trains,
How I loved them! All day the sea lay shackled
Under a merciless sun, allowing people
To sprawl on its back, poke into its flanks,
Treat it like a tame pussycat until

Without warning it rose up, threw off its chains,
Scattering people in fright and amazement.
I had a favorite perch, high on a cliff,
Where with a pair of binoculars I could detect
Far out to sea the storm preparing itself.
For a time I would observe two different worlds
Side by side, one the future of the other.
One—innocent, ignorant, and utterly
Powerless; the other—the huge muscle
Of their fate, the hammer descending on
The thin surface of their self-absorbed pleasures. . . .
Kurt, I will be the storm to this banal
Backwater of a place, this—Tennessee!"

Kurt stirred even more uneasily still,
A sharp stabbing pain at the base of his spine
Suddenly straightened him erect, a twisted
Grimace of utter agony wrenching
His face into a gargoylelike expression
Half-rage, half-fright. As the pain subsided
His face assumed its former troubled mien.
For Victor was worrying him. Raging about
Was not what was needed. Quite otherwise.

"Adolescent twaddle! That's what I *was* then,
A skinny, nervous kid imagining
Triumphs of courage and brute strength. Those storms,
However, held a lesson for me. A deep
Wisdom was hidden in them. The natural world
Draws out of calm, peace, and sunlight the strength
To cleanse, renew, give itself a fresh start.
As it scatters the sunbathers and swimmers
The storm rectifies, resets the clock for
Tomorrow. But most of all it summons
Passion, that sudden stirring in us of
Power and eros, kindling orgasm,

For which storms provide the perfect metaphor. . . .
They are withholding power from me, Kurt.
No. They will not allow that the power
Is mine already. But enough of that.
Envy is the most destructive sentiment.
But I will not get started on that, Kurt . . .
The fact remains that ever since my return
From California, I have not been myself.
I think you know that. It's why I undertook
This analysis—a crazy enterprise.
It's of a piece with my anxiety
On the plane—to seek the strongest medicine
In the disease itself, rekindle my anxiety
On this couch, lay myself open before you. . . . "
He felt himself stiffening, growing rigid
While inside all seemed at once to be melting.
He felt his head roll sideways and then snap back
As if slapped. Behind his navel, curling
Deeper inward and spiraling, twisting,
Fanning out and spreading upward, reaching
To his gorge where it hammered and choked,
The same dark unfurling, the same brute stoking
He had felt on the plane that now summoned him.
Outwardly he was calm, his stare fixed, stony.
Behind his marble eyes his mind folded
Inward, its energy sinking swiftly
Through a black funnel-shaped velvet past
That seemed immediate and unremembered.
He had forgotten how to move, to talk.
Square cagelike boxes, fluorescent, turning,
Changing into diamond shapes, collapsing
Into triangles, receding into a well
Of laughter, echoing mockingly
And then pinging against a smooth white door,
Louder, thinner, a distancing siren
Assaulting his ear and then giving up,

Leaving a little high-pitched tail of sound
Twitching in his ear. He waited and he watched,
His arms folded, his lips a firm thin line
Of cool mirth. All she had to do was ask.
Not beg. Oh, she thinks of it that way, he knows.
But she must finally, finally believe
He mattered. Unto death that door stays closed. Until
He mattered. Until he hears, "Victor, OK.
Let me out." *Victor* will let you out. Of
Course Victor will let you out! But first say,
"*Victor*, let me out." Rage shakes his eyelids,
Scalding tears blur his gaze trapped by the door—
Smooth, big, metal, white, cool to the touch.
No voice. Unto death. Unto . . . death. Freezing
Into white numbing rage, he melts as fright
Burns in his throat, the melt refreezing into
Rage, retaining in its smooth solid drops
The shape of fear. *No voice.* A muffled bump,
A weight letting go, loosening itself, dropping
Down shapelessly, a marionette unstrung.
Anna! What are you doing! Shameless girl!
A cool draft of air stings his cheek where tears
Cling unflowing. Inside, the crumpled brown leaf—
Stiff, mottled—shakes as the motor hums
More alive than she. He cannot risk moving.
He cannot risk speaking. He sees enough.
He knows enough. And then pouncing
On the prostrate form, he pummels her alive,
Making her move to his blows, grow red
With squeezing and pinching, taking liberties
With her thin flanks. She still refuses him,
Preferring death. And he raises his fist,
The fingers white with clenching, and strikes toward
Her pale frozen face to shatter its peace.
And his fist smashes against the stone floor.
The risen Anna floats before him, a pale

Shipwreck moon, light years from his disaster.
He joins his limp fist on the cool stone floor,
Hammering his forehead hard against it
In enraged prayer before his idol.
"I'm sorry, Vickie. But you asked for it,"
The idol speaks, rekindling hope, relief,
Revenge. He could not raise his arm or head.
The great pain in his once small fist now entered
His larger fist but out-sized it once again.
His eyes refocused on the sound-proofed ceiling,
The small pores in its symmetrical squares
Jumping crazily about until they settled
Into obedient rows. He found his voice.

"Kurt, I cannot continue with this. Never."
Victor wasn't sure he knew what he meant—
The analysis, his reverted past,
His current predicament, or all of them.
He ached with an unrepentant longing,
His fate unfinished and unclarified,
A man suspended in one stunning leap.

Kurt, in agony still, was greatly relieved.
He too had had enough. *La commedia*
E finita. It was time to leave this
Closet drama for the real, miserable world.
Yes, it had been a crazy enterprise,
An attempt at a virtuoso cadenza
Played for each others' delectation.

Victor sat up, dizzy for a moment,
Stood up, and made his way to the chair across
From Kurt.

          "It makes no sense, Kurt, to stay here
Any longer. I have an offer from

California. I'm sure you and Greta
Could join me. There's a new hospital
In LA. They want me as director.
It's a rich place. Jewish philanthropists
With guilty Jewish consciences
Are ready to give handsomely for any
Research we have in mind. And California
Is not Tennessee. Abundant culture
And a marvelous climate. Let's do it."

"Why have you waited so long to tell me
All this? Why have you been fighting so hard
For something not worth as much as you have
Already been promised? Are there problems
In California you're not telling me about?"

"No, Kurt, no problems, only opportunities."
He was getting annoyed at Kurt. Why these
Paranoid questions? There was a new path
Ahead for both of them. It only remained
To take it with vigor and resolution.
This place would be a shadow without them.

"I'm not sure California is for us.
We prefer the East."

                Victor stretched his cheek
With his tongue, considering his friend's rejection.
Perhaps it was time for going separate ways.
Kurt found it hard to bend as he stood up
To usher his friend out of his office.

Part Six

Paul Dreyfus
and
Josef Fouchault

36

It was forever peaceful and serene
In Fouchault's office. A mild darkness like
Twilight, Dreyfus thought, settled around things—
The couch, his chair, the desk, his mementos.
When Fouchault arose from his desk to cross
Over to the couch, he would be in shadow.
Or when he found him already seated
Behind the couch it was as if he had
Always been there—a presence in the void,
A pale indigo or mauve emptiness
And a darker thickening at its center—
Fouchault.

        "I had a funny dream last night.
It was barren and dark—a strong wind howled,
But I was sitting down playing with sand,
Unmindful of the storm. A man shouted at me.
I kept on playing. That's all I remember.
What a rotten, empty dream."
                      He fell silent,
And turned his face toward the wall. He was crying
Softly.
        "I wish I could play and ignore
Everything as I once could so easily.
I remember as a kid getting up

Early before anyone else was up,
Stealing quietly into the kitchen,
Lining up the toy train my father bought me,
Not using the tracks, they were too limiting,
And circling the kitchen with it. The tile
Platform under the stove was my station,
The beveled wooden border was perfect
For the station edge along which my train would stop.
No one up yet. The whole world mine. So much
So I didn't even have to *think* it was.
It was. All I did was move that little train
Around the room. One stop at the tile square,
Under the kitchen table and then back home,
Under the kitchen table and then back home...."

Again his tears came quietly, the drops
From his left eye salty between his lips,
Those from the right falling on the pillow.
There was in fact a photograph of him
Playing in the sand, totally absorbed,
Wearing a red-striped two-piece bathing suit.
His mother was still alive then. But she
Was not in that picture. Vaguely he recalled
A photo in which they were cheek to cheek.
Was it real? She was wearing a twenties cloche
Molding her head and he was so small,
So pale, blond—something like his father was
Years ago.   "I'm thinking about that photo
I've mentioned of me playing in the sand.
But then I thought of another photo—
Of me and my mother cheek to cheek but
I can't be sure of it. Now I'm thinking
Of something entirely different—a girl
I danced with once in Germany, wearing
A white angora sweater. I was drunk

On brandwein, my head spinning, my feet unsteady.
She was beautiful. Her teeth blinded me
With their brilliance. As we danced she laughed
At my clumsiness and her flashing teeth
Were like bolts of repetitive lightning
Dazzling me so that I had to squint. I
Never saw her again, only that one dance. . . .
Rembrandt is like that—a whole world appears,
A person in full perfection emerging
Out of a dark, hazy brown murkiness,
Vividly there but with a sense of transience,
Like a circus tent full of excitement
One night as if it could contain the whole world
And then the next day collapsed, shriveled,
Spineless, lying on the ground like an old skin,
The world it gave house to totally gone.
Rembrandt's people look as if they too could
Vanish leaving behind a barren space
Into which that hazy murk seeps slowly.
His paintings strike a blow for personality
Against impersonal chaos."
                                        His tears
Had dried.

              "You are trying to mourn for her,
Your young mother, but that toothy girl friend
Appeared suddenly in your thoughts as a
Warning, a fearful sign not to continue.
And then you let your poetry take over."

"That man shouting in my dream—a warning?
No. More like a scolding, 'Stop your playing!'
That's what I feel—you can't enjoy yourself,
You can't be alone with your games, your thoughts—
Even with your wife—Kleinman is listening."

"Am I not listening too?"

                              "Yes, I think that too.
I feel my words sink into something soft,
Lose their echo, disappear like water
Seeping into sand, an ocean swallowed up
By a great depth—quicksand, and I am alone.
No words returning. Strange, I hear you talk
But your words lose their sound and drift like feathers
Silently to the ground before they reach me.
How strange. It's all like a silent movie,
Slowed down. There is also something sacred
About it—ritualistic. As if
It has all happened exactly before.
But how? When? And where?"

                         "Like quicksand, you say?
There is so much danger for you in this
Exchange with me. I am that haziness
Into which your words disappear, the sand
Into which your tears disappear, I am
That mother with whom your hopes disappeared."

"But I can remember so little of her,
All my memories are like old photographs,
Brittle black-and-white squares, all motionless.
They may really just be photos. I've seen
Some of them many times over. Horrible!
No real memories. Just photos. Photos!"

He felt Fouchault shift in his chair and sigh.
He was disappointing him. Just too bad.
His mood was shifting. It was mutinous
Now. He thought of a line from Joyce. About
Mutinous waves. He was sick of thinking,
Associating, reflecting, talking.

"Do you know what's happening in research?
Victor and Allan are having at it.
A plague on both their houses. But why Victor?
He knows nothing, absolutely nothing
About research. Allan at least does research.
Kurt and Greta Denkman are behind this.
How cosily they work together—two
Stormtroopers—on that damned search committee.
Kurt and Greta, the only man and wife
I know who have a homosexual
Relationship. I hope you hate them too.
You don't like me to talk this way, I know,
But it all stinks—your whole damned Institute.
Victor should have been a four-star general,
Kurt—a gauleiter in the Austrian Alps,
Greta—a gun moll in a thirties film,
But instead they are all training analysts,
Their ambitions souring in their hardening
Arteries as they sit on their fleshy asses
Dissecting transference neurosis all day
While they ache to conquer 'die ganze welt.'
Kleinman, Kleinman, über alles. Today
Tennessee, tomorrow New York, and then—
The entire English speaking analytic
Freudian-Kleinian-Winnicottian world!"

Another speech. Another flop. Who cares.
Good for his thriving sense of injustice
Only. Fouchault seemed as helpless as he
In that somehow he felt a bond of kinship.
Two Cassandras in this two-bit drama.
But why didn't he take a stand against them?

"How your mood has changed. Have you been
    aware?"

Again that timeless, bodiless soft voice.
Is he untouched by all this? Uninvolved?

"They're out after your hide as well, you know.
Oh, hell! Why should I get upset by this.
If you're not why should I be? My patient
Is not doing well. At least I don't think so.
I find it hard to know what to say to her.
Too early to interpret. She's acting out
Sexually, looking back at me, asking
Questions I can't answer. She's upsetting."

"What do you feel toward her?"

                                        "What do you mean?"

"Well, what I said."
                    "You mean sexually?
There's something wild and mad about the girl,
Something dangerous."

                    "You mean, like lightning bolts?"

"Lightning bolts? Oh, the German sweater girl?
Maybe." He felt himself start to shiver.
"Is it cold in here? No . . . it must be me. . . .
I'm not thinking anymore. No thoughts at all.
Me without a thought—quite impossible.
Easier to take my clothes away from me than
My thoughts. But you've just done it, haven't you?
Wild and mad, poor girl, with a weak-kneed
Analyst who goes blank when sex comes up
In his own analysis."

                        "You really
Ignore what I say but then react to it,

As if you are fearful of agreeing.
Again it seems you are fearing something."

"It was that same feeling now as with her—
Be careful, look both ways before you cross—
Where in hell did that come from!
I might say the wrong thing, ruin everything.
When I was a kid I loved to make
Houses of cards. I'd stack them carefully,
The first two like a tent in the middle,
Then the four side walls and then the flat roof—
Eight cards in all—six stories high and four
Left over for an open roof garden.
It looked like a pagoda. And then I'd
Stand far off and start to blow softly toward it.
The eaves would begin to flutter and then
I'd move closer, blow harder. The roof cards
Collapsed first and then the wreckage traveled
Downward floor by floor in such slow motion
That at times I could arrest the damage
By quickly removing the guilty cards.
I would feel triumphant, start to rebuild
As if I had saved the world."

"Why guilty?
How are the cards guilty?"

"Did I say guilty?
If anyone was guilty it was I."

"Yes ... well ... we must stop for today."

He left.
The bright sun outside was blinding for a time.

37

Waiting downstairs before coming up, Paul
Was eager. Once on the couch he was tense,
Expectant, entertaining the wry hope
That this time it would start. He knew better.
Again he had that sense of space between
Them, not a void today but somehow charged,
A field of force between two similar repelling
Magnets.
        "An interesting weekend," he said,
Tempting him with a transparent come-on.
Silence. Paul discovered that he welcomed
The silence. Like a wave in a silent movie,
It washed over him soundlessly, slowly,
Its blank white head leaning over his form.
"Again I am thinking of that shot of me
At the beach, playing in the sand. Grouchy—
That's the way I look, poking at my navel,
A two-year-old grouch. I knew what I wanted,
Though. My father used to tell the story
How for my birthday (third, I think) he took
Me to this factory showroom full of toys
And, in a moment of weakness (bravado
More likely) promised to buy me any
Toy I would pick. I chose the biggest there—
A car you could sit in, peddle, and steer.

He bought it. I remember the car all right
But not the showroom. That car was my pride.
I tooled around in it like a big shot—
It was much better than my trike on which I
Also tore around. You know, I was active
As a kid, always going. . . . "
                                His voice trailed off.
She had been horrible. "Victor's back today.
Downstairs I really wanted to see you.
Now I don't know. It all seems futile . . . flat . . .
And last night I decided I was a zero—
Not a therapist, not a scientist,
But a cipher, a nullity, a goose egg—
A bowlegged balloon about to go pop.
When I said bowlegged I had an image
Of those comic balloons attached to flat
Cardboard imitation shoes that made them
Waddle when you blew on them . . . pleasure bent,
That's what a bowlegged girl is called—
Bernice Witkin—blond, breasty, and pleasure bent.
Strong-legged Bernice, she frightened me
Because she was so eagerly after me—
I hid behind indifference. . . . "

                                "You said
Something about a weekend—a great weekend?"

"No, no. Not great at all. Interesting."
Suddenly he didn't want to go on.
Not start the weekend.
                                "You misheard me.
I didn't say great. What gave you that idea?"

"You want to have a tiff with me today?
What's going on with this weekend business?"

"We had a big fight. She stayed in bed all day
Saturday. She wouldn't cook or clean or
Look after the kids. Just sniveling in bed.
I told her she better straighten herself out,
Get out of bed, dry her eyes and hop to it.
Whenever Victor cancels that's what happens,
She goes into a tailspin and I get mad.
But later that night she let me have it.
Dry-eyed, thin-lipped, pale, she lit into me,
Calling me cruel, unfeeling, self-centered.
If she had known all that before we married
Nothing would have made her do it. But still
She doesn't have to put up with it. No,
She will get a divorce. When I remained
Silent, not caring to look at her face—
Her grim certainty frightened me—she flung
A scissors at my head, barely missing.
Scared half to death and mad, I leaped at her
Grabbing her wrists and shaking her roughly.
She drew back in disbelieving horror,
Screaming, don't you dare touch me again,
And I said lamely, don't throw things again.
She then threw herself at me with full force
Knocking me across the bed, jumping free,
And making for the closet, scrambling there
For a suitcase. In a frenzy she threw
Her clothes from the drawers into the suitcase.
When I asked her where she was going,
She said, away, far away, as far
As I can get from you, you cold bastard.
It was true. I *was* cold. I *felt* cold.
I was shivering. The cold in my character
Had become an actual cold. I needed warmth.
When I saw her grab the suitcase I panicked.
It felt as if she were grabbing my guts
And wrenching them loose. She was emptying *me*

Into her suitcase. Although she was only
A few feet from me she might as well have been
Ten thousand light years off. I felt myself
Curl up into a ball. I couldn't stand it.
I flung her across the bed. She fought me off.
I scissored her around the waist between my thighs
And kept her in that vise until she quieted.
Exhausted, we eventually fell asleep
Locked together like stick-legged grasshoppers.
I slept always on the thin edge of waking,
Sensing her every move with uneasiness,
Tightening my grip when she would budge.
And all the while—sleep or no sleep—feeling
Shame—a deep, searing, agonizing shame."
Paul suddenly started hiccupping, the first one
Loud, shrill, and far down his throat. Crazy,
He thought, crazy, crazy. Another hiccup.
And another. He would have to stop the hour.
The hiccups were convulsing him. Another.
Now they were coming rapidly, clicking
Off, one right after the other until
Imperceptibly hiccups turned into sobs—
Wrenching, body-heaving, mouth-twisting sobs.
He felt close to vomiting and clamped his mouth
Tightly. The sobs now—like something strangled—
Struggled upwards in uncontrollable snorts.

"What's going on with you?"

                    "I don't know—
I'm nauseous—close to vomiting. Should I
Leave—perhaps I better." But he made no move.
Paul clung to the couch dizzy with the effort
Needed to keep the retching dry and quiet.

"You are showing how hard it was last night."

"Hard!? Yes . . . oh, yes . . . hard . . . horrifying."
Words, words. He couldn't cope with them right now.
They were no longer of interest to him.
And in the midst of it all—an erection.
Exactly like last night. This was too much.
He felt like shouting and mauling his cheeks.
"Why am I sexually excited now!
Am I some kind of fiend—a stinking pervert?!"
He beat his fists on the pillow alongside
His head, wanting to strike himself instead.
"Do something, you must do something now—please!
I am a penitent huge fish, scoop me up,
Clobber me on the head for Passover.
I am going stark raving mad—help me.
Your silence is like a sentence. I can't
Face the rest of the day—the hours, the patients."
The carp slithered the length of the subway car.
He was cold again, his forehead quite damp.
"I could kill you for your heartless silence—
You bastard, you French, frog-legged bastard!"
His anger made him feel whole again.
The enemy was there gathering behind him,
Its forces poised to crash around his head.
But he would hold his head high, unvanquished.
Fighting against tough odds. That's what he'd done
All his life. What had Fouchault once told him?
"Hungary, you said. I lived in Hungary. Yes.
A Hungary of the mind, a dismal place,
Small, bleak, oppressed, out of the way, forsaken—
But mine, altogether mine. Happy lands
Are for others. I can be fierce, defiant
In my god-forsaken Hungary."

                                        "You want me so
To punish you for your sins, to kick you out
For your rage and your clutching and your sex—

Then all would be quiet again in Hungary.
Quiet and empty—like a tomb. For sure."

The mutinous bile drained out of him, tasting
Quite bitter on the tongue. How could he leave,
Summon his strength, to make it out the door?
He was one raw wound, an ugly cleft
Spanning the full length of his spent soul.
He awaited the hour's end with dread.
How much easier anger would have made it,
Self-righteous anger at injustice—
Wrongful punishment.
                    "I don't feel sinful.
I feel misunderstood, left to myself."

"As when your wife threatened you with leaving."

"No, then I felt panic, my world collapsing.
It was when she took to bed and cried—
Then I felt isolated and alone,
Angry at what he had done to my wife,
Angry at her for being so affected
By his leaving. Leaving ... leaving ... always
Leaving—I will need to leave here soon.
My wife wanting to leave me. Victor leaving
Her. I know ... I know—my mother leaving me.
Isn't Hungary better? No leave-taking there.
In Transylvania the heart is staked
To the ground—impaled forever, no flight
Possible." He heard a sigh.

                              "Well, it's time."

Outside the door the world walked by shrugging.

38

"Well, I hear there was a little gathering—
At the Kleinmans' last night—eine kleine
Nacht Schauspiel. Or, less bar-oque and more bar-
    room.
Eine Kleine Bierstub Putsch. Don dropped a word
At coffee about it, a bit shamefaced, mumbling
Under his breath about lesser of two evils.
When I hear that spineless phrase, I think of
Those terrible twins from Lewis Carroll.
Let's call them *Tweedledon't* and *Tweedledamn*.
Tweedledon't is Fabrikant and *Tweedledamn*
Is Kleinman. Yuh puts yer money down and
Yuh takes yer cherce—the only game in town
And the house always comes out ahead.
Well, the tall dark stranger in town has blown
The whistle on them. I saw the president
Last week and told him how nefariously
The Denkman committee was doing its job,
How Austro-Hungarian its nasty intrigues—
A bit of mittel Europa in mid-
Tennessee. I told him Kleinman was all wrong
For Research—it would destroy the department.
Fabrikant is better but had his problems.
Mainly I urged a real national search
And a new committee to undertake it.

He raised his eyebrows at that and recalled
That the committee *had* undertaken
A nationwide search. Some search! For the nose
On their face and a big one at that! Nice,
How very nice all this decorum is.
And you at your castrated ease forbear
To enter the fray at all. You tilt up your nose
At it as if smelling limburger too close.
But we shall all pay for it. . . . Oh, I'm so
Everlastingly tedious. . . . She was afraid
That she might be boring me. I'm so busy
Walking a tightrope behind her, I've no time
To be bored."

        "What's this tightrope?"
                          "Made of gut,
My own. She is a waif and a wastrel.
The waif I want to take up in my arms,
And the wastrel I want to fling from me
As something unclean. Now there's superego
And ego for you. But where you say is the id?
Hiding in my comforting arms? You're right.
See how capable I am of self-
Analysis. Ready to terminate
Like Donald, that Irish Wagnerian.
I swear to you he is both Isolt and Tristan
All rolled into one ball, prepared to die
Of and for his love. But who can she be?
The real Isolt? Will the real Isolt please
Stand up! The other two will prove to be
Ruthie Prescott and Dr. Paula Veroff.
Francie would love me for talking like this.
So catty gossipy and rumor-ridden.
So I'm envious of Don for finishing
Soon, and of Michael for graduating,

And of Victor for publishing garbage,
And of Freeman for his facilitation,
And of Kurt for his Viennese venom
Like schlag laced with strychnine, fattening and fatal,
And of Marlena for her second place
Finishes right behind Victor. Watch out
If she ever hits the tape first. Victor
Will be parceled out among the sisterhood
Like so many Colonel Sanders chicken parts. . . .
Did you know I had the gift of prophecy?
It is given mainly to the blind and halt
As fair compensation for powerlessness.
When the present is a charred battlefield
And the future is a pregnant black hole
It is time to visit the erring kings—
And queens—to prophecy downfall and defeat.
Woe, woe unto Ahab and Jezebel!
The priests of Baal triumph in the land,
God is gone into his deepest black hole,
Like an anchorite to whom the daylight
Itself is too much remindful of pleasure
And of promises made to smile benignly
On a prideful, sinful, out-of-joint world. . . . "

"You say you are torn about what to do
With your patient, Emily—is that her name?"

"What? I don't remember—Ah, yes! Emily!
Each hour follows a ritual unveiling:
She finds it hard to start, she hints at dire
Events beyond her control, she provokes
Sexual feelings, she feels utterly lost,
She turns to me for help, and I am on
My high wire keeping alive and tongue-tied—"

"What's stopping you? You have an understanding

Of the case—that 'ritual unveiling'?"

"What do I say? Each hour, dear Emily,
You ritually unveil like an innocent
Psychic Salomé? My words must be crisp,
Concrete, lifting the preconscious flutter
Of unnamed presences into consciousness.
Let's face it. I'm a klutz of an analyst
As I am in everything else. Just look
At my work, my marriage, and this analysis.
I engage in devastating gestures
Like an operatic tenor. Like my
Visit to the president. What a joke!
The die is cast. Maybe your way is better."

Paul fell silent for the first time, his words
Echoing hollowly in his head like
Reverberations from a bell, vibrating
On after having been struck some time before.

"Gestures are safer than true actions when one
Is so fearful of doing something wrong,
Or committing an error. And I become
For you the epitome of inaction."

"I *do* act. I *did* go to the president.
I restrained my wife from a harebrained act.
I *don't* hide my attitude toward the Bund.
I speak up even when not spoken to—
Sinful in an analytic candidate.
No, the fault lies in my ineffectiveness.
You're right. I fear failure and I act too late,
Or not at all. I see clear as a bell
What Kurt, Victor, Greta, and Marlena
Are up to. I know Fabrikant and Freeman
Are opposed to them. I'd take Fabrikant

Over Victor as director, but neither
Fabrikant nor Freeman cares much for me—
Or I for them. To them I'm the kid cousin,
Smart, a bit of a pain at times, but not
To be taken seriously."
                     Paul made a face
At nothing in particular and grew
Disgusted with himself.
                 "All this is crap!
So much pure unadulterated crap!
My marriage is coming apart at the seams
And I'm worried about a directorship
And a recalcitrant patient. My wife,
In a wild snit, threatens to leave me flat,
Caught up in some stupid transference tangle
With an analyst whose skill I respect
And whose slimy guts I hate, while I—"

He broke off, a sudden anguish causing
A catch in his throat and he couldn't go on.
The room seemed to become immense and dark.
The unnoticed ticking of a clock now grew
Louder, dividing the silence into
Augmenting increments of emptiness
Which he shrank from filling. Instead he drew
Inward seeking a calm place and found a street
Deserted in the early A.M. hours.
Those walks, taken to solve only the greatest problems,
To air the head through and through as if the ears
Were vents through which a fresh wind, perhaps
With a hint of rain in it, would blow
The clean good sense of the commonplace
Right through his turgid noggin. A lonely
Ventilation, a purgative taken
Privately for a distended cerebrum,
Surcharged with accumulated grievance.

But now he was seeking another space
And a different sort of wind altogether.
He found it as an eagle finds an updraft
While fretting over the fringes of treetops.
He was borne upward as a dark open space
Gathered him, welcomed him, featurelessly.
He heard Fouchault's slightly drawled "Yes?"
The one he used when Paul was too quiet
For too long. He ignored the prompt. Nothing
Was on his mind except sheer existence—
Breathing, keeping warm enough and motionless.
The merest tingle of an idea
Would send him crashing.

"Well, it's time to stop."

39

Paul returned to the couch as one condemned
To an unjust punishment. That live carp,
Slithering and flopping the length of the subway car,
His grandfather in hot pursuit, flashed through
His mind. Dutifully and without interest
He mentioned it. Somehow all color had
Drained from his perceptions. Black-white semblances,
Smudges, trafficked through his mind, displaced
    persons
Trudging listlessly. Then the carp again,
A silver slash glistening, twisting, seeking
An ocean on the IRT. Perhaps
The mica glinting in the floor awakened
Hope and the dash for freedom.
                                    Paul said,
"Useless. I feel all effort is useless.
Like that carp—hurl yourself against your fate.
A solid wall, been up for years, waiting
For your desperate assault to flatten you out,
Soften you up for the sacramental meal—
Gefilte fool."

            "What's this about the carp?"

"That time my grandfather and I went to buy

A fish for Passover at the old market
Down at Fulton Street—for gefilte fish
My grandmother would prepare for Pesach."

And Paul crouched down in silence as in a cave
Where the darkness without words deepened, creeping
Up walls, arching overhead, like a cocoon,
Furry and comforting.

             "So you retreat
From pain into yourself, a withdrawal
Because you fear, not weakness, but too much
    strength."

As from the bottom of a well Paul looked up
And saw Fouchault peering down.
                "Too much strength?

I have no idea what you mean."
                    "Yes, strength.
Leaping from grandfather's grasp, swimming on
Dry land, flinging yourself against hard walls—
Yes, strength."

            "Mad useless courage is more like it."
Despite himself Paul felt something stirring
And then a wave of nausealike despair.
He could feel himself grasped and held immobile.
Involuntarily he hunched his shoulders
So he fit more snugly into the grip
Of a powerful machine lifting him
Away, far away, swinging its powerful
Arm wide over an abyss. Then stopping.
The grip he knew would not loosen. He was safe.
Encapsulated. His heart beat strong and slow,
His breath came in short, shallow drafts, his eyes stared

Until the paneled wall blurred, while inside
In a vacuum alarm bells vibrated
Mutely. Molecules of thought drifted apart,
Increasing the void, widening like a cosmos,
Great and pure, itself a supreme standard
Against which to inculpate existence.
His whole being hung in exquisite balance,
Bearing no weight. Motionless. Inviolate.
An eyelid flicking would smash it all. A rush
Of chaos would blow through like a storm
Sown with the debris of uprooted memories
Which could grind him up as in a bird's crop.
He saw—with a jeweler's precise eyepiece—how
One could crawl into oneself and disappear.
No "self," no "other." A state of intractable
Being, a mystic break in communion.
He heard his own voice speaking: "My grandfather,
Doctor Fouchault, was an amiable man.
He died at eighty, choking for breath, while I
Stood in the corridor staring at the sight. . . .
What was there to do? There are times when the world
Shakes a finger at you, or dies right under
Your nose and you cannot move or will not.
Does it matter either way?"

"Your tone has changed.
Are you here?"

"I don't know what you mean. I'm here—
As always." Now he was lying. Let him
Discover it for himself.

"Your voice sounds
Remote. You are not talking to me at all."

The porous ceiling tiles seemed to absorb

The softly spoken words, like smoke vanishing
After escaping from some underground
Fire raging along the seams of a deep mine.
On the surface a geological peace
Reigned. Dreyfus lay straight, motionless—
As if on a slab. He was an alien
In a world mocking him with its familiarity.
Again his voice issued from and into
A void:
      "There is nothing more to be said.
People are looking away from each other.
Words can't undo locks. Poor Emily knew that.
She wanted a bum to mouth her name so
She could feel the warmth of false recognition.
She didn't want to come to her hour at all.
I can't blame her. So she could cry barren tears?
So she could see her deaf and dumb misery
Turn into words? So she could hammer at me
And nothing open up or shatter? Damn, damn—
All of it! I am through with analysis.
Doing it, undergoing it, studying it.
I am sick of talk. I am sick of myself
For squandering the seed corn of so many years
On such used-up myths. Enough."

                       Fouchault hummed,
Or was it a kind of moan, Paul wondered.
The ember of the last silence crumbled
Into a fine ash. Bitterly he was through.
This hour was like a wind in the desert
Blowing sand like a fine sleet into one's pores,
Filtering through clenched teeth, bruising sore eyelids.
He felt a lethargy spreading through his limbs.
He could easily fall into a deep sleep
Which would have frightened him another time.
But now it was like waiting for a drug

To take effect. When Fouchault cleared his throat
Paul was startled as if he had already
Been asleep.

       "Yes, yes. Are you still with me?"

"I'm not so sure," Paul replied more honestly
Than before. "I might have been fast asleep
There for awhile."

       "What's wearying you so?"

"This whole fucking business I'm not good at."

"Yes, I agree it is the fucking business
You are having trouble with. What's going on?"

In a daze, Paul found a thin voice with which
To say, "I can't get a hard on anymore,
So I'm finished every which way. Curtains."

"When did all this start?"

       "The weekend Victor left
When Frances winged scissors at my head and
Threatened to leave. But before all that happened
We started to make love. . . . I couldn't perform.
It was lifeless, exactly as I felt.
Someone had thrown a switch and the current
Had gone dead. . . . Lights out. When Francie asked
    me why
I became furious at her without warning.
At myself too. I told her to leave me
Alone. She broke down into woebegone tears
Like a child keening in a wilderness.
Odd. How I yearned for isolation, she

For closeness. I couldn't give her what she
Wanted and she couldn't give me what
I wanted. Then I triggered the explosion
By saying what I thought was consoling,
'You'll be OK once Victor's back in town.'
Shortly after scissors were flying, luggage
Packed. I discovered I was in agony
Watching her furiously prepare to leave.
The house around me was collapsing like
A tent in a high wind. My life would be
Going out the door. That's when I grabbed her.
The rest is sordid."

"Your life, you say?"

"Yes.
It wasn't love I felt, losing it, but
Terror. . . . I can't explain it any better."
Recounting it had reinstated the pain
And he twisted on the couch as if skewered.
Again he felt a shroud of silence fall
In which he could wrap himself.

Fouchault spoke,
And his words were like a slow shower of sparks
Dying out quickly in a black sky.
"Notice
How you draw away totally from me too,
Hardly speaking to me, shutting yourself up.
What do I have to do with it, tell me?"

The sparks had left their after-images
Glowing for a split second. There was no
Warmth in them.
"I can't say. Does it matter?
The *world* was going out that door. What's left

Behind when the world goes? Nothing. Not you,
Not me."

"But you fought to keep her with you
And succeeded."

"Some success. Yes, she stayed.
But for all I can do for her she might
Just as well pack up again and take off."

"Well, we must stop for now," Fouchault announced.

Dreyfus rose stiffly from the couch as from
A bare rock exposed to the high places.

40

As he waited downstairs, the dusk-filled room
Above floated in another world, alien
And removed, an unpopulated star
Whose spiky brilliance dazzled to no good end.
His stomach contracted into a tight fist.
Nuts! He really did not need to do this.
No power on earth could bend him to this yoke.
He need only say, "That's it. I've had it.
I quit. Buzz off!" And it would be over.
But he couldn't quit and he didn't know
Fully why. The call came. As he climbed
The steep, narrow stairs he was enveloped
In a cloudy twilight through which he rose
Sacrificially, unready for what had to come.

Fouchault, seated behind the couch, where a weak
Light, stenciled by the blinds, partitioned
His figure into narrow pale rivers
And broad banks of dark featureless terrain.
Paul knew he couldn't bring himself to talk
About what most he needed to. When he tried—
Futility and fear.

                    "Nothing's on my mind,"
He lied and yet told the truth. Nothing mattered

So whatever was on his mind was nothing.
Maybe I can amuse myself out of
My misery, he thought, while Fouchault waited,
A presence, a field of undefined force,
No edges, or center, no vector out
Or in, an evenly distributed charge
That could grow or shrink, enveloping or
Vanishing. He toyed with these ideas,
Marking time, wasting time, fast becoming
Impatient with himself and Fouchault.

                                        "Yes?—
You are with me today?"

                            He was startled
By Fouchault's voice but managed, "So where else?"
In a sharper tone than intended.
                                "Would you
Believe me if I told you she was doing
Better, by her own account of course?"

                                    "Who's that
You mean?"

                "My patient. My glorious patient—
Emily Patterson." This was good for a while,
Paul thought. "And much transference material,
Just like a real analysis."

                        "You are
Being too sly for me. What's going on?"

"Nothing. Absolutely nothing. Zero—
Ground-level zero."

                        "Ground level, you say?
Isn't that something with atomic bombs?"

Paul stirred uneasily. "What I meant was—
Ground—level—zero—flat."

                              "Oh, I see.
Well, so that's that."

                    He's playing with me, Paul thought,
Or trying gently to budge my fat ass.
For a swift moment he felt sympathy
For the old man back there dragging his net
Through an empty sea. Not a carp in sight.
Paul slipped over a precipice, straight down
He hurtled, having lost his last hold. His voice
Sounding strangely in his own ears, distant,
As if trailing behind him, a comic-
Strip balloon streaming from his lips, his words
Encapsulated and separated from him,
Existing on their own, not his at all.

"Something terrible is happening to me
And Francie. We are going in opposite
Directions—she up and I down. Suddenly
She is full of energy, ambition—
And sex. And I just want to disappear
Entirely, nothing seems worthwhile to me.
Everywhere is a wall, a sheer stone wall,
Dark and glistening with a strange perspiration—
Clammy, slippery, hard. I go around
With a knot in the pit of my stomach as if
Something terrible has happened. Once I saw
These photos in a newspaper, horrible,
And I had that feeling then. . . . Five, maybe—
Or maybe I was six—a soldier was
Aiming his rifle at a fleeing man,
He fired, the man dropped—that's all. I kept
Looking and looking at the photos. In the first

He was alive, in the last he was dead.
I was told it was a war. I studied
Those photos as if they held the mystery
Of life and death. And a dread took hold of me
As it has now. I was haunted by
A black knight mounted on a huge black horse.
As soon as my head hit the pillow, he came—
Emerging from the wall to my right, moving
Slow and stately across the foot of my bed
And disappearing through the wall to the left.
His armor shone with dark light. He never
Looked at me, always straight ahead. He never
Stopped, slowed, or speeded up. Always the same
Stately, measured pace. Every night he came
For weeks and weeks. Oddly, I felt no fear.
I was awestruck and . . . possessive. No one
Must know of my black knight. He was my private
Apparition. He was meant for me and
No one else. I had no idea that I
Had made him up. Just like the photographs
He was in a reality apart
From ordinary reality, much more
Important than breakfast and school. He was
A messenger—he came to tell me something
About those photos. I never knew what.
After awhile he stopped coming and I
Missed him."
                    Paul felt the dread feeling returning
That had vanished as he was picturing
The black knight—just as had happened back then.
But soon too much of the present swept in
Like a thick cloud of dust, obliterating
The tangible dimensions of memory,
Defacing the clear identity of feelings
And choking him with bewilderment and pain.

"I can't stay married. It's unfair. Not right.
She needs another man. Not me. I'm wrong
For her. I'm moody, sullen—lash out at her
For no reason . . . and sex doesn't interest me.
That's the truth. I don't want to be aroused.
I lie straight in bed, on my side, stiff—
Don't want to touch her while deep inside I . . .
Yearn for her to reach over and stroke
My body—not my penis—no, not that.
Just a soothing stroking of my shoulders,
Chest, stomach, legs. But of course, she wants
It all—that caresses should lead to sex.
I can't. Once she touches my penis—lights out,
The dread returns. I knot up and die a little.
She becomes confused, angry, then enraged,
Threatens to call you up, complain, I guess.
I say go ahead, feeling relieved somehow
By her telling you my troubles. We each
Fall asleep eventually, like prisoners
In adjoining cells. Incommunicado.

"Why do you dismiss your patient's progress?"

Paul felt jolted back by Fouchault's question.
"Because I don't know what's going on with her."

"You said there was much transference material.
Like what?"

            "Something about wanting me there
Beside her in the park. And . . . and it was
In a park she witnessed intercourse as
A kid . . . after deciding to run away
From home because she felt no one wanted her."

"That's all?" Fouchault chuckled. "You don't see it—

The connection?"

                        The last thing he wanted
Was connections. He remained silent, wanting
and really not wanting him to go on.

"You cannot tolerate the excitement
In her for you, in you for her *or* Francie—
Or anyone. Why? Because excitement
Leads to death, yes death. Connection means death.
Your great black knight was Death himself marching
By you—not making connection either
So you would live."

                        Fouchault's voice held a rare
Tension in it, a pleading to be heard,
To reach him. Paul felt himself turning away
As from an invitation he couldn't
Accept. He felt that same suspension
In a vast space beyond fathoming in which
He yearned to rise up ever higher, further.

Fouchault's voice intruded, "You are so quiet."

His words were thin invisible threads, drawing
Him down. He resented them, welcomed them,
But could do nothing with them. Soon the end
Of the hour would come and it would all
Vanish, this world where things stood still or revolved
Slowly, giving you a good look over
And over at the same things. If only
He could keep between times, not ripen or
Crumble as life proved to be too much for him.

Fouchault lifted from his chair, saying, "Well. . . . "
And Paul rose from the couch hardly capable
Of finding the door a few feet away.

41

"Jungle Jim is hoisted on his own seesaw."
He considered this one-liner, perceiving
That detached, jaunty sarcasm aimed at
His own despair, a kind of schadenfreude—
If you can't cry, laugh; if you can't laugh, joke.
He had no clear idea what he meant by it.
The words captured an image, a feeling
Of passive, forced elevation that kids
Knew well.
               "I gotta be cute. I can't begin
Flat out, spitting up gray marrow and guts.
You don't get it. Let me read you the score card.
Jungle Jim equals me, lost in miasmic
Vegetation—broad leaf, sticky, prickly stuff—
The kind natives stitch into magnificent
Jungle skyscrapers for their large naked
Families. They also milk them for sustenance,
And ground up they cure tse-tse fly disease.
Only recently has science discovered
The intuitive wisdom of these crafty,
Bowlegged, blow-gun, sharp-shooting geniuses
Who perish at twenty-eight from fast living
And the inroads of civilization.
And now for the seesaw. Please bear with me.
What else can you do, poor man? Emily

On one end and Francie on the other.
When one is up the other is down. And I
Rise and fall with each. The case is now up,
I mean Emily. It's turning around,
Miraculously. But Francie's way down.
I am losing my wife."

                              With that the gee-gaw
Burst, scattering its glossy splinters which turned
Salty and wet. He felt crushingly humbled,
Like in those cartoons when a huge safe falls
On the villainous cat, flattening it out.
Only he won't spring back into shape that quick.
Yet another time he felt a spurt of rage
At Fouchault, so cold that it felt searing.

"I have to get myself out of this quagmire,
Or everything will be lost, everything."
His tone contained the demand, not his words.

"She shrinks from me as if I were leprous.
All I am is impotent—it's not catching."
And he fell into a stupefied silence,
As if suddenly the space around him
Had filled with feathers, softening and
Deadening the livid pain burning in his face.
He was so good at alienating people—
A moat of disdain with the drawbridge up,
And beyond a forest thick with enemies.
Now Francie was among them. But not Fouchault.
He could not risk that—not Fouchault. Then again,
Why not? Damn it, why not? He was better off
Alone, totally on his own—a fierce knight
Solitary in pursuit of—what? Collapse.
He had delivered a blow to his own
Solar plexus. It was sheer emotional

Solipsism. He began to feel how the long
Lever of his intellect was ratcheting
Him up into connectedness. His mind
Cleared, like an island rising above a sea
Roiling with volcanic heat, emerging
Dark and glistening—like something newly hatched.
"When I lie down next to her, I—"
There was no way he could go on, no way.
Everything in him rebelled against going on.
His words would carry bits of him across.
A divide once crossed there was no going back.
He wanted to stay put in that sanctuary
Of mute being, that state of slow revolving
Motion to the rhythm of deep breathing,
Feeding on self-provided sustenance.
Even the self was an unwelcome magnet
Polarizing the scattered strands of memory
Into vectored, decipherable meanings
Ready for words, those inadequate laundered bits
Which could make news out of wounds and glories,
Once suspended mutely in cellular depths.

"When I lie down next to her, I—
Am overtaken by a sense of . . . sense of
Something . . . it's hard to believe . . . how often
Had I . . . I had . . . lai . . . been near, next to her.
Ordinary daily stuff . . . But this . . . one time
Something happened . . . different . . . it was me . . . it. . . . "
His lips seemed to have become puffy and
Entirely apart from him, his voice
Came to him as an echo.

                              "Something . . .
Something terrible was about to happen . . .
In my chest, in the pit of my stomach—

I felt . . . my head, the skin became tight . . . and
    chilly. . . .
I started to shiver. No . . . I thought . . . the flu, yes
The flu—I had caught a flu—a flu bug
Suddenly got me. Shut my eyes and go to sleep.
All better by morning. . . . No way . . . it got worse
Like a warning you try to ignore.
I had to get out of there—or what? Die?
Downstairs in the kitchen no more flu—cured.
What a relief! It goes away, thank god.
Just stay down in the kitchen. Then I knew
That it was something about the damn bed—
The bed! *My* marriage bed . . . it was . . . killing me.
I must be mad with fever and not know it.
That once happened to me a long time ago.
I ran one hundred and six for awhile
And didn't know it—felt great, actually.
But my bed began to shake on its own
It seemed. My father was sitting on it,
Looked surprised and then saw that I was shaking
All over—and I still didn't know it.
They said it was an acute pneumonia.
There in the kitchen I started to shake
But no fever. I told myself I had
To go back, get into bed, see what happened.
I did. It started again. I said to myself,
'You're staying here. Don't wake her up. Be quiet.'
It was like when I was a kid, really small,
When I'd get sick. I did run high fevers.
I'd have the strangest experiences, and yet
They weren't frightening, but fascinating.
I didn't know the name for them back then—
Synesthesias. Great heavy-footed elephants
Would appear to me sounding like deep gongs.
I could taste colors, smell with my fingertips
Like ten noses. The world rushed at me from

Every corner. I could feel my brain expand.
Well, I had no fever but things began
Happening as I lay transfixed and frightened
Alongside the rise and fall of my wife's
Breathing as she was moored in deepest sleep.

I wanted to kill someone—wanted is wrong.
I felt it in my fingertips, my nails,
My fists, my guts, my teeth. It tasted
Acidy, tart, making my lips curl, my
Tongue stick to the roof of my mouth. My jaws
Began working. I couldn't lie still. But the dread
Was gone. The anxiety was gone. I was free.
For one exquisite moment I knew I could kill.
A great humming power swelled up in me.
You! I could drive you into the ground
With my fist, stuffing your mouth with earth.
Everything seemed etched in merciless clarity.
The darkness around me was lucid, transparent.
Was this the song trapped in me? A song of hate?
I rather liked it. It was a goddamned dream.
I'll shake and beat the whole goddamned world.
Send it on a forced march until it sank to its knees."
Paul knew he had to stop. Words had triumphed,
Carrying him as on a shield, exposed.

"Yes, you are strong, as you have always felt.
Powerful, with a humming—how did you say?—
Swelling up in you. What is it you would do?
Drive me into the ground? Yes. Stuff my mouth
So that I won't talk nonsense anymore.
And above all, no more unexpected
Dying. You will be master of death.
OK. You will blow down the house of cards
Before it collapses. And, oh yes, then
You are guilty, very guilty, either way."

What in god's name is he talking about?
Paul wanted to shake off Fouchault's little speech,
As a dog shakes off water.

                              "What do you mean—
Either way?"

                    "Yes. Either way. What's puzzling?"

"Well, it's not clear at all—at least not to me!"
Paul was vastly annoyed.
                              "I can see that
I'd be guilty if I got rid of people.
But if they just died on their own, why then?"

"Why then? Because it's the same. You still did it."

"I felt I killed my mother?"

                              "Yes. At least
You felt responsible. What was it you said,
Joking at the beginning? . . . Yes . . . the pygmies—
Those bowlegged geniuses with the blow-guns
Who perished at twenty-eight—"

                              Paul's annoyance
Vanished. Twenty-eight. He knew now where *that*
Had come from. Where did Fouchault get pygmies?
He hadn't said pygmies. He was engaged in
Fighting a rear-guard action, he knew that.
Fouchault had continued, "They're like little boys
Who take such pride in their growing powers,
But always must end up defeated,
The swelling down."

                    Paul felt a curious itching

Behind his ear, like after a bee sting.
Fouchault's words were settling on his flesh like rain,
The first touches cool and surprising.

                                        "Well,
We must stop now." Fouchault sounded satisfied
To Paul who left thoroughly bewildered.

42

It would be too easy to turn it all
Outward, he thought. Rumors were flying thickly,
The whispers in which they were uttered, like drafts
Of air currents lifting them higher, blowing
Them further than open talk would. But Paul
Questioned himself, doubted his motives, torn
Between his personal turmoil and the rich
Irony of what he heard was going on:
Serey hospitalized, the gang of three
Thwarted, at an impasse of their own making.
With which voice should he start the hour—
A voice he couldn't trust, it was so foreign,
Strong with unspent rage and an odd resolve.
It was a puzzle to him. The other voice,
An old friend, its tone of bitter, insider's
Savvy, unsurprised and uncharitable, rang
False in his ear.
                    "Who am I to talk.
I'm as much an opportunist in my heart
As they, only I don't act. I nourish
Ambitions I disdain and counterfeit
My passions as high-minded contempt—of you
For letting this sorry affair go on
Without even a peep of protest, of them
For their betrayal of their own professions,

Of this place for its casual acceptance,
Its passive letting itself get screwed by those
Who defile what they say they value most."
By then his voice had modulated into
Its minor second key of the bled prophet
Drained white before fate, finding strength only
In "I told you so's." He enjoined silence
On himself. No more squealing like a pig
At the sight of others at the trough he yearned
To snuffle at himself.

                    "I can murder.
I discovered that one night and thought it was
The flu." The words escaped his lips
As if born with the breath that made them. Paul
Hesitated no longer.

                    "One damned picture
More than all the rest. I didn't know what
It meant to me until the other day.
An item in the paper with a photo.
This strange young man asked after an actress,
Where she lived in this neighborhood. No one
Told him, or at least no one said they did.
But he found out. Rang her doorbell. Shot her
Once in the chest and fled. She died instantly.
The photograph was of her as a bride—
An old fashioned bride, her bridal cap more
Like a broad lace band across her forehead,
Extending into her veil on either side.
She wore a joyous wide-lipped smile, showing
Glorious teeth, her head tilted up in sheer
Orphaic triumph, her face pale with illness
Or too much powder. Perhaps her last role.
I was stunned. Not by the story, I mean,
But by the resemblance in the photograph."

He could feel his pulse quicken, becoming
Thunderous in his ear. A streak of pain
Shot diagonally through his ribs, leaving
An acrid taste in his mouth like heartbreak.
He felt illuminated by pain as if
A giant klieg light made daylight of his
Suffering, clarifying its deepest trenches,
Nullifying its ambiguous shadows.
He talked on, confused, sorrowful, ignorant
Of where his words were taking him, like a stick,
A blind man's stick, that could feel out only
A step or two ahead.
               "A silent movie—
No not really a movie. It's still—
A bunch of silent stills *from* a movie
With all the movement taken out, leaving
Something on the sand, like tides when they
Run out. Once you have the story, the action,
The photo looks . . . different. . . . "
                      Riveted by
A sudden blurred image, his mind's eye changed focus.
Thoughts ceased. Talk lapsed. He was alone, staring
And not seeing, feeling and not knowing.
He twisted on the couch as if some force
Was exerting a slow brutal torque on his
Body, and through his body, on his soul.
He felt a lift that he resisted by
Pressing urgently against the couch,
Resorting to words to restore sanity.
"Five, six stills—photos—of my dead mother."
Again his body seemed to twist of its
Own accord. "The one of her . . . of her . . . self
In her wedding gown, just like the actress.
The same smile, the same pale, sick powdered face,
The same joyous triumph. . . . "

                                                 That same head,
Autumnal hair spread on a pillow, in sleep,
Pale beyond grieving. Only the rose-tinted breasts
Living in the morning light, rising and
Falling.

          "At my father's second marriage
I sat right in front of the bride and groom.
My stepmother had a large head, circled
By a lacy veil, her face like a full moon. . . .
My father's head—." He had to hold his breath
And as he did so anger rose in him
Stealthily like a periscope scanning
For a target. But he was tired of that game.
With a sudden ache he imagined Francie
Lying on Victor's couch, her face at peace,
Not like her face alongside his in bed
Where it was tense with confusion and pain.
He could see her smile sweetly, but then it changed.
Her lips parted wide and her smile grew harsh.
She's talking about me, he thought, ruefully.

"I've been a miserable husband, not so
Great a father either, as a son—
I don't know." Unthinkingly a curse
Formed on his lips: "Fuck my father! Fuck him
For a rotten son of a bitch bastard!"
And with the words the feeling vanished.
Instead a curtained stillness enshrouded him,
Transparent and impenetrable,
Making it hard to breathe, sharpening vision.
He was not to move. It was an enchantment.
A mythic tableau at the start of his life
As son to both his father and mother.

"I rose early one morning in my crib

And saw through the bars my mother's bare breasts
Rising and falling as she slept, her lips parted
In a dreamer's smile. Beneath her right breast
My father's head rose and fell like a boat
At anchor on the sweet tide of her breathing.
I stared and stared sounding depths I couldn't
Fathom. *That* still photo is not in the album."

The words flowed out easily, quietly,
Bare unadorned tokens of a lost wealth.
"I feel that same wonder now before my life,
The same profound sense of an enigma
I should know the answer to but never will."

"You were, are still afraid to move. If you do
It would be in anger or in lust. Either
Way and the loving tableau is shattered
And it would be your fault."

                              Fouchault's soft words
Dissolved the stillness and he felt a rush
Of anguish for all that was passed and no more,
For the moments he had lost, for the head
He had not laid between her breasts, for the rage
He had not spent against *his* head that lay
So vulnerably exposed, so lovingly sustained,
For the blanket he had drawn over them
For so long, fixing in his own deathless time
Two lovers who were his life's protagonists,
For whom he filled his bare world with actors
Playing their roles badly but bringing life
To old lives and letting him try again
And still again to see into the depths.
But each time he had closed his eyes, choosing
Stillness, blindness, and each time knowing the end,
Above all, the betrayals, the sweet damned betrayals.

"What will happen, I suppose will happen,
With Serey, with Victor, Kurt, and Greta.
They've made their bed and will have to lie in it."
They both chuckled at the double entendre.

Part Seven

Donald Prescott
and
Paula Veroff

43

He liked the roar in her voice. Even when
Quiet it was like summer thunder gathering
Strength, grumbling and maybe booming or not,
Depending. So unlike other women he'd known.
He knew it was a smoker's voice. Her cough
Disturbed the physician in him. He said,
"I like the deepness in your voice and yet
It worries me. It's a strength and a weakness
At the same time. . . . Two weeks without these hours
Unnerved me. I retired even more into my
Usual calm. My wife irritated me,
My kids are barely tolerable, my work
Was a reminder that you were still gone. . . .
I had a strange fantasy yesterday,
So obvious I smiled as I had it.
I was in the outdoors somewhere, maybe
Northern California, tall trees—redwoods
Possibly, large Douglas firs—the forest
Alternately dark and light, an unspoiled
Cathedral. The silence filled me with pure joy.
It was my kind of silence, the silence
Of natural being, of things breathing, growing
Without egoistic fanfare, without shame;
Virtue and sobriety without conscience.
As I sat at my desk, I could sense it!

My silence was at one with that silence.
And then my fantasy took an odd turn.
I heard drums—a bass drum and a snare drum,
One booming, the other rasping, conversing
Across the forest. I tried to imagine
Who the drummers were. When they emerged
They were both you! A small, elflike you
Playing the bass and a huge, giant you
Playing the snare drum. I couldn't help laughing.
I had provided myself with two you's
For the one I had not been seeing two weeks,
Each making a noise in my silent country,
Each a caricature of you, my revenge
For leaving me."

                    Paula was pleased by Prescott's
Modest yet useful self-analysis.
Sadness sweetened the fatigue she felt so
Often now. Her work would soon be over
With him. Another few months. This summer.
"Why the bass drum and snare drum?" she asked.

"Your voice, of course. Rather your two voices—
Deep, booming, and then sometimes harsh, rasping.
My mother's voice is shrill, high pitched, piercing.
How I hated it as a kid. One gift
Of the analysis is to know how
My hatred hid from me the siren call
In her voice, 'Donney, Oh, Donney! Where are you,
My own Bonnie Donney!' I never heard
Or let myself hear the cooing in it.
All I knew was I had to flee from it.
You could say that in my analysis
I lashed myself to the mast and listened,
Heard the siren call at last of that
Young lonely woman with her small, downy boy.

How she must have dreaded my growing up.
My father was as much her father, being older
By twenty years. . . . She's so sick now, my mother.
Her mind addled. The siren's busted.
Every now and then a young smile flits across
Her otherwise wrinkled up, perplexed face—
The light I hid from that I regret so
Now. Analysis can be so cruel.
It says to you, 'Where were you, wise guy,
When life was in its first full ripeness,
When your mother was young and calling to you
And you hid and hated out of fearfulness?'
I wish I could have acted otherwise.
Now when I see her I cry for the lost time.
I take her hand and kiss those leathery fingers
And her eyes open wide as if alarmed.
She withdraws her hand and sticks out her tongue!
Would you believe it! Poetic justice!
My father runs his hands up and down his cane,
His nose leaking a little, his eyes staring.
Where are my parents gone! Those giant athletes
Of life who broke all the records I knew of.
Tall, strong, handsome, making the world go round . . .
And now I worry about you. What were you like
As a young woman, I wonder? Sly, I bet,
Sophisticated, not so easily had.
Also candid, fresh, and exhilarating.
I wish I had known you then. How marvelous! . . .
My thoughts turn on regrets. This summer we stop?
Almost five years. Am I really ready—
Things are not right with my wife or children—
I'm not the family man I once could be.
Work means more to me, writing, thinking.
I see them all from a distance, small-sized
Like through an inverted telescope.
What have I done with my life? I'm forty.

Young if you're sixty, old if you're twenty. . . .
Funny how I think of changing buses.
Transfer in hand you climb onto the new bus
And don't pay but hand the driver your transfer—
A yellow slip printed black with conditions—
Such a simple act, so many conditions;
Void if used another day, another time,
On another line, et-cet-era, et-cet-era,
Watch your step, move to the rear. Don't talk to the
Driver when the bus is in motion—
Use the rear exit please. No smoking or
Spitting on the floor. All that just for
Sitting on the bus for fifteen minutes!
What's all this about?"

                              Paula heard his complaint.
High time for a free ride. No conditions
Here in the analysis, the old bus
Left behind. Off in a new direction.
The old driver dismissed, the new driver
Young, accommodating . . . yes, his wife was
In danger as she felt herself to be.
All this hypocritic talk of knowing her
When she was young! How about the present?
But what danger was she in, the analyst?
Absurd. She could not disavow the thought
However. He had reached her. . . . Yes, she knew.
Her own son off somewhere, a wanderer
Continuing to wander as she had once,
Country to country, city to city
And no transfers. Sneaking across borders,
Escaping from hell as hell with its flames
Leaped closer—Vienna, Prague, Warsaw, Paris—
A few years here, a few years there—and then
Forty! Ah, to be forty and in Paris!
Nonsense! She was sixty-seven and in

Tennessee. Without Hitler no such miracle.

The long silence had deepened between them.
Prescott had dropped his inquiry and found
Himself bedded down in silence, or
Riding like a boat at anchor, rolling
Gently with the tide. A voluptuous
Interlude to be savored in its own right.
Words were the shrill seagulls reconnoitering
The shore. The real meaning was in the tide,
Powerful beyond tongues or estuaries;
It rides in or out on its own timetable.

"My sister has a way of singing her
Own tunes. She'd say to me, 'Listen to this,
Donney. I made it up!' I wish I could
Sing my feelings now. How did we, you think,
Discover singing? Quite astonishing,
Imagine! A singing analytic hour!"

"Yes, you like the deep forest with young birds
Singing and not this old crow chattering—
Or beating her empty drum." A bit too much,
She thought, her pique was showing.

                                    "Not at all!
You're wrong there. Or perhaps I hurt your feelings
A little with my talk of youth and transfers.
I'm sorry. I don't know what I'm reaching for.
Your two-week absence is clearly the silence.
But come this Fall—Summer, the silence will last.
This forest here will be forever silent.
Fall? You see how I try to stretch it out?
I mention problems with my wife and kids,
A come-on for you to pick up, explore."

"Notice how you gave me a fancy fantasy
On my return—forest, sunlight, two drums,
Fat and thin analysts—and now singing
Instead of words. You are embroidering
My going and return and this termination
With Wagnerian stitches—a liebestod.
And you are enjoying it."

                              He felt crushed.
She knew how much he loved Wagner's music.
But she was right nevertheless—cruel and right?
Smart, shrewd, tough women were baffling to him.
He knew that. She always threw him off balance.
But when he righted himself things looked different.
Yet he felt the blood rush to his face and neck.
He was angry and humiliated.

"What's wrong with my fantasy and Wagner
Anyway? I know, like Freud, you have a
Tin ear for music. Silence can be eloquent
In music. Yes, I tried to fathom your absence—
There it is again! To measure its depths.
Yes, I did enjoy doing it. So what?
Did you want me to greet you with a bat
In my hand! That two weeks missing of you
Was an innoculation against the en...."
His voice trailed off. He was upset again.
The world was erupting in loud clashes
Of cymbals. "Against the disease of ending...."

Paula took in a deep breath. "We stop now."

44

Donald Prescott approached the couch frowning,
Not wishing to look at Paula and with
Only the curtest nod of greeting. He was
Still angry at how the previous hour
Had gone. She had been unfair. So unlike her.
Donald composed himself on the couch, pursing
His lips and fixing his eyes on the bare wall
Opposite.

        Paula observed his ritual
Settling into position, his body
Defining, then possessing the space. Goyish.
Jews ignored space because they lived in time
Only. Jews crowded together, hunched over
Food because space belonged to the goyim.
In their tomes crowded with text and commentaries
Jews lived their past for an eternity.
Paula did not like that either. Who wants
To live forever, or should? She was aware
In herself of a certain natural leaning,
A sense of difference, a taste that was not
Her own, perhaps like another language.
Neither worse nor better, simply foreign.
At the same time she felt an affection for
Prescott, partly of course because of his

Success in the analysis, but also
For his sturdy, reliable character
Seasoned by a pinch of Irish wildness—
One could not note his pale blue eyes suddenly
Intensify without responsive delight.
She would miss him.

                    Prescott saw images
On the wall, his favorite pastime when
His thoughts failed him and silence drizzled slowly
Down on both of them creating a sobering
Dampness and it seemed as if she were strange
Altogether to him instead of someone
With whom he had lived though five years of chaos,
Passionate unsettlement, and despair
In which nothing was secure from challenge,
From being toppled and turned inside out.
The image was of a kettle—a large
Iron kettle. Of all things, he thought, why that?
"Why should I be imagining a kettle
Right now? A large iron kettle, nothing
More, no fire, no contents—just a kettle
On the shelf. Have I put myself on the shelf
Today? Perhaps I have. The fire's out.
Nothing cooking but a lot could be in
Such a large kettle. Yes, you insulted me
Last time, so I will refuse to bubble
For you. Go stir up your own trouble for a
Change."

              "Maybe you've terminated already
And on a sour note."

                  Prescott had to smile
At the "sour note" jibe. Wagner was back
And the liebestod. He could get angry

All over, but his feelings softened instead.
The season of his analysis was
Drawing to a close—an irretrievable
Voyage across an uncharted ocean.
Once wrong-headed, proud, ponderously serious,
Which he had to say he missed right now. Why
Couldn't he stay angry at her? Once he could—
Sullenly, simmeringly mad. He heard
Those heart-rending, drawn-out Wagnerian chords
And then he frowned for he had remembered
Dreyfus's smiling dismissal of Wagner
As so much music to masturbate by.
It must be Paul's Jewishness that leads him
To hate Wagner. Ah, maybe. . . .
                                    "I understand
Your crack about Wagner now. He's German
And an anti-Semite. Analysis
Is a Jewish trade. Jung was the shabbos goy,
The one who was going to light all the lights
All over Europe for Freud when he couldn't.
Jung was supposed to make analysis
Acceptably unkosher, fit for gentiles. . . .
Jung was to Freud as Paul was to Jesus.
Jung objected to Freud's heavy emphasis
On sex. Paul freed the pagans from observing
The Mosaic code. Had Jesus lived He
Well might have driven Paul out of his new sect
And we would have had Paulians as well
As Jungians."
                Prescott's pale eyes were twinkling
With mischief. His anger had faded away.

"You want to confuse a simple woman
With all this theology. Are you
Drawing up sides for a fight? Jew against
Gentile, Jung against Freud, you against me,

With Wagner presiding over everything?"

"You mean über alles?" Prescott interrupted,
Immediately regretting his riposte.

"What do you mean by 'über alles'? Wagner?"

"You said 'over everything.' Isn't that
Über alles in German?"

"Yes, so what?"

"Oh, you know the Horst Wessel song—the Nazis. . . ."

"You must be furious with me over
Something to drag in the Nazis. . . . Is it
Wagner still?"

Prescott grew quiet. His jaw
Tensed. He felt himself become combative,
Even aching for a little hassle.
Once and for all to get this Jew–Gentile
Business out on the table. But she had
Suffered terribly because she was Jewish.
He knew that. Already he sensed how quick
She had been to assume he was furious
With her because he had mentioned the Nazis.
"Wagner wrote great music. He was German
And prejudiced. Freud was Jewish and a great
Scientist. He hated music. Should music
Lovers dismiss psychoanalysis?"

Paula was growing impatient and puzzled.
He was misusing his fine intellect.
And then the true message clarified itself:
She was angry at him because he was

Dismissing her and the analysis.
He, the music lover, she the Philistine—
The appearance in her thoughts of those ancient
Enemies of Israel confirmed her hunch.
It always delighted her when rich, thick
Meanings bubbled up in her associations,
Evidence that her unconscious was fully
Participating. And then she recalled
His slip at the end of the last hour—
The "disease of ending," her two-week absence
The inoculation against that disease.

"Again you play at intellectual games.
You are fighting my return because it hurts
To welcome me back only to terminate.
My absence was an inoculation
Against the 'disease of ending.' "

                         Prescott
Heard his own words as if on a recording
When one wonders, "Is that my voice. I know
I said that, but was it me?"

                         "I said that,
Didn't I, although I find it hard
To own up to it. Strange how foreign it sounds.
You inoculate against smallpox—that
Old scourge of mankind. . . . "

                    No further words would come.
Instead his mind skipped to Serey and their talk.

"Ran into Serey downtown on Saturday.
How can one person be so relentless
And charming at the same time? She's transparent,
And yet manages to be intriguing.

Her voice is musical yet her face hard.
She dresses stunningly, yet strides
Like a man. Her figure is full of promises
Canceled in advance by her tough bearing.
As we talked I found myself comparing her
To Frances Dreyfus. More woman with less plot.
Never hard to know how Frances is feeling
About you. In fact since her analysis
She wears her feelings more openly on
Her sleeve. So different from Paul who tucks them
Up his sleeve and can't shake them loose when he
Wants to show them. . . . Serey let me realize
That I was growing beyond my Ruthie.
She complimented me for the great changes
I had made in analysis. I was
Even handsomer. She's stirring up trouble
So that I won't challenge Michael—that other
Shabbos goy . . . and she wants me to know it,
And knowing it will make me think of her
As shrewd and dangerous. She is so involved
With Victor and Kurt; I worry about
Her analysis with Greta. How can
Analysis survive such politics?
I suspect you are caught in the middle
Between respect for Victor and distrust
Of Kurt. Why I could never understand.
Do stay out of it. They are all bloody minded.
Myself I think Victor would make a good
Research director. Certainly better
Than anyone else. Fabrikant is shallow,
Dreyfus is bright but too young, and troubled,
And the rest of them are nonanalysts.

Paula Veroff felt her dander rise. Awful!
This destructive invasion of treatment
By all this feuding and politicking!

Victor and Kurt were neither to be trusted.
Although Victor had a bright future ahead
And would accomplish something, dear old Kurt
Was a leftover still clinging to a tree
From which the first strong wind would dislodge him.
Kurt knew it and had to keep any wind
From blowing too hard. How she longed to be
That wind! Prescott was right to warn her off.
She yearned for a cigarette. And as happened
So often when an appetite was keen
She leaped ahead.
          "You wish to protect me
From my own impulses, but also from yours,
And you must protect yourself against your own
Wish to hold onto me or be rid of me,
Or better still that I be neutralized
Like a virus by inoculation."

Prescott felt both assaulted and reproachful
As he had last hour. Be rid of her!
How could she say that when even his slip
Was meant to refer to the *ending*, not her!
It was the *ending* that was the disease
Against which he wanted inoculation,
Not her.
        "I don't want to get rid of *you*,
Dr. Veroff, but of the pain of ending,
Of not having you as my analyst,
Of . . . of . . . *losing* you."

           Paula felt uneasy.
She was the unused kettle on the shelf—
Of that she was sure. She was the Ruthie
He was growing beyond, the senile mother,
And what he could not know would have to hurt him
And several others . . . unless. . . .
        "We stop now."

45

As she awaited Prescott's arrival
Paula Veroff was unhappy with herself.
Her damnable tongue had run away with her
And she knew it. It was at a meeting
Of the training analysts yesterday.
Victor and Kurt had taken out after Dreyfus,
Raising questions about his training status
After Freeman had given a poor report
Of his progress with his first case. Paula
Quickly perceived the reason for the animus—
Dreyfus opposed Victor for research head,
A foolishness, to be sure, but courageous.
Paula had a weakness for the foolhardy,
Those who fought unwisely but bravely
For lost causes. She herself had followed
Her share of tattered banners in her youth
To know that a lost battle could still be
A good battle. Before she realized it,
She had said, "Let's leave politics outside
And attend only to analysis in here."
She looked full at Fouchault's impassive face
And he very faintly nodded agreement.
Victor did not take kindly to reproach,
And he bridled at the insinuation.
"We *are* talking about analysis, Paula.

Are we wasting our time with this Dreyfus?"
Paula could not restrain herself, "And how much
Analytic time has been wasted on
All this stupid politicking, tell me!"
And then dear Kurt put in his two cents worth,
"Paula, Paula, we are all mature enough
To render unto Caesar what is Caesar's
And unto Freud what is Freud's."

The phone rang.
It was the receptionist. Doctor Prescott
Would be arriving late—an emergency.
For a moment her brow creased—something bad?
But likely it was a hospital patient
Of Prescott's requiring his attention.
Paula was grateful for the brief respite.
She was not feeling well, coughing all night.
Ben Zeitler wanted her to have an X ray.
That old woman of an internist
Was as usual much too worried. One survives,
Oh, how one survives, despite one's wishes.
How often death would have been gladly welcomed.
She pictured how at the circus a clown
At the end sweeps up the spotlight into
A smaller and smaller circumference
Until it disappears. Her throat felt raw.
Automatically, she lit a cigarette
And relaxed amidst startling reminders
Of past excitements. Life will not subside,
She concluded. That's beyond her control
For good or ill. The old party persists.
She welcomed the phone's renewed ringing—
To work.

When Prescott arrived he looked at her
Before turning his back to lie down.

He had the diagnostician's calm eye
Which takes in and sorts out at the same time.
He did not like her appearance today.
And when she started coughing his concern
Deepened.
      "You don't look well to me," he said,
Knowing that she would not respond. But he
Also knew she would have heard. "I'm sorry
I'm late. An urgent message to call Serey
Right away. I was very puzzled,
As you can imagine. When I called her
She answered in a whisper, saying
Someone could be listening. When I asked who
She startled me by saying Michael could.
I thought she was joking, you know, flirting
A little as she could. She burst out laughing
And said, 'April Fool!' I reminded her
It was January and in any case
Why the urgent message? She turned serious.
She had to talk to me about Victor.
Things may not be going so well for him.
The president is being indecisive.
I interrupted her, quite peeved, telling her
I had an hour and had to hang up.
This didn't sound at all urgent to me
And then she shouted, 'Hang all your hours!'
And slammed down the phone. It's all very
    strange. . . .
I can't rid myself of my worry for you.
Maybe it's to make up for the anger
Last time. But there's something else on my mind.
I had a dream and I can't figure it out.
It's so banal that it must be hiding
Something of great importance. A washboard—
An old-fashioned washboard, corrugated.
The kind old Irish washerwomen use

In all the cartoons—bent over, perspiring,
Limp strands of hair falling over their faces.
Only this washboard was shining like a
Jewel, surrounded by a bright aura.
It was new and dry as if never used.
What in heaven's name is that all about!
I think I recall a picture of a harp
I saw somewhere—a harp floating in the sky
Also surrounded by an aura. . . . Silly!
The whole thing is silly. I want so much
To dismiss it. Clearly, one of those highly
Condensed dream images, one image
Doing the work of many like Erikson's
Dream made up entirely of the word *Seine*.
A multilayered dream, the one word
A complex anagram from which one could
Derive the French for *breast*, the Paris river,
The German for *his* and *one*, the English *sin*.
Breast, river, his, one, sin—
Some collection. And now washboard and harp."

Paula, alert and sad, noted that his
Long absent obsessiveness was back
And with it extremes of dirt and divinity.
The end remembers the beginning
In analysis. He was folding time back
Like those crazy mathematical curves
In which you go from inside to outside
Without going over an edge, Paula thought.
She learned this from her son, the scientist,
Who now measured the earth with his restless strides
Which moved in all directions except home.
She knew, she understood, the pain persisted.
Yes, she had a spiritual son in Donald,
As she had in other candidates.
An analyst's work is like creation itself.

Not *ex nihilo* but a tangible, palpable
Transformation of a living being.
This brilliant physician on the couch—
His mind once crippled into pretzel twists
Of tortured thought, always a yellow light
Flashing, reducing his actions to cautious
False starts. Now he could be bold, straightforward—
Perhaps a little too much so. She thought
His present retreat might also signal
Retrenchment to guard against impulsiveness.

"The corrugations of the washboard remind me
Of ripples on a lake, or wavelets whispering
On a beach, the shining metal of a sword.
Yes! *Excaliber.* I remember now.
My kid, John, was reading a comic book
Last night retelling the Arthur legend.
It showed King Arthur's sword glowing in the sky
Like the washboard in my dream. And the harp
I guess connects with old Irish legends.
God! This all reminds me of my childhood.
I envied John his excitement."

                              "The washboard—
What of *it*?" Paula inquired.

                              "Oh, I think of those
Hillbilly musicians who play on saws
And such like."

                    "You are still so full of music—
Soaring Wagnerian helden music
While you make this old lady scrub away
On your dirty thoughts."

                              "What dirty thoughts?

Why do you keep on knocking Wagner's music!
What's wrong with heroes? Or celebrating them?"

Paula knew she was pushing hard, harder
Than was timely or necessary. Her heart
Was beating fast. *She was feeling too ill
To wait.* This thought had suddenly appeared
And disappeared like a blazing comet
Leaving behind it a dark trailing cloud.
Involuntarily she waved her hand
Quickly back and forth before her eyes
As if scattering cigarette smoke.
She squinted distractedly and put
The fingernail of her left small finger
Between her lips as if meditating
On a thought already gone. She then said,
"You are twisting your thoughts into pretzels
Again—soggy, dirty pretzels and wanting
Me to straighten them out and clean them up—
Just like at the beginning. What's up your sleeve?
What's going on with Serey? Why does she
Call *you*? Perhaps you are to be her hero?
And you can end the analysis
In a blaze of cheap romantic glory
Like you want to rescue your old mother
From your decrepit father, and this crone
From death itself."

                    He was seized with longing,
A desperate, unfathomable ache
Which broke finally into a soft evenly
Spreading sadness. There was no one to save
Except himself, he concluded mournfully.

"You ask why Serey called *me*? How should I know?
Although I admit I had a vicious fantasy.

I'd take her up. Conspire with her. Destroy
Michael and then blow up this whole awful place.
Run off with her and hate her for making
Such a fool of me. And I am sick, sick
With worry. What will happen when I'm finished
And have finally to confront my life
For what it's worth with no further hope
Of what I can still make of it—ever!"

He had no idea where this bile had
Risen from. He was angry and bewildered.
Paula still saw the same pattern in this
Wild vision: to rescue an undeserving
Mother from a disappointing father
And to end in despair—unrewarded
And demeaned. Old guilts always find their shadows
Even when all is bathed in the brightest
Light the present can afford.
                            Paula said,
"You wish to rescue me from Kurt and Victor,
Save me only for yourself and as we both
Expire, the flood waters rising around us,
We both sing hooray at the top of our lungs.
So—you have me and pay for it all at
The same time. Of course, it isn't so good
For me either—all this singing and drowning,
And I might add—all this carrying on
About my voice, my coughing, my appearance.
You seek a catastrophic finale
For having fared so well and for so much
Life that lies ahead of you."

                            Donald grimaced.
No more loitering in the harbor of her
Good will. She was mad and he was furious.
If she wanted a fight, she could have it.

"Damn it, there *is* something very wrong with you.
That *is* a terrible cough and you *do* look awful.
But why should I give a damn! Save yourself.
I'm sure you've done that countless times before."

But his anger was quenched quickly by its
Excess. He succumbed to dull moodiness.
Paula was sorting the real from the unreal
With pain and foreboding. The hour was up.

46

She noted that his face was expressionless,
Almost as if he were wearing one of those
Hoodlum stockings over his head. But she
Also knew that was precisely the time
When the strongest feelings were stirring
Behind his bland exterior. For it was
A discreet curtain securing privacy,
Not a blank window with nothing to reveal.

"Something terrible is going on. Almost
I don't want to know what it is. More than
Enough is going on right now in my life—
Like ending this analysis. And after
All that talk last time about heroes, I'd just
As soon sit this one out. I ran into
Michael yesterday in the parking lot.
He talks in asides so you figure out
His real meaning by what he doesn't say.
He stared intently at his shoes, mumbling
'My car is acting up' and then a moment
After, 'Where are you going on vacation
This summer—going abroad again?' From that
You guess that *he* is having the hard time
And wishing *he* were going on vacation.
I had in mind the wild call from Serey

But was reluctant to come out with it.
Instead I asked him how Serey was these days.
His reply was vintage Michael, 'The work
Around here is getting tougher and tougher,'
By which he meant he's staying away from home
As much as he can because Serey is getting
Tougher and tougher. Finally I asked him
Point blank if she were well, which caught him off
    guard
And he said, drawing in his breath quickly,
'No!' But when I asked him what was wrong,
He recovered and said, 'The weather, you know,
Is a great problem.' I could only shake
My head in disbelief as he walked off. . . .
By this time everyone had expected
The president would have made his announcement
On the directorship. What's holding it up?
Well, enough about these trivial matters.
On to the world shaking affairs of Prescott,
Donald, forty-one, father of four,
Husband of one, physician to too many,
Friend to all, ex-analysand-to-be
And self-appointed nonhero, his lance
Stowed in the attic along with his beer stein,
Dueling sword, plasticine scar, and gauntlet."

"Ah, you are full of fun today like an
Undertaker at an execution.
Again you are laughing at me—and again
These German allusions. Who now is talking
In asides?"

         Swiftly his mind shifted. He scowled
And closed his eyes, nodding his head slightly.
What *were* all those German allusions about?
Had it all grown out of defending

Wagner's music against her prejudices?
He felt his nostrils flaring, his teeth gritting—
Angry—Yes, dammit, angry, a cruel anger.
She could not just sit back there and—and what?
Amazingly his mind went blank entirely.
As if to fill the frightening void, his thoughts
Returned to Serey. Again the anger,
Cruel anger, like driving a nail into flesh.
He was possessed by a strange will to sneer,
To chortle aloud at some enigmatic joke.
He fought back the feeling as one would
A wave of nausea. He thought of his mother
And a sharp, agonizing pain returned
As if a hot iron was put to his flesh.
He had talked to her on the phone yesterday—
A weekly chore.
                    "I talked to my mother
Last night. It's getting harder and harder.
She wanders, forgetting who I am, saying
Suddenly, 'Is that you, honey? Don't be late.'
She thinks I'm Dad when they were young marrieds.
I don't have the heart to say it's me, Donald,
Because she gets so confused, saying, 'Donald?
Yes, of course. Where's your father?' And I—yes, I
Get angry at her. . . . That's finishing too.
Her mind is dying and her poor flesh is
Wasting. And I'm furious at—at what?
Mortality? No. That's too easy
Because it's she I'm furious at—and at you.
I'm offended by your incessant coughing
As I am by her confusion and decay.
And God knows what's happening to poor Serey.
Why I lump you all together, God knows.
But I do. I want to shake you all hard.
What's happening? What's happening to my world?
My mother's sweetness, gone! Serey's pluck, gone!

Your role in my life—going if not gone.
I become furious at the thought."

                                    "Furious
And helpless, and furious because helpless.
Endings are not diseases, Doctor Prescott,
That can be cured by a physician's care
Or prevented by living right. They are
Endings, and nothing more. That's what makes them
Hard for us. Desires don't end. They live
On and on, like your mother's for her man,
Like yours for her, and when the brain wearies,
Or the spirit flags, the old desires show
How young they still are."
                        Paula stared at her hands,
Hearing her own words as if another
Had spoken them. Prescott fought off accepting
Her words. His anger was now smoldering
But ready at the least gust of self-pity
To burst out in bright justifying flames.

"We've agreed to finish by September,
About half a year. Not so long a time.
Until recently I felt good about finishing,
Calm and settled about it. I could see
I was different. I wanted to get on . . .
But somehow since . . . I can't say when, but recently,
My feelings have changed. I'm not ready, that's it."
He was aware of his defiant tone,
A chip ready to be knocked off. He was
Alarmed by the strength of his disavowal.
He knew it was suspect—nevertheless
His feelings were clear and undeniable.

Paula listened as if she heard two voices—
One voice, her patient's, struggling with an ending,

Always difficult, the other voice, her own,
Sounding from his lips, chastising her roughly
For ignoring her own well-being, even
Her own health. She held a skeptic's attitude
Toward her own life. It had a bitter length
To it. She recalled her physics. One half
The trajectory you overcome gravity,
The other half you are mastered by it.
As you fall back to earth, nature takes over.
Enjoy the ride down. There is nothing for it.
She had reached the high point in thirty-nine,
In another land, another language,
Another husband, as if now she lived
A mirror image of her previous life,
The downward curve of her parabola.
At any moment, at any point, she could
Look across and see a comparable point—
A husband at her side, a son, a close friend.
But they were not at all the same as now.
Or was it the same play with two casts, one
A revival? Or was the main difficulty
Simply that across on the other arm
Of the curve, the direction was always up?
The bitter truth was that she would never know
Whether the curve had reached its natural height
Or could have risen higher, carried further
If not for the crushing catastrophe
Of war. Certainly there would have been no need
For changing players. . . . She had to stop her thoughts
Or the work at hand would suffer. Falling
Or no, propelled or sinking, the path itself
Must be followed. Life had its form or else
Chaos prevailed. And to her chaos was
The Gestapo crashing through a locked door.

The silence between them was of two worlds

Moving in their own orbits. Prescott sensed
The slackening tension in their exchanges.
She wasn't answering him, responding to him.
He fought against a mounting feeling of
Great personal insignificance. It was
Then he brandished his anger again, saying,
"I must assume your silence means you're not
Prepared to change the termination date."

Paula discovered the other voice and listened
With all her being to Prescott's entreaty.
She had to separate the self she was
From the self she had to be for him alone.
Not the woman playing out her few years,
But the young–old mother crossing her eyes
At her son's insistence that she be his
Forever, when he himself could never
Fulfill his end of the bargain. Paula
Said, "Like your mother I live in my own time.
But you want us both to live in yours. Why?
So you can be safe against your own desire
To grow beyond us both—to graduate?
Why should we change what our work together
Has made possible?"

                    Donald's face went blank
As he seemed to hear in himself footfalls,
Eerie echoes of his own departure.
He knew that she would soon announce the end
To this hour as long as a lifetime.

47

The couch stood only a few feet down the hall
From where Donald waited in the large room
Among other patients. It could have been
A dentist's waiting room, or a real doctor's,
He mused, still at times stung by his colleagues'
Condescension toward psychiatrists.
But these were eddies in the main current
Of his thoughts, a current roiled up
By an outpouring from a sudden storm.
Again it was Serey. Another call, wilder
Than the previous one. But he had resolved
Not to entangle himself. He saw an image—
His couch on a high grassy slope above,
High above, a turbulent plain below.
He had his own business, his own sad fate
To work out as best he could—job enough.
This calmed him and prepared him.

                         "Doctor Prescott."
All eyes turned toward him—a doctor, here?
He strode from the room toward Veroff's office.

"You are right. The original agreement stands.
We stop in September—beginning or end?"
He added jokingly, knowing it was

The first. And then became aware of more
Than dates in his joke, beginning or end.
"I'm still struggling with ending. It's too much."

Paula welcomed the session for reasons
Of her own. With Prescott she could enjoy
The superb tart pleasure of her life's work—
Tart it was because you were always left
With a twist at the end, a sharp flavor
Reminding you that all was not smugly
Predictable. How had Freud put it? A navel,
An omphalos, a depth into which the dream
Sinks beyond reach, beyond interpretation,
Becoming again the quicksilver of life.
Just as well. She was weary and now knew
How ill she was from Zeitler's damn X rays.
'What is this fellow up to now? Some good,
Or not?' she mused, banishing personal thoughts.
"What is this struggle about?"

                                    "Nothing and
Everything. Nothing because our work *is* finished.
Everything because I fear. . . . What do I fear?
For a moment I was certain about what
I was going to say—and then the thoughts—
Or really the thoughts about to be thought
Vanished, and nothing came . . . only a void."
And Prescott tumbled into confusion,
A turbulence of spirit in which appeared
A floating shadow rippling on its tide.

"I can't get it out of my mind. It's nothing
To do with what you and I must deal with . . .
But . . . I put it in the same category
As my worrying over your terrible cough.
I refer to Serey. She called me again.

Wanted to have lunch. She had news for me.
Maybe I shouldn't, but for old time's sake
I did. It was a mistake, a big mistake.
For some outlandish reason she looked Spanish,
Flamenco Spanish! Spit curls, powdered cheeks,
And too red lips. I started to get worried.
What was possessing this woman? But when
I made some joking allusion to her
Get up and she said with a stiff, cold smile,
'I am *La Seriosa*'—I think that's what
She actually said—and she added,
Knowingly that there was much to tell me
Since I was—I'm not sure I remember it
Right—Secretary of all Secret Affairs,
I burst out laughing, absolutely stunned.
She joined in the laughter. 'This is some joke,'
I said. 'Now let me in on it.' 'Yes, a joke.'
She replied, 'But on whom? Yes, Donal, on whom?'
She had dropped the final D in my name.
I shifted gears, believe me, quite quickly.
I thought it useless to pursue any
Explanation. Clearly she was disturbed.
I told her I hoped she was talking about
All this in her treatment where, I added,
It really belonged because people could
Easily misunderstand. But then she said
I was the best at keeping secrets, better
Than the general—whoever that was.
God, something was happening to this woman.
I knew I had to get out of there without
Upsetting her. She picked this up, saying,
'Before you leave here's another secret.'
And before I could stop her she informed me
That Victor was going to be the next
President. It had all been decided.
She had let the president know of this

So he could put his affairs in order
Before resigning. I didn't know what to say.
I just told her I had to run and took off.
What's going on? For a moment I thought
Maybe she does know something. Maybe Victor
Is going to be the next president.
But why would she then need to notify him?
No. It was crazy. Poor Serey is crazy!
What kind of world are you sending me into?—
That was the thought before! I'm afraid of
All that is awaiting me out there afterwards.
Yes, it was always there but I had you—
This chance to second think, to repeal my thoughts
Before they tyrannized me. An oasis
Of real sustenance in the midst of . . .
Mirages."

          "*I* am sending you?" Paula said,
Aware that her own world had once again
Assumed its old gray pattern. It catches up
With you, sooner or later. You hope later.
Like tying a shoe day after day without
A thought. And then one day the shoelace snaps
In our hands and it strikes us as a surprise.
But everyday the lace was growing weaker
Exactly because we *were* tying it—
That's how it was. One uses up the string
As one has to, but then why be surprised
When it gives out? Because what one needs must
Last forever, again like our desires,
Immortal as the gods who *are* our desires.
But this old string is giving out at last.
That is his worry, a worry long present,
Having nothing to do with the wearing
Out of things—not at all. Much too rational
A thought and much later than the worry.

No. It is desire's innocent demand
For its object to stay forever fresh that
Quickened guilt. If desire cannot keep
Its object fresh it must destroy it. And so
It guiltily perceives the object's end
As its own doing and sometimes tries hard
To make it so, thus denying further
A mortality it cannot master.
A shoestring broke because I yanked it.
How even now she wished to light up, to
Reaffirm that the same old lace still works
Even though it broke in her hands. Even though it
Had to break again and again in her hands.
So Serey made her own reality
In which desire moves in a vacuum,
Without friction, nothing rubs, nothing wears out—
Nothing happens. Satisfaction becomes
Illusion, but remains always possible,
Immortal as the gods in their marble
Eternity. She hated the Greeks for their
Arrogant way of separating desire
From mortality. They made us all Greeks—
But maybe we are all Greeks to begin with.

Donald had sunk into his wordless thoughts,
That state in which faceless images and
Feelings lie masked, draped figures articulate
Significance in a language of silence,
Of gestures purely mental. It was Serey
Who first removed her mask and crossed the threshold
Of speech, and quickly behind her, Ruthie,
Who seemed to take advantage of the chance
Provided by Serey, and then Francie—
All seeming to be one and still separate.

"I feel so sorry for Serey. It's so

Wrong for her to be the one to crack.
And isn't it fitting in a sad, strange way,
That it should be about the directorship.
I suppose that's what she means by Victor
Becoming president. Ruthie and Francie
Have been seeing a lot of each other.
They're cooking up some scheme about a teashop
Over a bookstore. All they need is money.
God, I feel so distant from all of that.
From Serey—sorry, yes—but not ready
To do a thing; from Ruthie—what world is
She in these days, after all she is my wife;
From Francie, whom I've known for years . . . But not
From you—" as one but last of the figures
Crossed the threshold. "And you're the one I must
        leave
And then I worry. What will happen to you
Afterwards . . . and to me."

                    "What's worrying you
About me?"

            "You'll . . . die, grow old . . . get cross-eyed
And senile like my mother." She had slipped
Across quickly and was standing in the final
Sunlight. "I have good reason to worry."

"What reasons?"

                "You ask me that? For one you *are*
Old. You *do* have a chronic cough. You *are*
A chain smoker. You *have had* a rough life.
You *are* overweight. One more strike and you're out
Twice over." Prescott wondered if he had not
Gone too far.

Baseball terms were not strange to her.
She had learned them from her patients. She was out
Twice over? The X ray was that one more strike.
Zeitler had called her—a few spots, yes, small ones,
But a workup was called for. She knew for what.
He wanted her in the hospital soon.
She told him not until the end of August.
Zeitler tried not to sound alarmed. She could
Hear him throttling his protest and saying
Finally, that he could order a few tests
In the meanwhile. But he warned her that if
The tests indicated he would *order* her
Into the hospital. She said sure, knowing
She'd not change her spots even for those other spots.
She knew the odds. She was always good at that.
She had survived not on gambler's luck, but
On quick, shrewd sizing up of her chances.
Once done, she acted, never looking back.
She knew what it meant to be turned to salt
Like Lot's wife—it was to be frozen in
A backward glance, one's mouth filled with bitterness,
One's eyes forever fixed in grief and terror.
Not for her. And the same way now. She had not
Been able ever to give up smoking—
A piece of unanalyzed neurosis.
So be it. Nothing is ever finished.
No analysis. No life. Things end
But are never completed. Only stories
Have resolutions. But no matter
How things end, it's the finality,
The clifflike drop into nothing, which can
Crush one's spirit on the rocks below
When we are supposed to start over again.
No. Like analysis provides a place
For dealing with endings, for sighting the cliff
Before we drop off, for landing more softly

Therefore, so her illness would be *her* place
In which to work out her life's end—to leave it
Without a violent fall, perhaps in pain
But not in anguish. She couldn't ask for more.

Prescott fidgeted, unusual for him,
A person of slow, sure, polished movements.
But once again he felt a powerful surge
Of fantasied heroics lifting him
High over his earlier resolves. Why him?
Why did she always pick on him to tell her
Stories to? Beneath the crazy talk
Was a mute appeal, a throttled scream for help
A friend and physician could not ignore.

48

It was the last hour of a hard day.
She lit up. Five minutes before she must call
For Prescott. Until then she would enjoy
Forbidden fruit—the taste of bitter truth
Curling down her throat into her lungs
Where new life took its own way, nosing
Where it did not belong, somehow hers and
Not hers, of her flesh and alien to it,
A wild, blind, enigmatic fetus
That could not grow itself a soul or body
But multiplied itself over and over
As if looking in reflecting mirrors
Were enough to create countless replicas . . .
Like a multitude of soldiers or ants
It foraged across her green countryside,
Invading, destroying what sustained it,
Its triumph ensuring its undoing.
The exquisite harmony of bodily parts
Becoming a bedlam of competing pains.
And thus begins sickness and death. Old Freud
Had it exactly right. Thanatos disperses,
Eros rises up and binds—for awhile.
That was the truth in her patient's wry slip—
Ending *is* a disease when it severs
Not only people from one another but when

It severs past from future, banishes
Memory itself, and installs hatred
Like a furious Cerberus guarding
Our own personal horde of terror that
Multiplies in darkness, and like a flame
Consumes all that is worthwhile within us,
No one atom left clinging to another
To form a double star no matter how small—
She started. Sooner or later physics returned.
Her son, that wandering star in his strange orbit
That must swing through emptiness, circling her
From afar. . . . A child like any child once,
Born after a brief labor, quick to emerge,
Slow to cry, but furious at the breast, suckling
With such vigor he made her nipples raw.
A child at forty! Healthy, enchanting—
She stubbed her cigarette in the ashtray,
Putting out the onrushing thoughts with it.
She could explain—Ah how she could explain
But she could never understand. Never.

Prescott entered slowly, pursing his lips,
His eyes squinting so that their blue was dimmed,
His head tilted to the side and down.
He arranged himself on the couch as if
Preoccupied with the lay of his trousers.
He cleared his throat several times and passed
His slender hand over his creased forehead.

"I have just come from the hospital where
I spent most of the day attending Serey.
She is psychotically depressed, maybe
Manic as well. Right now she simply sits,
Head thrown back, eyes rolled up, jaw slack, teeth
    bared.
I've had her started on medication. . . .

Oh, god! I didn't ask for this. I know
You won't believe me. Greta telephoned
This morning as I was about to leave
On rounds. Only a minute later and
Somebody else might have had the lucky break,
Although I doubt it. Greta wanted me,
Telling me I had to be her doctor. . . .
It's so hard to see her this way. Poor Serey!"

Paula was lifted out of self-regard
Into the spinning world of accident
And chance. Serey psychotic? Amazing . . .
True there had been a few recent hints, but—
Psychotic? Had Greta missed something?
Or had she herself not been hearing what
Prescott had been saying about Serey—
The phone calls, that luncheon? It was quite true.
Analysts like herself busy themselves
Within the four walls of their demanding work,
Like laboratory scientists at their
Microscopes, eyes glued to the minutia
Of their preoccupations—one small life
Darting through the currents of its obscure
Existence, important only to itself
And a few others like itself. Why the fuss
About analysis, a tribute only
To singularity. But once look up
From the eyepiece and one is taken aback
By the stormtroops of a reality
Always there, stationed at one's door, ready
To stave it in with their hard rifle butts.
Paula frowned at her reflections. Was she
Reverting to her teutonic origins,
Lapsing into vain abstractions, rising
Above the plane of real being on hot air?
Serey. Safely in analysis, now where?

And Prescott? He was now on stage again
Facing a cruel demanding audience ready
To blame him if the play did not end right
And to shrug if it ended as they wished,
Convinced there was no other way to end it.
What of Victor now? Kurt? And what of Greta?
That poor woman. Of course there are failures
In any profession. She had had her share.
But it was how it was all enmeshed, knotted—
The personal, political, professional.
Analysis was not meant to bear such
Added weight, to serve so many masters.
The shoemaker must stick to his humble last.
She frowned again. This time at her pious
Sermonizing. Perhaps it was the toxin
In her blood going to her brain; perhaps
It was a substitute for worry and work.
Cancer might yet make her a philosopher
Where all else had failed. Right now she'd better
Attend to that mite in her microscope
Commanding a battleship in a thimble.
We do not pick our stage but are thrust on it.
She frowned again. This time it was bad Shakespeare.

It was not easy to hold back the habit
Of years that ordered his thoughts and actions
As a physician. He had a patient to heal
And he must do no harm. She was hedged in
By an iron wall of resistances—
Her own, her husband's, yes, her analyst's,
And of course her import for Victor's hopes.
Already he knew of the president's role
Who had called him at the hospital, wanting
To know whether he could help in any way,
While telling him what had happened earlier.

Both analyst and patient were caught up
In their silences. Each felt a new world
Had risen above the horizon, filling
The widest range of their vision with surprise,
Dwarfing the nearby reasons of their own concerns.
Only Paula worried about this confluence
Of chance and character. Prescott dismissed
As coincidence his sudden new role
And the sword it placed in his ready hand.

"I have to keep in mind I have a patient,
A very sick patient, who needs to be
Walled off from all that is going on. Greta
Agrees. I talked some with her just before.
She herself believes it is a severe
Transference reaction. I'm not so sure.
But she put the case entirely in my hands.
I'd have it no other way. Michael cried,
Saying something about Serey being
A foolish, heartsick girl. Her father should
Be told all about it. He'd have the cure
For her poor, restless soul. I can't fathom him.
Nor would he explain further what he meant.
He left saying sadly, 'Do what you must.
I'll see to the children. They are hungry.'
This is all too much for me. I've enough
On my hands. . . . You're not coughing as much
Today. I hope you have stopped smoking . . . I'm
    lost . . .
Becalmed would be a better word for it.
I'm waiting for a wind to fill my sail."

"Perhaps there is a wind already blowing
Strong but you hesitate to spread your sails,
I mean that wind that would blow you out of
This harbor and onto the high seas again—

The wind stirred up by Serey's sad decline."
Paula had been ruefully amused by
Prescott's comment on her absent coughing.
Oh, well! Why cough any more. The damage's done!

"I don't know what you mean. What wind stirred up
By Serey? What harbor? And what high seas?"

Why had she fallen into allegory,
Paula wondered. She was having trouble
Today in staying plain and simple, direct
As was her way. . . . Even in her own mind
She was weaving fuzzy thoughts intricately.
Has her brain already been infiltrated?
Nonsense! She was wrapping the pain away
In wordy poultices, not taking it raw.
Not so good for her own thoughts, and bad for his
Analysis.
          "You have a job to do,
A hard job. But you are a physician
Used to such hard jobs. Why all the fuss?"

"Why all the fuss? She's not just any patient.
I suspect a lot is riding on what
Happens to her . . . on how I manage things. . . . "

"What has all that to do with your patient?
She's gotten sick for whatever reason.
Now you must help her. You have other patients
Worse off and you know how to help them, no?"

"No! I mean, yes. But that is all beside
The point. She is no ordinary patient."

"You remember your dream, Excaliber,
Sword in hand?"

"Yes."

                    "You will save us all—
Mother, me, and now Serey, not only
From herself but from her good friends as well
So there is never any good-bye to
Anyone. Only another hello."

"I did agree to saying good-bye to you—
In September. . . . Maybe you're not as sick
As I thought."

                    "So, you've already saved me.
I'll be around in any case, you think,
So it's O.K. to say good-bye, fingers crossed."

Prescott suddenly felt woefully sad.
It was a feeling of waiting for someone
Who promised to return and the promise
Itself became an aching remorseless void.

Paula waited the few ticking moments
Until the hour ended in heavy silence.

49

She watched her cigarette smoke curling
Upward, blossoming into a fuller shape
As it rose. Like in the films, she mused,
When the genie emerges from the bottle
And hovers hugely over the poor fellow
Who unstoppered it. No doubt hers was an
Evil genie, but not altogether.
It had brought much pleasure and how was it
To know, or she—Ach! The same tired script.
No wish can ever be granted fully.
Every wish must have its embedded hook
For those who must swallow their wishes whole.
A little munch at a time is wiser.
But we are never convinced after a munch
That the rest will still be there. So we swallow
Whole hog, hook and all. Hook and all. Enough,
She counseled herself, noting again how
She had to wax philosophic before
She saw Prescott. She knew, she knew too well
That these musings were efforts to allay
Her pain at their parting and what it meant
For her. He was the last patient she would
See through to the end. Her last candidate.
With a broad smile, a sudden thought appeared.
Yes, and I want to swallow him all up.

Let him ride inside me like a fetus
Never to be born. A better fetus
By far than this cancer that doesn't know
How to grow into a human being.
Its signals are all wrong. Maybe
Its wishes are more diffuse, its urges
Vaguer. It is what it can only be,
As we ourselves. Enough of this. If I
Keep this up, I'll ask him to take my pulse
When he comes in! He has enough to deal with—
This ending, Serey's treatment, his keen
Intuition that something is wrong with me—
That is also the wish keeping him around.
She called for her patient.

                              With not so much
as a glance at her he lay down on the couch.
She missed that initial diagnostic look.
"Serey is getting better. It may not be
The medication either. It's too soon
For it to work. I had her see Greta,
Although she was hesitant to go.
I felt she wanted to, if only to show
Greta she was better. She kept on talking
Continuously of how terrible she was,
How destructive, malignant, obsessed, sick—
Constantly threatening to choke herself, or slash
Her throat. Greta had tried to save her and
She wanted to save Greta, Kurt, and Victor
From some unclear danger—and she had failed
And didn't deserve to live. Poor Michael!
She didn't want to talk to him. Ashamed,
I suppose, or angry—it was hard to tell.
I benefited from an intensely
Positive transference. She confided
To me that it was I she wanted to be

In analysis with because I knew French.
No idea where she got that from. Well,
In hindsight analysis was not for her.
Is it for anyone? Is it for me? Or
Did old Freud create a scientific
Counterpart of purgatory, a place
Where souls simmer before they're saved or damned.
I tell you nothing new when I say that
Analysis for me has been like that.
It goes so well I think I am ready
For an earthly paradise. Life without
Hitches. And then—like recently—it turns
Abruptly sour, agonizing, hopeless,
And I feel damned to an eternity
Of neurosis—that thick, pitch-black despair.
Nothing can ever change. I will end as
I began."

       "But you are smart enough to see
That that's the wish—to still be sick enough
To begin again, with nothing really changed.
We both five years younger, Serey healthy,
Your youthful wishes as strong as ever.
Nothing given up, nothing accepted.
You turn back the clock not to stop time but
To defy it. All this purgatory talk
Is like your King Arthur mythology.
Draw the sword from the rock and be powerful
Forever. Fail and stay weak forever.
Maybe it's that analysis is too
Much like life itself with its ups and downs,
And you want to have a Great Experience
With Heaven and Hell hanging in the balance,
And you always hovering in between,
Never settling one way or the other."

"Don't get me wrong. I am still ending this
In September. . . . Now you have made me sad."
He chuckled at his wording. *She* had made
Him sad!

       "I guess I still blame you for this
Ending. As if it were your idea, your
Doing. But I have had enough. I'm better.
Even though it's hard to pinpoint exactly
How. I am happier. Not always and when
I'm not, I blame you and think I should stay.
You're right, though, to stay is to return,
Or try to return again to an earlier
Happiness—no, not happiness but
To a state of unconditional yearning,
A yearning—how to capture it—a yearning
Like . . . an erection . . . seeking, seeking its
Place—when it still has no idea what
And where that is. But wherever and whatever,
It is blessed . . . innocence. Is that what I am
Describing? Innocent of the world, but
Wise in itself?"

      "An eternal erection,
Is that what you want of me?"

        "Is that what I've
Been saying? So I keep arriving at
The same destination. But the world itself
Is circular. We're bound to end up where
We started if not close by. . . . After we end
Will I never see you again? Of course
I will. . . . But never in the same way. Never.
I will slip into the envelope of
My life and you into yours. And the letters
Will have different addresses."
        And he

Grew sad again. A twilight of silence,
Descended in the midst of which he heard
Her voice, but he knew she hadn't spoken.
It was a voice he had often imagined
In her absence, speaking to him, saying
Harsh things sometimes, soothing things other times.
Strangely it was the quality only
Of her voice he now experienced, its timbre,
Like music, like a voice heard from afar
That we can recognize before we can
Make out the words. When she did speak it jarred.

"Where are you now?"

                            "Nowhere. I mean, right here.
But I'm thinking of hikes I've taken
Alone or with friends in the wilderness, far
From civilization. And realizing that
The stillness, that special wholesome stillness
Is created by intervals of sound—
Birds calling, the wind blowing, your own footfalls.
Sounds that don't last long but seem to be
Nestled in the stillness, like seeds in the earth."

Her eyebrows raised. Another fetal image.
They were both giving birth, each in their own way.
She to finish with his training analysis,
Her last. He to become an analyst
Himself. And then inside her something never
To be born. She coughed, coughed again and again.
She wanted no more of that and dropped a lozenge
Into her mouth.

                  It was as if a train had
Suddenly torn through the middle of his woods.
"You still have a bad cough. Take care of it."

"I shall do my best. It's time for us to stop."